A COLD
HIGHLAND
WIND

ALSO BY TASHA ALEXANDER

A COLD
HIGHLAND
WIND

A LADY EMILY MYSTERY

Tasha Alexander

MINOTAUR
BOOKS
NEW YORK

First published in the United States by Minotaur Books, an imprint of St. Martin's Publishing Group

www.minotaurbooks.com

Designed by Omar Chapa

Library of Congress Cataloging-in-Publication Data

Names: Alexander, Tasha, 1969– author.
Title: A cold highland wind : / Tasha Alexander.
Description: First edition. | New York : Minotaur Books, 2023. | Series: Lady
　Emily mysteries ; 17 |
Identifiers: LCCN 2023025372 | ISBN 9781250872333 (hardcover) |
　ISBN 9781250880970 (ebook)
Subjects: LCSH: Hargreaves, Emily, Lady (Fictitious character)—Fiction. |
　Murder—Investigation—Fiction. | LCGFT: Detective and mystery fiction. |
　Novels.
Classification: LCC PS3601.L3565 C65 2023 | DDC 813/.6—dc23/
　eng/20230530
LC record available at https://lccn.loc.gov/2023025372

Our books may be purchased in bulk for promotional, educational, or business use. Please contact your local bookseller or the Macmillan Corporate and Premium Sales Department at 1-800-221-7945, extension 5442, or by email at MacmillanSpecialMarkets@macmillan.com.

First Edition: 2023

10　9　8　7　6　5　4　3　2　1

For Al and Muffy, with eternal gratitude for friendship, martinis, and Sunday lunch.

Wee, modest, crimson-tippèd flow'r,

Thou's met me in an evil hour;

For I maun crush amang the stoure

    Thy slender stem:

To spare thee now is past my pow'r,

    Thou bonie gem.

        —Robert Burns, "To a Mountain-Daisy"

A COLD
HIGHLAND
WIND

1

Emily

Cairnfarn, Scotland
1905

At first glance, blood doesn't stand out on tartan. At least not on the tartan worn by the dead man sprawled next to a loch on the Highland estate of my dear friend Jeremy Sheffield, Duke of Bainbridge. It blended into the red wool of his fly plaid, hardly visible until I looked closely. Looking closely wasn't pleasant. The man's face, bloody and bruised, offered a chilling vision of his final moments, which must have been brutal and painful. I would've given anything to have kept my sons from seeing him, too. This was not the way we'd expected our holiday to start.

The pastiche of Scottish culture popularized by Queen Victoria never appealed to me. I don't object to a riot of brightly colored tartan or the skirl of the bagpipe, but rather to the idea that English royalty should be Scotland's cultural ambassadors. The region, rugged and sublime, deserves better. It's full of contrasts and complication, its beauty simultaneously harsh and soft, a place better understood by its native population than imported aristocracy.

I grew up on my parents' sprawling estate in Kent, next to Farringdon, the seat of the Duke of Bainbridge. The duke's elder son, Jeremy, and I were inseparable as children. We raced horses. We climbed trees. We caused no end of trouble. Although I primarily spent time with Jeremy at Farringdon, it was not the family's only domicile. Among their other possessions were Bainbridge House in London; Woodsford, a cozy two-hundred-room hunting lodge in Yorkshire; and Cairnfarn Castle deep in the Scottish Highlands.

I'd always loved the castle. The idea of it, anyway. I hadn't seen it because Jeremy's father despised the place, for reasons that were never articulated in my presence. It had something to do with the thirteenth duke, Jeremy's uncle, who'd refused to marry and, hence, never provided an heir. When he died, his brother inherited the title and, after installing his aunts there to live, the fourteenth duke never went back. Jeremy and I hatched periodic schemes to flee north and use Cairnfarn as a base to fight unruly Highlanders (we were convinced there were still bands of them hiding in caves, ready for battle), but they fell apart for a variety of reasons, not the least of which was a lack of train fare. We rarely argued, but when I read Sir Walter Scott's *Waverley* and became less sympathetic to the English response to the Jacobite uprisings, Jeremy showered unexpectedly harsh words on me. For two weeks we avoided each other. Then he read the book. Shortly thereafter, accompanied by his nanny, he went to a tailor for a complete set of Highland dress fashioned from the Bainbridge tartan his uncle had designed. His father, offering no explanation beyond muttering something about troublesome children, forbade him from wearing it.

When at last I found myself at Cairnfarn, it was because of some equally troublesome children. My own.

My husband, Colin Hargreaves, and I have three boys. Most people assumed Richard and Tom were twins; their dark curls and eyes mirrored Colin's own, but it was Henry, with fair hair and blue eyes, who was Richard's twin. Tom, short for Tomaso, was our ward, and we loved him as dearly as we did the twins, who were only a few months younger. While his brothers were well behaved, Henry did his best to entangle those around him in one outrageous scheme after another and often succeeded. He was catastrophically persuasive.

Which was why we were all now in Scotland. Last year, Colin and I had been investigating a case in Egypt. Henry was desperate to come, but we wouldn't allow it. The wretched boy convinced Jeremy to bring him and his brothers to meet us there. In the course of making the arrangements, Jeremy mentioned that he owned a Nile crocodile, who lived in the menagerie at Cairnfarn. Henry dubbed the creature Cedric and insisted it must come to Egypt as well. During the journey, the child became concerned about the conditions in which its animals lived. Upon our return home, he penned a sixteen-page document—all of it very badly spelled—on the subject. Jeremy, utterly charmed by it, insisted that we all come to the Highlands so that Henry could see for himself that the creatures were well cared for. And so we did.

Cairnfarn Castle, a towering stone building whose construction began in the fourteenth century and was completed in the eighteenth, perched overlooking a loch in a verdant glen surrounded by towering mountains. Silver fog danced through patches of deep purple heather, and when it rained—which it often did—it felt mystical, like something sent by the fairies. It was a place of splendid isolation, so far north and so distant from any towns of reasonable size as to make it quite difficult to reach without ordering a special train.

On our second day in Cairnfarn, the village was hosting a

ceilidh to celebrate the arrival of a new doctor, hired to replace their long-standing physician, William Cameron, so that he might retire and focus on writing. A consummate storyteller, he'd published several novels, all of them well-received, and was lauded both as a stylist and as having a talent for unforgettable plots.

I knew little about ceilidhs beyond that they included dancing, but was always game to immerse myself in the culture of a new place. I'd donned a tartan gown and dressed the boys in kilts, but failed to convince Colin to wear one. Jeremy, kitted out from head to toe in Bainbridge tartan—a flamboyant concoction of bright turquoise, scarlet, and yellow—moaned when he saw my husband in ordinary evening wear.

"You've never been fun, Hargreaves, but this is distressing, even for you," he said. "Get in the spirit of things, man! You can't dance a Highland reel in that."

"I've danced more Highland reels than I can count in similar dress," Colin said. "Our late queen's affection for Scotland made it one of the most popular dances in London for years."

"I suppose I've done the same, although I can't recall the details," Jeremy said as we approached the village hall. He turned to the boys. "One must be very careful when it comes to consuming spirits while attending balls. Too much and you'll remember nothing, too little and you'll remember everything."

Henry's eyes nearly popped out of his head. "You're the only grown-up who ever bothers to give us useful information. Would you provide more details?"

Fortunately we arrived at the village hall before Jeremy could respond. Almost as soon as we'd stepped through the door, a comely young woman with dark auburn hair pressed a glass into my hand.

"Welcome," she said, her bright blue eyes flashing as a broad smile split her face. "I'm Maisie Drummond and I work for His

Grace." She bobbed a curtsy in Jeremy's general direction, winking at him as she did it. "This is Mrs. Pringle's famous punch. Go easy with it or you'll regret it tomorrow. Dinnae say I didnae warn you."

Another woman approached. Maisie muttered something under her breath, stepped back behind the table with the punch bowl on it, and started filling more glasses. The newcomer looked to be in her early thirties, but she was still handsome, still aglow. Her hair, so fair it was almost silver, was piled on her head in a fashionable Gibson girl–style pompadour. Her eyes, pale grayish blue, lit up when she smiled. Her complexion was perfect pearl, with just a subtle hint of rose on her cheeks. Her dress, made from a fine lilac fabric, was simple and elegant. Delicate lace fell from the cuffs and embellished the bodice.

"Maisie, dear, that's not the way one ought to speak to a lady." She turned to me. "I'm Caroline Pringle, the vicar's wife, and can assure you my punch is not nearly so lethal as you've been told. Maisie thinks rather a lot of her opinions but would be better served keeping many of them to herself." Her amiable tone softened the words, but Maisie—still in earshot at the table—rolled her eyes and shook her head. Then, with no attempt at subtlety, she turned to Colin, looked him up and down, and smiled, apparently pleased with what she saw. Mrs. Pringle sighed. "I promise you she's harmless, only so distressingly spirited. At times I wish I could tame her, but at others, I envy her youthful lack of concern for the niceties."

Jeremy leaned toward me conspiratorially. "If anyone could tame her, it would be Caroline. She's the glue that holds us all together. We'd be lost without her. She organizes everything—including myself—and is an extraordinary seamstress. Keeps all the young ladies in the village dressed to the nines. And listen to how cultured she sounds. You'd never guess she grew up here, would you?"

"Don't embarrass me, Your Grace," Mrs. Pringle said, blushing. "Cairnfarn could do perfectly well without me. Mr. Pringle is far more essential, and Mr. Sinclair is proving an asset as well, his influence stretching far beyond the castle park. I've never seen a man so dedicated to setting a good example. He's taught the boys in the village everything they could ever hope to know about the local wildlife, made them see that poaching is an affront to all decent people, and has them so thoroughly convinced of the necessity of performing good deeds they're in a constant contest to outdo one another. I can't think when I've last carried a parcel home from the grocer or the post office. There's always a youngster ready to lend a hand."

"Sinclair's my gamekeeper—ghillie, I suppose I should say, but I rarely remember. He's an absolute treasure," Jeremy said. "Thank goodness he decided to return to Cairnfarn. He'd been living in Edinburgh."

"You hired a gamekeeper from Edinburgh?" Colin asked. "Sounds very like you, Bainbridge."

Jeremy huffed and the ostrich feather on his cap fluttered. "It's not what it sounds like. He grew up in Cairnfarn. His father ran a prosperous croft, but Sinclair never had much interest in farming. When his parents died of influenza, he took the opportunity to flee. Left not three hours after their burial and went in search of a better life in Edinburgh. Not that anyone was aware of it then. He explained when he returned. At the time, it caused quite a scandal."

"Primarily because he was only eleven years old," Mrs. Pringle said. "We all thought he'd joined the Royal Navy and never expected to see him again. Ties here run deep, though, and he returned a year or so ago, two decades later. He'd become a solicitor, but grew tired of city life and wanted to return home."

"Which is not to suggest he was any more interested in farming than he'd been when he left. His father's croft had long since been taken over by someone else, so I offered him the position of game-keeper," Jeremy said. "He's cracking good at it."

Someone tugged at my arm. I looked down and saw Richard. "Mama, please do come at once. The first part of the evening is meant to be dedicated to storytelling and Dr. Cameron is about to regale us with a tale about kelpies, the shape-shifting water horses that inhabit nearly every loch and river in Scotland. It's much more interesting than what I'm told he shared at the last ceilidh, some-thing about a princess tricking a man into falling in love with her by feeding him some sort of magic cake."

"That sounds perfectly dreadful," Jeremy said. "I far prefer kelpies."

"The doctor's seen several, one only yesterday," Richard said. "He's going to take me out in the morning to find another. Mr. Fletcher, who lives in the village told me there's nothing more dan-gerous than kelpies. They lure their victims to the shore and then drown them. He's a bit terrifying, Mr. Fletcher."

I let my son lead me to a circle of chairs in the center of the room, where we sat and listened to Dr. Cameron detail the trickery of the kelpies, the gravelly burr of his voice at once thrilling and soothing. He certainly knew how to keep an audience spellbound.

When he finished, cheers and applause filled the hall. He waved his hands to silence them. "Enough, enough, or you'll make me just the sort of arrogant fool we all despise. You're kind to have indulged me telling my little tale, and now I must beg your attention for a little longer. Some of you have already had the pleasure of meeting my new colleague, Dr. Genevieve Harris. She trained in Edinburgh, and I've never seen a more competent physician. Aye, she's a lady, but we in the Highlands know it's skill that matters above everything, and she's got that in spades. I wouldn't feel comfortable turning over my prac-tice to anyone else and I know you'll trust her just as much as I do."

An undercurrent of discontent rumbled through the crowd, but no one voiced a discernible objection. A tall, whip-thin woman in her late twenties who'd been sitting near him rose to her feet. Her countenance was serious, but there was warmth in her otherwise nondescript eyes. She looked utterly capable as she gave a little smile and waved. Before I could make her acquaintance, a young man moved to the center of the circle, made a perfunctory-sounding statement welcoming the new doctor, and began to recite a poem. Another followed, and then an elderly woman recounted a lengthy story about a ghost said to inhabit a cave not far from Cairnfarn's loch. Almost the instant she finished, people stood up and started lining the chairs along the walls in order to make room for dancing. I lost sight of Dr. Harris in the ensuing commotion.

"Lady Emily, I'm glad to see you." A well-built man with broad shoulders, flaming red hair, and chocolate brown eyes stepped in front of me. He was dressed in Highland kit, sporting a bright red kilt with a green interval and blue and white stripes. His doublet and tam were fashioned from dark green wool that matched the shade of his knee-high argyle hose. A fly plaid draped over his shoulder and a long rabbit fur sporran hung from his hips. "Forgive me for being so bold as to introduce myself. I'm Angus Sinclair, the duke's game-keeper. Master Thomas has expressed a strong interest in shooting, and I'd like to take him out tomorrow if that's amenable to you."

"Of course," I said. "I can't say I expected him to have a passion for ptarmigan and grouse, but I'm happy for him to learn the sport."

"He's a little gentleman, your son," Mr. Sinclair said, "and shooting's a proper activity for a gentleman. I'll collect him after breakfast. If either of the other peerie lads want to join, I'll be ready for them as well."

"Thank you, Mr. Sinclair."

"You're most welcome. Now, might I be cheeky and ask for a dance?"

His smile was so engaging, so affable, I could hardly refuse. Many of the dances were new to me, but Mr. Sinclair proved a talented partner, teaching me the steps as we went. It proved to be rollicking good fun. Colin and I stood up together for the Highland reel. The joyful music, the enthusiastic company, and the punch that was as potent as Maisie had warned made for a raucous evening.

The hall, crammed tight with people, grew warm, so when the reel finished, Colin took my hand and pulled me outside, where the crisp Highland air cooled us in an instant. Clouds hung heavy in the sky but parted just enough to reveal the glowing full moon. Mist was settling in the valley. An owl hooted and some other night creature sounded like it was calling back.

"I've always liked seeing you bathed in moonlight," Colin said. "It makes me wish we had more privacy. Perhaps tomorrow we should take a nocturnal stroll to the loch so that—" We heard heated voices and he stopped. Looking around, we saw no one visible in our immediate vicinity, so we followed the noise until we saw Mr. Sinclair and Dr. Harris standing near a patch of towering trees, arguing. I couldn't make out what they were saying, but the tone and the sharpness of their gestures made it clear this was no friendly conversation.

"Perhaps he objects to the presence of a female doctor," I said.

"I'd put money on the argument being about something entirely unrelated." Colin tilted his head. "This looks to me a squabble far more personal. We should leave them to it."

We went back to the hall, where all thoughts of what we'd seen rushed from my mind as soon as we started dancing again. Little did I know our holiday was about to take a dark turn.

2

Tansy

Cairnfarn, Scotland
1676

Rossalyn was crying again. Crying and wouldn't stop. Not that it mattered. I'd grown used to the sound. It was something I was all too familiar with, having heard it coming from my own mouth—and deeper, from my chest, from my heart, from my soul—throughout the journey that brought me from North Africa to the cold, rainy island I now inhabited. I wasn't raised to be a servant. My father was a man of education and culture. He insisted we learn to speak English and French. We were Moors. Muslims. The kind of people who could be sold as slaves to Christians. Although I wasn't a slave anymore. Not literally. Not technically. In the end, though, I found the semantics didn't matter.

Nevertheless, I displayed appropriate gratitude (as expected) when Rossalyn freed me. She wasn't Rossalyn to me then, just Lady MacAllister, mistress of Castle Cairnfarn. A privateer from Glasgow—pirate, more like—kidnapped me when I was on my way home from the market in Tunis. I thought my religion would protect me from such a fate. It would have if my abductor had followed Islam, but he was a Christian and he liked what he saw when he laid eyes on me, so he took me. Kept me for his own private amusement. When he was tired of the novelty, he sold me. My new owner, who changed my name from Tasnim to Tansy because it was too hard to pronounce, gave me to his friend's wife as a wedding gift.

Gave me as a wedding gift. Like I was a silver salver or fine linen.

The wife—the aforementioned Rossalyn—displayed appropriate horror at this (as was not expected) and immediately set about the business of granting me my freedom. Everyone around her lauded her while she basked in what she viewed as appreciation for her virtue, but without the means to return to my home, it didn't make all that much difference to me. I was still a servant, unable to live a life I'd chosen. As the ensuing months passed, I became accustomed to living at the castle. Growing more comfortable with my mistress, I asked her to post letters I'd written to my family, explaining what had happened and begging them to send for me. She agreed, and after that, we became friends of a sort. The sort you can be when one of you once owned the other and remains in charge of her. I became her companion. I read to her. Embroidered with her. Said witty things when her friends came to visit. I was a novelty. Apparently having Moorish attendants was fashionable, or at least it had been ages ago. James IV's daughter Margaret had two, but that was more than a hundred and fifty years ago. This far north in the Highlands, fashion ran more than a little behind. All of which is to say that instead of scrubbing floors or working in the kitchen, my job was to be entertaining. I considered my role to be something like that of a pet.

Nice for a dog; not so much for a human.

The maids toiled at harder tasks, but they had come to their positions voluntarily, seeking employment. I'd had no choice. Was I cynical? Bitter? Unhappy? Yes, to the first two. As for the third, unhappy doesn't begin to do justice to my state of mind.

I'd always been bright. Quicker than my brothers at learning to read. I wanted to study science. Astronomy, to be precise. I would have if I hadn't been kidnapped. So while I acknowledge that certain aspects of my plight could be worse—Roman slaves in salt mines come to mind—doing so provided little salve for my psyche. Still, we learn to live with our misery. I refused to wallow, but equally I refused to forget. Rossalyn freed me, but she didn't send me home.

From the time I first landed on its shores, Scotland revealed herself to me as a strange, exotic place. Which was exactly how Rossalyn talked about North Africa. "Endless sun and endless sand," she said to me on a rare day when the sun was shining at Cairnfarn. "With the scent of spices wafting through the air. That's how I picture your home."

I cringed at the word *home*. How could she mention it, accept that I had one, and not lift a finger beyond posting my letters to help me return to it? "Tunis is on a lake and it's not far from the Mediterranean. You're conjuring up images of the desert."

"Let me have my fantasy, won't you? Sometimes I wish we could go there together."

She'd started talking like this not long after her husband died. The loss of him had gutted her. Duncan MacAllister had stood nearly as wide as he was tall, the sort of man who looked more comfortable holding a claymore than a book, an observation that sums up his personality rather neatly. He was considerably older than his bride, thirty years at least. If I'd been her, I would've been horrified, but the difference didn't seem to bother her. She gave every appearance of liking him. This was the first thing about Rossalyn that surprised me. The second was how she reacted when the laird's son from his first marriage threw her out of her home.

3

1905

Nothing went as expected the day following the ceilidh. First, Dr. Cameron sent word that he would not be able to embark on the promised search for the elusive kelpie. He'd been out on an emergency call most of the night. Richard, disappointed, followed Colin, Jeremy, and me to the castle's library, where he consoled himself by reading. Jeremy's uncle Albion had amassed a magnificent collection of fiction that ranged from rare first editions (many signed) to a complete set of the works of Mary Elizabeth Braddon, my favorite author of sensational novels. He'd had no interest in pandering to anyone's taste but his own. He also had an astonishing number of truly important volumes, one of which Jeremy pulled down and handed to my husband: a Shakespeare First Folio.

"You ought not have it sitting on a shelf as if it were nothing special," Colin said. "It's not good for conservation. There are clear signs of water damage on it. Do you know—"

"You can't blame me for that, Hargreaves," Jeremy said. "It happened during the Cairnfarn witch trials centuries ago. Before them, actually. An accused witch stole it from the castle's library and was accused of using it to cast a spell on some unfortunate girl. I don't know precisely what happened, but somehow in the course of it all the book wound up getting wet."

This caught Richard's interest. "I don't believe a witch would have much use for Shakespeare," he said, closing the book he'd been reading and crossing to his father.

"There are witches in *Macbeth*," Jeremy said. "Even I know that."

"Be that as it may, any witch worth her salt wouldn't use spells penned by a playwright. It's inconceivable."

Jeremy grinned. "You're a bright lad. My understanding is that she was acquitted of all charges. Perhaps the book proved her innocence." He pulled a small polished stone off a shelf and placed it on the table next to us. "This had something to do with the trial as well. There are Viking runes carved on it. My uncle always claimed it and others like it were used by witches to identify each other."

Richard picked it up and inspected it. Before he could comment, the door opened and Tom entered the room, his face writ with worry. "Papa, Mr. Sinclair and I had arranged to go shooting this morning, but he's nowhere to be found. I've looked everywhere."

Richard perked up. "A kelpie might have got him, although that seems unlikely. He's well aware of the danger. There's always the possibility of fairies, though. They can be rather tricky—sometimes friendly, sometimes not. They could have kidnapped him; but if so, it's probably nothing serious, just a bit of a laugh and they'll return him again soon." He was so very serious as he spoke that Colin and I both nodded solemnly.

"He may be on the trail of poachers or busy with some other

urgent estate business," Colin said. "Why don't you plan to go shooting tomorrow, and for now the both of you can round up Henry and look for kelpies?"

"It would be quite dangerous," Richard said.

"I've absolute faith in you." Colin crouched down in front of the boy. "You know how to be careful and I'm certain your knowledge of the subject at hand is at least as comprehensive as Dr. Cameron's. Your brothers couldn't have a better guide."

Richard looked quite pleased. He and Tom ran off; Colin and I turned our attention back to the First Folio while Jeremy dozed in a chair near the fireplace. About an hour later, the door flung open with such force that it slammed into the wall with an alarming thud. Richard, bathed in sweat, his face drained of all color, ran into the room.

"You must come at once. We've found a body. A dead body. Very dead. Extremely dead. The most dead it's possible to be." His voice was shaking. "Tom's gone for the vicar. There's no sheriff in the village nor any police, but he felt it was essential to report the incident to someone official without delay. Henry's standing guard at the site. Kelpies don't usually attack in this manner. Perhaps the ones local to here have adopted tactics never seen elsewhere, but I suppose—"

"Slow down, old man," Colin said, "and tell me exactly what happened."

"There's no time for that, Papa. We must go at once. We didn't like to leave Henry alone, but we thought someone should stay."

The commotion had woken Jeremy. "It's quite likely the work of errant kelpies," he said, crouching down so his face was even with Richard's. "Will you tell me more about their usual methods? I'm afraid my education in these matters—as with all others—is sadly lacking."

He took the boy's hand and walked with him, keeping him distracted the entire way to the loch. I'd never before seen him have such a calming influence on anyone. It didn't last, however. When the body came into sight, Richard pulled away and ran to his father, who put an arm around his shoulders and held him tight. I continued to the shore. There, at the edge of the water, was a corpse, a mess of blood and gore. I moved closer until I could see his face. It was Mr. Sinclair, Jeremy's gamekeeper. He was still dressed in the Highland garb he'd had on at the ceilidh, minus his tam, which must have fallen off when he'd been attacked. It now lay some twenty feet away. His face was covered with bruises, his temple bashed in, and his chest was full of what looked like stab wounds. It was a horrific, bloody sight. Lying on his forehead was a single stone, small and polished, with what looked like Viking runes carved on it.

Jeremy came to my side. "Bloody hell." His voice was a gruff whisper. "The poor man."

"Where's Henry?" I looked around but did not see him. I called his name.

"I'm over here, Mama," came a small voice, sounding distinctly unlike my unruly son. "Behind the trees, so that I could observe anyone coming to cause mischief without being seen myself."

He was perched on the trunk of a fallen tree, looking most forlorn and brushing tears off his cheeks. "My dear boy." I sat next to him and pulled him close. "It's quite an awful thing you've seen."

"I wasn't brave at all," he said. "Instead I was sick and now I'll be forever mortified. I couldn't bear to stay close to him. I didn't want to look anymore. I've always thought I'd make a good soldier, but now I know I can't stand the sight of . . ." His voice trailed off.

"No one can stand such a sight. A soldier may become necessarily hardened to it, but that doesn't mean he's not affected, only that he's learned how to best deal with it." Colin and I had investigated more than a dozen murders. I was as accustomed as one can be to stumbling upon corpses, but this was not something I'd expected my sons would ever face, particularly when they were only nine years old. "Let's return to the castle. There's no need to stay here. Your father will have the matter well in hand."

"No. I'd rather face it," he said, his voice shaking. "To do anything else would only mean more humiliation."

He refused to take my hand as we walked back toward the body. Colin and Richard were still standing some distance away, with Richard turned so he was not facing the corpse. Jeremy was next to them. Approaching from the village were Tom, the vicar, and Dr. Cameron.

"Oh, dear." Mr. Pringle went a sickly shade of gray and his knees started to buckle. Dr. Cameron steadied him. "This is . . . this is . . . beyond anything I could ever imagine happening in Cairnfarn." He began to pray. *"Heavenly Father, into whose hands Jesus Christ commended his spirit at the last hour: into those same hands we now commend your servant Angus, that death may be for him the gate to life and to eternal fellowship with you; through Jesus Christ our Lord."*

We all stood still and silent for a moment after he'd finished. Then the doctor spoke.

"I'm sorry you're facing this after the difficult night you've had."

"She's doing better this morning, but still struggling." Mr. Pringle closed his eyes.

"Your wife?" I asked. "Has she fallen ill?"

"She'd prefer the general population doesn't know, but I know she's in need of some female companionship and sympathy, so I'll tell you," he said. "She was with child, although she was not aware of the fact until things began to go horribly wrong. It's why she left the ceilidh when she did."

"I'm so sorry," I said. I knew too well the pain of losing a child in such a manner. "Would it be appropriate for me to call on her when she's feeling better?"

"I'm certain she'd very much appreciate it, Lady Emily, and I'd say the sooner the better. She's lived in Cairnfarn all her life, but I don't think she has anyone she'd consider a close confidante."

"I'll go as soon as possible," I said.

"Thank you. Would it be a help if I were to take the boys back to the castle? Young Tom informed me that you and your husband aren't strangers to dealing with matters such as this. I believe your presence here would be more useful than mine."

None of the boys protested when I told them to go with him. Instead, their shoulders sagged with relief. After they'd left, Dr. Cameron knelt by the body and began to examine it. "He's been dead nine hours at least. I'll need to perform a full postmortem, but initially I'd say it was the blows to the head that caused his death. The stab wounds appear to have been made after he was dead."

I shuddered. "A deliberate mutilation?"

The doctor looked bewildered. "I'm afraid so. It's grisly."

"Could this be the knife?" Colin asked, gingerly holding a knife with an antler handle in his handkerchief. "I found it not ten feet away." He passed it to the doctor.

"I recognize it. It's Angus's own, his skene-dhu, which he would have worn tucked into his hose. It's the right size and shape to have caused the wounds. His killer must have removed it after Angus was dead, bent on doing even more damage to the poor man."

"Unless Mr. Sinclair was using it to defend himself," I said. "After he fell, he might have dropped it."

"Either way, the details are sickening. This is not the way I wanted to end my professional career." Dr. Cameron grimaced.

"I imagine not," Colin said. "We'll need to contact the police in Inverness. Is there a telegraph office in the village?"

"In the post office." The doctor looked down at Mr. Sinclair and sighed. "What a tragedy. A senseless, useless tragedy." He set off for the village to prepare for the grim task he faced. Jeremy sat on a boulder far away from the body, looking rather ill. Colin and I began to search the area, looking for the object used to strike the dead man's head. The ground near the loch was strewn with rocks of various sizes, from rough boulders large enough to stand on to tiny pebbles, smooth and shiny. Colin marked the spot he'd found the knife with a tall stick around which he tied the cravat he'd pulled from his neck.

"Look here," I said, stooping down to get a closer look at one of the boulders. "There's blood. It could explain the wound on the back of his skull. If it was the first of his injuries, he might have been unable to fight back, even if his attacker was physically weaker than him."

"You're thinking of Dr. Harris?" Colin asked.

"We saw them arguing. I'll go question her while you finish here." I squeezed his hand and got directions to her house from Jeremy. As I followed the path along the edge of the loch, the sun came out, showering the woods and mountains with golden light, wholly incongruous with the grisly scene I'd just left. When I reached the village, I sent a telegram to the Inverness police and then knocked on Dr. Harris's door. She answered promptly, welcomed my introduction, invited me inside, and offered me a cup of tea.

"I've come bearing terrible news," I said, taking the seat she offered in her small sitting room. The furniture was unremarkable, but had simple, pleasing lines, and the fire roaring in its stone hearth perfectly warmed the space. "There's been a murder by the loch. Dr. Cameron is preparing to conduct the postmortem."

"A murder? In Cairnfarn?" Her eyes widened, and her mouth hung open. She gave every appearance of genuine shock. "A tiny village that gives every appearance of bucolic perfection is the last place I'd expect to find that sort of violence. Do you know what happened?"

"My husband and I have begun to investigate," I said, "but as of yet, we're not certain of the details."

"You and your husband?" She smiled. "Dare I assume that you, too, have embraced a profession not usually allowed to us ladies?"

"It's not a professional pursuit, but I do have a reasonable degree of experience when it comes to bringing murderers to justice."

"Tell me what you've discovered so far and let me know how I can help."

"The victim was viciously attacked, bludgeoned—possibly with a rock—and his body was mutilated after death."

"Who is he?" she asked.

"Angus Sinclair, the gamekeeper at the castle," I said. "I believe you spoke with him last night."

She shifted in her seat. "Angus Sinclair was not at the ceilidh."

"He most certainly was," I said. "I saw you speaking to him outside."

"You saw me with a man, but he was not Angus Sinclair, the man who fled Cairnfarn for Edinburgh. I was engaged to Angus for two years and can tell you, unequivocally, the duke's gamekeeper is not he."

4

Tansy

1676

Wealthy people spend most, if not all, of their lives happy in the knowledge that bad things won't happen to them. Extraordinary bad things, that is. Their relatives will die, their fortunes at court may fall, their reputations may suffer; but on balance they feel confident assuming that the broad strokes of their existence won't cause them all too much pain. My family possessed no great riches, but we had enough to be comfortable. Comfortable and then some. I didn't think that would ever change for me. Nor did Rossalyn. How wrong we both were.

Duncan MacAllister passed from this world unexpectedly. Choked on a chicken bone at dinner during a clan meeting. I didn't see it happen, but it sounded gruesome. Nothing dignified about it. The other men there tried to help him, but to no avail. His son, Ewan, the new laird, didn't have much sympathy for the young woman he viewed as having replaced his mother. It wasn't the fairest of accusations. His mother had been dead for more than a decade before Rossalyn came to Cairnfarn as a bride. Still, I suppose no one's likely to be ecstatic at having a stepmother younger than his own sister.

When Ewan inherited, his first act was to order Rossalyn out. The loss of her husband left her all alone in the world. Her parents had died some years earlier, and her only cousin had succumbed to childbed fever only two weeks before Duncan expired. We had nowhere to go, no one who would take us in. Which is how we wound up in the cottage. Might as well make the best of the situation. Because I had technically been a wedding gift to her, the new laird agreed to let Rossalyn take me along. Chattel even when I wasn't chattel. Not that I had any interest in staying at the castle. I'd never wanted to be there in the first place.

"It's not so bad, is it?" Rossalyn looped her arm through mine as we stood in front of the cottage she'd taken for us. It was in the village of Cairnfarn, not far enough away from Ewan to satisfy either of us, but it was all she could afford. "It's not as if he'll give us any trouble. He never wanted me to exist. Now he can pretend I don't."

The house was small—snug, to give it a positive twist—but adequate. The roof didn't leak. The fire didn't smoke. There were two good-sized rooms, thick walls, and a neglected garden. All in all, it would suffice. It didn't take more than an hour to unpack our meager possessions. That gave us the rest of the day to enjoy being objects of fascination to our new neighbors.

They didn't know what to make of us. Rossalyn had been the mistress of the castle for seven years. They were keenly aware that she outranked them. Yet now she was living here, in the village, not in the dower house on the castle grounds. She didn't even have a particularly nice cottage. So maybe she no longer did outrank them. Either way, she didn't quite fit in. How could she?

The truth was, she'd never really belonged at the castle either. She'd grown up in Inverness, the daughter of a moderately successful tradesman. She was a city girl, through and through, not a Highland lass. She met Duncan when she was visiting her cousin who'd married another MacAllister and was hosting a clan meeting. By all accounts, her future husband was stupefied upon seeing bonnie young Rossalyn. Speechless, they say. Captivated, as if someone had cast a spell on him.

Witchcraft references never endear a person to unwelcoming in-laws.

She looked more like a Viking than a Scot, at least to my eyes. Her hair was so pale as to almost be white, her eyes gray. Duncan called her his *lochlannach*, which meant something like fearless Viking warrior. For reasons beyond my comprehension, Rossalyn returned his affection. They were married less than a month after they met.

Short engagements never endear a person to unwelcoming in-laws.

Yet the marriage was a success, so far as the couple was concerned. They genuinely liked each other. Which made things all the harder when Rossalyn was widowed.

The first week of our residence was surprisingly quiet. As I said, no one was quite sure what to do with us, so they kept their distance. Then, one rainy morning—the ordinary state of affairs for Cairnfarn—there was a knock on the door. I opened it to a young woman, probably of an age with me, certainly no older than twenty, holding a basket.

"Apologies for not coming sooner," she said, walking into the house before giving me a chance to refuse her entry. "I wouldn't say we're an unfriendly lot, but . . . well, we're used to Lady MacAllister coming to visit us. She's very good with sick children, you know. It's generally her bringing the baskets."

"I'm Tasnim Faraj," I said. "Lady MacAllister's companion."

Rossalyn poked her head into the corridor. "Cora! How lovely of you to come. Do sit down and have tea with us. Tansy, this is Cora Brodie. She's the daughter of the most obstinate farmer in all of Cairnfarn."

"Obstinate doesn't begin to cover it," Cora said. "I've brought biscuits and eggs and some of Mrs. Glendinning's notorious marmalade. It tastes like something a sheep might find interesting. Horrendous, truly, but well-intentioned and better than nothing should you find yourself in the midst of a famine."

"Sounds like high praise," I said. I already liked Cora.

"Too high. You'll know that the minute you taste it."

I made tea while Rossalyn arranged the biscuits on a plate. We passed a pleasant hour or so. I'd never realized how much gossip there could be in such a small village. Cairnfarn might prove more entertaining than I'd expected. Then again, I wasn't sure how much I'd like being talked about myself. That's always the trouble with gossip. It's great fun when you're listening, not so much when you're the topic.

So far as I could tell, there were two types of men in Cairnfarn: those who raised sheep and those who grew barley. The barley could be used for various things, including making the strong, sharp whisky everyone in the castle loved. I liked the smell of it but not the way it burned my throat. As for the women, they did what women do everywhere. Kept house. Cooked. Cleaned. Did laundry. Bore and raised children. Weaved cloth. As I thought about it, I felt more content with my plight than I had in a long time. That is, relatively content. How could I ever be truly content? I'd been stolen from my family, a family that had replied to none of the letters I'd sent. Perhaps they blamed me for my kidnapping and assumed—correctly—that my virtue had been stolen. Perhaps they no longer wanted anything to do with me. If that were the case, I might as well focus on my new life. At least Rossalyn and I had more independence than the other women in the village.

It was that independence that got us both in trouble.

5

1905

Dr. Harris's claim that the gamekeeper was not Angus Sinclair stunned me.

"When I was introduced to him, I was taken aback at hearing his name," she said. "He launched into his history at once, explaining that he'd left Cairnfarn after his parents' death when he was eleven years old. He'd gone to Edinburgh and talked his way into a menial position with a solicitor in the city. He worked as an errand boy and impressed his employer with his diligence. The man sent him to school and supported him through university, where he studied law before going into practice with his former master."

"And then he grew disenchanted with city life and decided to return to his roots." I frowned. "I've heard the story."

"It's the truth about Angus's life, but the gamekeeper is not Angus," she said. "I realized that at once and asked him to come outside with me so I could confront him. As I told you, Angus and

I were engaged. We met in Edinburgh and planned to marry after I'd completed my studies, but he disappeared two weeks before
the wedding, without saying a word to anyone. Don't suggest he'd
changed his mind. I know him too well to give that any credence.
Running away was entirely out of character for him."

"It wasn't when he left Cairnfarn," I said.

"He was a child then. He grew into a man who would never
behave so recklessly." She crossed her arms. "I've searched everywhere for him, pursued countless false leads. I delayed starting to
practice medicine for more than a year so that I could dedicate myself to looking for him. I've combed every inch of Edinburgh and
gone through passenger lists for every ship leaving Scotland. All of
it was to no avail. I may not be able understand why he disappeared
or where he went, but when I heard what the gamekeeper claimed
as his own history, I knew at once that he must've known Angus.
Otherwise, how would he have known the story? For the first time
in ages, I felt hope. I thought he might be able to tell me what had
happened to my fiancé."

"Did he?" I asked.

"No," she said. "He denied everything and insisted the story was
his own. When I told him I was engaged to Angus, he blanched.
He knew his lies wouldn't stand up to my scrutiny. I threatened to
expose him to the village. That scared him. I could see it in his eyes.
He begged me not to and promised that he'd tell me everything, just
not anywhere we could be overheard. We agreed he'd come here
this morning. Obviously, he never arrived."

This stretched credulity. Why would she agree to wait until the
following day to learn what had become of the man she loved? If it
were me, I would've insisted on hearing everything at once. They

could have walked a short distance from the village and had plenty of privacy.

"So you returned to the ceilidh and pretended everything was fine?" I asked.

"No, I went home. I had no desire to return to the ceilidh."

"What time was this?"

"It was after eleven o'clock, but before midnight."

"Did you see anyone on your way home?"

"No. I'm fairly certain most of the village was at the hall half the night. I could hear the music from my house."

"You didn't leave again until this morning?"

"I haven't left yet this morning," she said. "I've been waiting for the gamekeeper and passed the time finishing unpacking my belongings."

Her home was remarkably neat for someone who had only just moved in. Dr. Harris did not seem the sort of person who had much patience for upheaval. She was all efficiency and competence, but I didn't quite trust her.

"If what you claim about the gamekeeper is correct—and I will find a way to prove or disprove it—it seems to me that he would have a more viable motive for committing violence against you than you would against him. Have you evidence for what you're saying?"

"Angus has a dark red birthmark just below the left shoulder blade. He always said it was the shape of Corsica. It won't be present on the gamekeeper's body. I never saw it, but Dr. Cameron might re-member it. He was already in practice here when Angus was born."

Because I knew Dr. Cameron was preparing for the body to be delivered to him, I suggested we go straight to the surgery. Dr. Harris led me to the high street, which contained a grocer, a butcher, a chemist, a pub, and the doctor's surgery. Dr. Cameron was inside, about to start the postmortem. He walked to his colleague and laid a gentle hand on her arm. "I hope this doesn't put you off Cairnfarn. I promise we're not a particularly violent lot."

"I shan't hold it against the place," Dr. Harris said. "It does, however, raise some questions of a personal nature for me." She gave a concise summary of everything she'd told me about her fiancé and Mr. Sinclair. Dr. Cameron listened closely, nodding as she spoke and making sympathetic noises at all the right moments. His concern was sincere. When she finished, he paused for a moment, as if to consider all that he'd heard. He then went to his office and returned with a file.

"I made note of Angus's birthmark the day I delivered him," he said. "This is all most alarming, Dr. Harris. You're quite certain it couldn't all be some bizarre misunderstanding?"

"I don't see how," she said. "I'll admit that part of the reason I applied for the position here was to be in a place that Angus had once lived. I can't claim he had a soft spot for it, but he spoke fondly of many of the people he knew here. I hoped I might possibly learn something from them that would lead me to him. It's foolish and embarrassing, not to mention unprofessional."

"I've heard many stupider reasons for choosing a place to practice," Dr. Cameron said, "and it doesn't affect your professionalism in the slightest. Now, to the matter at hand. It shall be simple enough to find out the truth about the gamekeeper's identity. None of us in Cairnfarn had seen the lad since he was eleven, so it's useless to claim we'd recognize him. Still, that striking shade of red hair and his familiarity with every detail of the Sinclair family's story are hard to ignore. I'm not suggesting you're lying, only that we don't know which Angus Sinclair—the duke's gamekeeper or your fiancé—was who he claimed. It's time we found out."

He drew the sheet back from the body and lifted it by the shoulders, exposing the back. There was no birthmark.

I left the doctors and started back toward the castle. When I arrived, I found Colin and we immediately went to the nursery to check on the boys. They were faring as well as could be expected, with Henry struggling the most. He was far more sensitive than he liked to let on. Colin sat with him for a long time, quietly reassuring him that his reaction to seeing the gamekeeper's body did not in any way mean he lacked courage.

"Perhaps you're right," Henry said, perking up. "After all, I'm the only one of the three of us who's willing to take care of Cedric. Richard and Tom are so afraid of him they won't even go into his enclosure in the menagerie."

"You shouldn't be going into his enclosure either," I said. "It's not safe."

"Cedric would never hurt me."

I frowned. "Cedric is a wild animal."

"He knows I'm the one who made it possible for him to visit Egypt and for that, he will be forever grateful. I've earned his trust."

"Crocodiles don't subscribe to the concept of trust," I said. "Stay out of his enclosure."

Jeremy looked less ill that evening, but he was still gloomy. "I say, Em, if I thought you'd bring murder to Cairnfarn I would never have invited you to come."

"You can hardly blame me for what happened," I said.

"You and Hargreaves are the only individuals I know who have people dropping dead wherever they go. No one ever got murdered here until you arrived. What other conclusion am I to draw?"

I scowled at him and then grinned. "Perhaps you should be keeping a closer watch on your employees so they don't fall victim to marauding criminals."

"Good heavens, you don't think I've got marauding criminals on the loose?"

"Don't be ridiculous," I said. "I was only poking fun at you."

"Poor Sinclair, or whatever his name was. It's devastating. I was excessively fond of him, you know. There's something very appealing about his story. Fleeing a life he despised but then not being too proud to return when he realized he'd made an unsatisfactory choice."

"Surely it was hard to believe," Colin said. "One doesn't abandon a thriving law practice in favor of working as a gamekeeper. It's no wonder he turned out to be a fraud."

Jeremy huffed. "I'm telling you, I recognized the man. That hair is unmistakable."

"There's more than one man in Scotland with hair the color of fire," Colin said. "What did he say to you when he turned up in Cairnfarn?"

"He claimed that he'd grown disillusioned with the professional life, but I got the sense that he'd had some sort of trouble," Jeremy said. "Gambling debts, it sounded like. Seemed as if he'd paid them off, but was left disgraced and with virtually no money. He wanted a fresh start and I was happy to give him one."

"When was this?" I asked.

"A bit over a year ago. You can check my steward's records if you want the precise date."

"Was any of his behavior unusual after you took him on?" I asked.

"Not in the slightest," Jeremy said. "I admit I'm not the most organized landowner, but I do know what it takes to manage an estate and I've always been close to my gamekeepers. They're essential to keep a place running in good order. Can't have poachers or bad land practices or everything would go to the devil in an instant."

"Had the real Sinclair any prior relevant experience?" Colin asked.

"I knew that as a boy he'd spent a great deal of time with the bloke who was then the castle's gamekeeper. Sinclair hated farming, despised sheep, and Kincaid, who'd been on the estate since the dawn of time, was no friend of Sinclair's father. He was all too happy to take the lad under his wing and teach him something other than a despised occupation. I believed that gave him enough knowledge to do the job."

"And the man who claimed to be Angus Sinclair fulfilled his duties with no issues?" Colin asked.

"Yes," Jeremy said. "He was an ideal member of the staff, the sort who requires no interference. Just what I like. Now, though, I'm bound to have a rebellion on my hands. Who wants to work in a household where people get murdered? It's a bloody—forgive me, Em—nightmare. Of course the worst of it is the poor man, whoever he was. He didn't deserve to die. I'm gutted, I tell you. What am I to do now? I'm the duke. Everyone here thinks I'm capable of fixing any problem, yet look what I let happen."

"Jeremy, no one who has even the barest acquaintance with you—be it friend, servant, or foe—would ever think you capable of fixing even the smallest problem," I said. "Furthermore, you didn't let this happen. You weren't negligent. You did nothing wrong. Colin and I are here and will take care of it all. I've wired the police in Inverness and picked up their reply on my way out of the village. They're sending up a detective posthaste."

"Police?" Jeremy looked at me with an expression of exquisite disdain. "Em, how could you? That's the last thing I need! Can you imagine the scandal? My mother will never forgive me."

"Scandal, indeed," I said. "Just the sort of thing to reduce your appeal on the marriage market. It ought to buy you at least six months of keeping the desperate mothers of desperate daughters at bay."

His eyes brightened. "You raise an excellent point. Still, I don't like it, even though I accept it must be done. I won't stand in your way. Anything you need, I'll make sure you have it."

6

Tansy
1676

It started innocently enough. That is, if there's any reasonable way of claiming theft to be innocent. As far as Rossalyn and I were concerned, what we did wasn't stealing. Technically, the books were hers; at least they should have been. I can't claim an expertise in the intricacies of Scottish law. Regardless, she had every right to take them. But I'm getting ahead of myself.

Rossalyn's father wasn't the sort of man in a position to provide his daughter with a dowry, but her Scandinavian good looks kept her future husband from caring about that. She married above her station. I'd argue he did as well, even if he was a laird and possessed a castle. Rossalyn was sharp. Engaging. Witty. Not to mention more refined than most of the other women I met in the Highlands. I don't mean to imply they were bumpkins; they were nothing of the sort. It was only that they'd never been exposed to the finer things one finds in a city, even one like Inverness. I'd never been there, but nothing

Rossalyn told me about it made me believe it could measure up to Edinburgh, let alone Tunis. The day of her marriage her father presented her with a set of books. Among them were *Ane Godlie Dream*, written by Elizabeth Melville, Samuel Daniel's *The Collection of the History of England*, a Bible, something called *Triumphs of Love, Chastitie, Death* by Anna Hume, and a book of plays written in verse that Rossalyn told me an actor friend of her father's gave him as a gift.

The day Ewan evicted his stepmother from the castle, he told her she could take all her personal possessions, which he went on to explain didn't include any jewelry except for the gold posy ring her husband had given her on their wedding day. The rest, the new laird insisted, belonged to the family. He refused to let Rossalyn stay while I packed, instead dragged her out of the castle, flung her onto the wet ground, and left her there waiting—not even allowing her to stand—as I gathered our belongings with two of his men standing over me, hands on their swords. It was unnerving and put me in a distressed state of mind that caused me to altogether forget about the books. They were in the castle's library, not in Rossalyn's rooms; anything I didn't see, I didn't consider.

We noticed the books' absence as soon as we started to settle into the cottage. The first few days were chaotic, both in a practical way and an emotional one. We weren't used to living in such close quarters or cooking for ourselves. We spent half a day speculating as to how one washed one's clothes. I had a general idea, but Rossalyn found the whole prospect daunting. I decided we ought to rescue the garden from its current state of disrepair. We could plant vegetables and herbs. I wondered if there was a way to get seeds for the spices that had seasoned the foods I'd grown up with: turmeric, cumin, mint, coriander, and *Corchorus olitorius,* from which came mloukhia.

Thinking about the flavors caused me to slip into a deep, hopeless melancholy that kept me from realizing we didn't have the books.

It was raining inconceivably hard. Although I far preferred the warm climate of Tunisia, I admit to finding the cold Scottish rain fascinating. I'd seen nothing of the sort before. Silver and glistening, with fog that looked like fine lace. To be fair, the fascination faded rapidly. From then, I recognized it as a nuisance. Now that we were in the cottage and doing everything without the assistance of a household staff, it became a dreaded obstacle. On this particular day, I'd trudged through the village to buy some chickens from a farmer's wife. We needed their eggs. I was drenched within seconds of leaving the cottage, even wetter when I returned home, and was still exceedingly damp that evening, when, after we'd dined, we sat in front of the fire.

"The books," Rossalyn said and then sighed. "We didn't bring the books with us from the castle. Tonight would be the perfect time to read aloud, wouldn't it? Something diverting, from the book of plays. Nothing serious or religious."

"They belong to you," I said, "so I'm sure Ewan won't object to you going back for them. He's not the sort likely to miss them." This was an understatement. Although I knew he was capable of reading, he possessed neither the intellect nor the inclination to spend much time doing it. The idea that it might be a pleasant way to occupy one's leisure time would be entirely beyond his comprehension.

"Ewan despises me. The fact that I want them will be enough for him to keep them from me."

She was probably right about that. I couldn't think when I'd encountered a more spiteful individual. Once, when a messenger arrived on a snowy night, he refused to allow the man to wait inside while he penned his reply, a reply he didn't bother to write until the next morning. The messenger spent an uncomfortable night in the barn. "Is there no one else in the household still sympathetic to you?" I asked. "Some of the maids were very fond of you."

"I can hardly ask them to steal for me. It would be too great a risk." She pursed her lips. "We could slip in and take them ourselves."

"Ewan would go no easier on us as thieves than his servants."

"That's true, but we wouldn't get caught. I know every inch of the castle," she said. "If we timed it just right, we could be in and out before anyone noticed."

"This is not a good idea."

"I wouldn't require anything of you except to act as a lookout. If we are found, I'll take the blame."

For an intelligent woman, her naïveté could be staggering. If we were caught, of course the former Moorish slave would take the blame, not the gentle lady, no matter how much the new laird despised her. I liked Rossalyn; I did. I'd almost started to believe that our friendship would grow now that we were out of the castle. I still believed it might, but not if she insisted on putting me in such a dubious position.

"I won't do it," I said, my voice firm. "I don't like to disappoint you, but it's too great a risk. I appreciate your willingness to take the blame, but if we were caught, it wouldn't be you in charge of deciding who was responsible. You'd bear a share of the laird's anger, but I could face something far worse. Crimes against property are taken seriously by the Crown. Some thieves face execution."

"I'd never allow that to happen."

"You wouldn't be in charge."

"Ewan's awful, but he's not a monster—"

I interrupted her. "I can't place my life in the hands of someone

38

you admit is awful. I will, however, offer an alternative way to get the books without putting ourselves in danger. You could apply to the housekeeper. Tell her you left a few things behind and that you'd like to collect them when it's convenient for her. There are numerous trinkets in the library that are of little value. Things the laird would have no interest in. You claim a few of them and while we're collecting them, we surreptitiously take the books, too."

"It might work." She sounded skeptical.

"We'll time it just right, as you said before, and go to the castle when the laird isn't there. I can think of three things that aren't empirically valuable we can tell her you want: a small wooden box, a polished rock your husband sometimes used to hold down papers, and a roughly carved statue of religious nature."

"I don't recall any such statue."

"It's an animal of some sort, rather lumpy looking."

"Then it's not religious. I think I know the one you mean. It's a horse." She looked into my eyes, held my gaze, and sighed. "We'll try it your way. I just hope it works."

She spoke as if she was giving permission to follow my plan. She assumed she still had authority over me. Time can be a great equalizer, but I wasn't sure it could correct the imbalances between us.

Three days later, the new laird was going out for a hunt. It was time for us to strike.

7

1905

The next morning, Colin and I decided he would search the gamekeeper's cottage while Jeremy and I called on the villagers, ostensi-
bly to offer support in this difficult time, but really to learn whatever
we could from them in the guise of pleasant conversation. The pace
we set en route to the village could best be described as leisurely, although the connotation of the word gives the entirely wrong impression. We were making our way through stunning countryside, but
this was no pleasant stroll. I could sense that my friend was struggling. He was grieving and dreaded speaking to anyone about the
murder. As if the environs understood, dark clouds rolled into the
sky, and the breeze stiffened.

"It's appalling, Em. Appalling," he said. "What good is being a
duke if one has to deal with things like this?"

"Who better to deal with them?" I asked. "I believe the original idea was to bestow dukedoms on individuals the monarch believed capable of rising to any occasion, no matter how daunting."

"That probably worked during the Middle Ages, but we're far from that now. I'd prefer not to be embroiled in any of this."

I decided this was not the time to deliver a lecture on the manner in which a hereditary aristocracy works. "No one wants to be embroiled in any of this, least of all the murdered man."

"Forgive me," he said. "I don't mean to sound awful, but I'm wholly out of my depth, incapable and useless. Yet at the same time, I'm somehow responsible for it all. If I hadn't hired him, he'd still be alive."

I stopped walking, just for a moment, and looked at him. His blue eyes were dull. He'd pulled off his hat; his sandy hair was wind-blown and disheveled. "Do you believe that?"

"Of course I do." He plopped the hat back on his head.

I looped my arm through his. "It's not your fault, and I will do everything I can to ensure justice is served."

"That's all I want, Em. It's the first time in my life I can't embrace feeling useless. It's unbearable."

When we reached the village, we decided to approach our task in a straightforward, orderly fashion. We would visit each house and place of business as we passed them on the street. Cairnfarn was well laid out, something that was no accident. Jeremy's uncle had a long-running feud with the sixth Duke of Devonshire. In the late 1830s, the duke grew disgusted with seeing village buildings from his windows in Chatsworth, so he ordered the village moved. Uncle Albion considered this outrageous; the audacity of uprooting scores of hardworking people so that His Grace needn't look at them rankled him. In response, he ordered his own village moved, and replanned Cairnfarn so that it would be in full view from the windows of his study in the castle. The irony that both sets of villagers were horribly inconvenienced was lost on him. He felt it proved he was a man of the people. Still, everyone agreed the new Cairnfarn was beautiful. The houses, built one up against the next, were finished with rough-textured harling—lime mixed with gravel—and brightly painted in shades of gingery ocher, yellow, white, and green. A few were a vivid cobalt blue. The village church, originally built in the fourteenth century, had been moved stone by stone to the top of a hill that offered spectacular views of the loch and the surrounding mountains. Behind it was a large field of heather.

Before long, I'd had eleven cups of tea, six biscuits, a scone, and had heard nothing of any use. I felt overstuffed and rather ill. It started to rain, but we pushed on, heading further afield, to the crofts outside of the village proper. It was only on our way back, when we ran into Callum Fletcher, a day laborer with black hair, dark eyes, and a permanent scowl etched on his face, that our fortunes started to change.

"That man was no saint, you know," he said, standing on the side of the road. "Forgive me, Your Grace, if I'm speaking out of turn, but I'm a man who tells the truth. I dinnae claim he deserved to die, only that it didnae come as much of a shock, did it?"

I am always skeptical of individuals who feel the need to characterize themselves as truthful. Most such claims were nothing more than protesting too much. "He was not much appreciated in the village?" I asked.

"Aye, though that's a prissy way to put it. He didnae belong here and he should've stayed away. I never liked him. Never liked the real Angus Sinclair, either, not even when we were wee lads. I supposed the imposter reminded me of him. Now dinnae go thinking that means I killed him. I'm just being honest, that's all. As I said, that's my way. I've no fondness for smug buggers."

I was shocked by his language. My face must have shown it; he laughed.

"Offended you, have I? I'm sorry about that." He turned from me to Jeremy, deep lines marking his forehead as worry crept into his eyes. "Dinnae hold it against me, Your Grace. I'm a hard worker, but a man of no education or refinement. I dinnae do well in polite company. I suppose it's why you gave that man the job as gamekeeper instead of me, even though he was an outsider."

Jeremy pulled himself up to his full height and crossed his arms. I hesitate to admit it, but he looked almost ducal. "There's more than a little truth to your words, some of them, at least. I know you're a good man, Fletcher. You're reliable, and, as you say, you work hard. Sometimes, however, those things aren't enough. Manners do matter. You've always seemed to set a store in being deliberately provoking, which is not a quality I seek out when employing members of my household. Were you to reform, we might be having an altogether different conversation. It can't have escaped your notice that I'm once again in need of a gamekeeper."

"Well, Your Grace, I dinnae ken there's much I can do to change the way I was made."

"Now you're talking rubbish," Jeremy said. "I've seen the other side of you. I know you're good to the children in the village. I know that, even though she's old and ornery, you visit Mrs. Glendinning because you can see that she's lonely. I know you're the one who pulls the weeds in the churchyard when you think no one's looking. All of which means reform isn't beyond your reach. I shan't mention it again. You know where I stand on the matter."

Both men were silent after this. I gave them a moment and then turned to Mr. Fletcher. "Did you see the gamekeeper leave the hall on the night of the ceilidh?"

"I saw him go outside twice: first with Maisie and later with the new doctor," Mr. Fletcher said. "I saw him dancing with Maisie a little while after he came back the second time."

"You're certain this was after he went out with Dr. Harris?" I asked.

"Yes. I was standing near the door when they left and was still there when he came back alone. Are you asking because you think the doctor killed him? I wouldnae have thought she'd have the strength."

"How do you know the crime required strength?" I asked.

"Everyone's been talking about it. My brother saw them bring the body into Dr. Cameron's surgery. Said there was blood all over the sheet wrapping it. Butchery sounds to me like something that requires strength. It was a man's doing, there's no question of that."

I wasn't ready to agree, although his conclusion did seem likely. "How long was the gamekeeper outside with Dr. Harris?"

"Long enough for me to drink two whiskies," Mr. Fletcher said. "Which I confess isnae a great deal of time. No more than half an hour, probably not even that. Twenty minutes, more like."

"You're certain?"

"As certain as I can be. He came in and danced with Maisie. They stood up together three times. Anyone would notice and remember that."

"Was there an understanding between them?" I asked.

Mr. Fletcher laughed again. "People like us dinnae have understandings, madam. When we want to get married, we get married. The man haedne married Maisie, which suggests he didnae want to, although I'll admit to having wondered."

His voice had softened, just a bit. I suspected he was rather sweet on Maisie. "What do you think Maisie wanted?"

"He's the sort of braw man the girls like, but I've never known what goes on in that lass's head and I never will. No point trying to figure it out. She's a nightmare, but a bloody sweet one." He drew in a deep breath. "I suppose that's an example of the sort of thing I ought not say."

"I won't object in the current context," I said. "How many times did you stand up with Maisie at the ceilidh?"

"Four." He grinned. "Once more than that bugger did. Apologies, Your Grace."

"You should apologize to Lady Emily."

"It's quite all right," I said. Mr. Fletcher looked directly at me every time he spoke in a manner unsuitable for mixed company. He wanted to get a rise out of me; I wouldn't satisfy him. "Did you notice anything at all during the course of the evening that seemed unusual?"

"A ceilidh's a ceilidh," he said. "They're all more or less the same, minus the details, at least in Cairnfarn. People drink. Tell stories. Recite poems. Play music. Dance."

"It's the details that interest me," I said. "Did anyone seem out of sorts or preoccupied?"

"Madam, with the amount of spirits flowing, no one had a right to be out of sorts. Thinking on it, though, Maisie wasn't her usual bright self. Couldnae tell you why. She's got those changeable emotions, doesnae she? More unpredictable than a Highland storm."

"And less congenial than them, too, when she's in a mood," Jeremy said. "My footmen are half terrified of her."

"Did you ask what was troubling her?" I asked.

"No, madam, I didnae," Mr. Fletcher said. "If I had, she might have told me and then I'd feel obligated to fix it. I dinnae need that kind of trouble, no matter how pretty she is. Figured I'd wait it out till her mood changed again. Usually doesnae take more than a few hours."

"And did it change?" I asked.

"Not before the end of the dancing," he said. "I went home soon after that. Had an early morning and didnae think staying out half the night getting blootered with the lads would've improved my outlook on the day."

"A wise decision, Fletcher," Jeremy said. It was something, watching him with his tenant. He was eminently capable of playing duke when he needed to. I couldn't imagine any other circumstance in which he'd come down against a late night with the lads. "Is there anything else we should know about the ceilidh?"

"Only that we all appreciated you putting it on for us, Your Grace. I'm sorry it ended so badly. I didnae like the gamekeeper, but I dinnae like murder either, especially when it comes on the heels of a person like Your Grace doing something nice and generous."

"I'm glad it was an enjoyable evening," Jeremy said. His voice faltered a little. "Where are you working today?"

"The grocer has a leak in his roof. When that's done, I'll be on to Mrs. Glendinning's. She insists her fire is smoking, but it's not. She'll have me in, admit there's nothing wrong, and force me to eat bread and cheese with that terrible marmalade of hers. Family recipe, they say."

"She mentioned the smoke when we spoke to her earlier today, but we saw no sign of it," Jeremy said. "You're kind to indulge her."

He shrugged. "It doesnae take much and seems to make her happy. Easier than most tasks I face. I remember my grandfather telling me stories when I was a wee lad about the grief her grandmother caused him when he was a young man, always badgering him to do something or the other for her. It seems there's always been a troublesome Glendinning in Cairnfarn. Probably because they insist on marrying their cousins." He smiled—a wide, pleasant smile that revealed a set of bright but crooked teeth—and winked. We thanked him and let him get back on his way.

"He's an interesting case," I said.

"You don't know the half of it," Jeremy said. "I believe that, on balance, he's a decent man, but he's quick to anger and slow to forgive. He'd be happier if he'd stop trying to stir up trouble every-where. It's as if he'd rather instigate it himself than worry about waiting for it to catch him unaware."

It was late in the afternoon by the time we'd finished speaking to the villagers. All, that is, with the exception of an herbalist who was away from Cairnfarn for the afternoon and the Pringles. I hated to have to question them—Mrs. Pringle in particular—given what they were going through, but it had to be done. When we reached the vicarage, a lively young woman answered the door. Lively, but utterly befuddled.

"Oh, Your Grace, what an honor to see you," she said, giving a little curtsy. "You know it's ever so long since you've called. I cannae remember the last time you were here. Mrs. Pringle would've had me make that special cake you like and it's been an age since I've done that, which means it's an age since you've come round." She turned to me. "It requires ginger, you see, which we dinnae always have on hand. I've not seen you in the village before. Are you walk-ing out with His Grace?"

Jeremy's eyes looked ready to pop out of his head. "No, Effie, she's not walking out with me. Heavens! This is Lady Emily Har-greaves. We've been dear friends since childhood and she's—" He stopped, looked to the sky, took a deep breath, and then continued. "Is the vicar in?"

"Of course, Your Grace," she said. "Come right inside and I'll fetch him straightaway. I'm afraid I dinnae have the cake you like— what with the ginger situation—but there might be some biscuits left, although the truth is—I must admit it to you, Your Grace, it wouldnae be kind not to—they didnae turn out all too well. Taste a bit soapy, though I can't imagine why." She led us into a small, comfortable room overlooking a neat garden. The furniture was decidedly old-fashioned, the sort popular in the middle of Queen Victoria's reign, with its surfaces covered by a jumbled assortment of knickknacks and lace doilies. An extraordinary collection of colorful butterflies hung on the walls in frames, and a small bookcase was filled mainly with volumes of sermons. Only the bottom shelf showed promise, holding a handful of novels and travel memoirs. I wondered if they belonged to Mrs. Pringle. On a table in front of the settee was a beautifully carved wooden box of a quality higher than any of the other objects on display.

Jeremy dropped himself onto a chair once Effie had gone to fetch the vicar. "She's utterly incompetent, but Caroline doesn't have the heart to get rid of her. Who else would give the girl a position? Although she's privately confessed to me she's less concerned about that than having to train someone new. She's learned how to deal with Effie's foibles. The devil you know and all that." He rose when Mr. Pringle entered the room.

The vicar was considerably older than his wife, but showed signs of having been a decent-looking man in his youth. Not handsome, certainly, but not unpleasant. His eyes were a bit too close together, and what little hair he had left he combed forward in an awkward attempt to cover his scalp. Yet he moved with an almost youthful agility and had just the sort of voice one hopes for in a man of God: resonant, deep, and authoritative.

"Sorry to disturb, Pringle, with everything your wife's going through," Jeremy said, shaking the man's hand. "Terrible business, all of it. If you need anything . . ."

"Aye, it's a great disappointment," Mr. Pringle said, "but we will come to terms with it. There's no way on but forward."

"Quite, quite," Jeremy said.

"Shall I have Effie bring tea?"

"No!" I responded rather more sharply than I'd intended. "Forgive me, it's only that we've talked to nearly everyone in the village today and I've had more tea than I'd thought it was possible to consume."

"Wouldn't be the thing to turn down hospitality, though, would it?" The vicar smiled. "Not when you've got an agenda to fulfill. Believe me, I understand all too well. I expected you'd call round, not only to see my wife but to ask me about the ceilidh, so I've been giving the matter a great deal of thought. Presumably, the things that will prove most useful are those that didn't ordinarily occur at such events, and there is only one that stands out in my mind. It may not signify, but the punch was notably stronger than it ought to have been. A small point, perhaps, and hardly anything to get upset about, but I am absolutely certain it wasn't like that at the beginning of the evening. My wife made it—she found the recipe a year or so ago—and has used it every time since, a version of Glasgow punch. It turned out we were a bit short on rum. We joked about how it would make for a less ribald occasion than a usual Cairnfarn ceilidh."

"Was more rum added later?" I asked. "Maybe someone else in the village had some and brought it for her?"

"No, no, there's not a household in Cairnfarn but ours that would have any," Mr. Pringle said. "Caroline orders it specially. Yet, clearly, late in the evening, someone put something in it. Probably noticed it was on the weaker side and added some whisky, which had a deleterious effect on the flavor. Hardly nefarious, but again, out of the ordinary."

I was glad I'd only tasted it before the whisky was added. "What about the villagers?" I asked. "Was anyone out of sorts or behaving unusually?"

"We're a fairly consistent lot in Cairnfarn," the vicar said. "Not boring, mind you, but implacable. Maisie Drummond flirts with every man she lays eyes on, Dr. Cameron blossoms at having an audience for his stories, Mrs. Glendinning sits and passes silent judgment on those she views as having too good a time, which you can take as everyone else present. Dr. Harris's arrival did have the effect of keeping us all on our best behavior. Perhaps that's not quite right." He paused for a moment and sat very still, a look of deep contemplation on his face.

"How would you describe it, then?" I asked after enough time had passed that I'd started to wonder if he'd lost his train of thought.

"It's difficult to describe," he said. "They were rather guarded. Generally, at a ceilidh, people let themselves go a bit, if you know what I mean. They indulge in some drink, some dancing, and say whatever comes to mind. It serves almost as a cleansing, I've observed, allowing one to purge oneself of bad feelings, anxieties, that sort of thing. Some might view it as a primitive sort of ritual, dismissing it as a thing suited only to rural savages, but I'd argue we all benefit from a good catharsis. Very healthy indeed."

"And that was lacking last night?" I asked.

"Yes, I'm afraid so." He turned to Jeremy. "I'm confident—

absolutely confident—that Dr. Harris will eventually be a valued member of the community, but we shall have to be rather more patient waiting for that day to come than perhaps we'd like. Change can be difficult, and there aren't many left in the village who re-member a doctor other than William Cameron. I'm grateful he's not leaving altogether. You are generous to have offered him a cot-tage on the castle grounds. Keeping him nearby will help ease the transition."

"It's nothing, really," Jeremy said. "One takes care of those who have served so ably." Once again, he sounded like a duke. Truly, it was a sight to behold. Astonishing.

"I hope you don't object to me mentioning it, but your uncle would be proud of you," Mr. Pringle said. "You're the sort of duke he liked. I half expected him to marry simply to ensure his brother didn't inherit. Not much warmth between him and your father, was there?"

"I should say not." Jeremy squirmed ever so slightly in his seat.

"That's families for you," Mr. Pringle said. "We squabble the most with those we care about deeply. They put on a good show, but I know they loved each other very much."

"Right, well, of course, there's that," Jeremy said, sounding more like his usual, bumbling self.

"Is there anything further you can to tell us about the ceilidh?" I asked.

"I'm afraid not," Mr. Pringle said. "I do wish I could be more useful. If something else occurs to me, or if I hear of anything—you know what village gossip is like—I'll let you know straightaway."

"I do appreciate it," I said. "Now, if your wife doesn't object, I'd very much like to look in and see how's she's doing."

"She'd be most grateful, Lady Emily, more than you can imag-ine," the vicar said. "I'll take you to her."

We stepped into the corridor, where Effie was standing very close to the door, making no effort at disguising the fact that she'd been listening. She tugged on my arm. "When you're finished with my mistress, could I have a wee word with you? There are things I noticed at the ceilidh that others might have overlooked. I'm very observing. Is that the right word? It doesnae sound like it. Observic. Observy. What is it?"

"Observant," I said, smiling. "I'll come find you when I'm done."

"I'm likely to be in the kitchen as there's supper to prepare. You're not staying, are you? It's only that I was doing chops and there are just the two of them. It's possible Mrs. Pringle won't want to eat as she's feeling poorly, so I could cut hers in half for you and His Grace. Of course, really, His Grace should have a whole one, but Mr. Pringle needs it or he'll never be able to keep up his strength, and you know that if a vicar—"

"Thank you, Effie," Mr. Pringle said. "It will just be Mrs. Pringle and myself for dinner."

"Right, then I suppose there's no need to slice either of the chops in half, is there?"

"Correct," Mr. Pringle said.

"I'm off to the kitchen, then, to start cooking."

"Oh, there's no need to rush." A flash of frustration crossed the vicar's face. "We won't be eating for hours."

"I could slow roast the chops," Effie said. "Yes, that's what I'll do. Thank you for the suggestion." She walked away, talking to herself.

The vicar, a look of despair on his face, watched her go, and then led me up the stairs. When we reached the top, he tapped softly on the bedroom door before cracking it open. He popped his head inside. "Caroline, darling, Lady Emily is here—" He stopped, pushed

52

the door open the rest of the way, and rushed to his wife's bedside. Her face was ghastly pale and covered with sweat, her head rolling from side to side. Mr. Pringle turned to me. "Would you be so kind as to fetch the doctor? Something isn't right."

8

Tansy
1676

Late on the evening before the scheduled hunt, I carried a message to the castle. The moon was nothing but a sliver, so my way was lit only by a tin lantern, whose light was barely adequate to cut through the increasingly thick fog that was settling into the valley. I pulled my cloak tight around me and wondered if the strange sound I was hearing in the distance was wolves. I wasn't sure if there were any of the creatures left near Cairnfarn, but now was not the time to encounter any lingering stragglers. The first week after I'd arrived at the castle, Duncan's ghillie told me a horrifying tale about how they liked to dig up bodies from the cemetery in the churchyard. He said if you couldn't afford a coffin fashioned from heavy stone, you were doomed to have your corpse torn apart by the beasts. It was such a problem that the king ordered his subjects to hunt them three times a year. This sort of thing was something I'd never had to worry about in Tunis.

I heard what could have been furry footsteps and started walking more quickly. Ordinarily, I wouldn't have chosen to leave the village after dark, but in this case, Rossalyn and I had agreed it was essential. We wanted to catch the staff late in the day, when they were most likely to be tired and, as a result, unlikely to think much about the request we planned to make. When, at last, I arrived at the castle, the maid who opened the door told me the housekeeper had already retired to her room. I insisted that I couldn't leave until I'd received a response.

"You know how the gentry can be," I said, realizing that Rossalyn might no longer technically be included among the gentry. I didn't suppose it mattered. "They don't like to wait, and Lady Mac-Allister is particularly impatient tonight."

The girl let me in. I sat at the long table in the servants' hall while she took the note to the housekeeper. Only a few minutes passed before she returned. "I'm to instruct you that Lady Mac-Allister is welcome to come tomorrow as she requested, but says that as there's to be a hunt that day, to please not arrive until after they've all left."

"Of course," I said. "I know how chaotic it will be. Thank you so very much for helping me. It's greatly appreciated." Excessive kindness proving a generally useful weapon, I gave her a small tin of biscuits Cora had brought us the day before. None that I'd yet baked were fit for human consumption, although my latest batch was a significant improvement from my first. Biscuits weren't, perhaps, the best gift—the castle's cook could rustle up countless sweet treats— but it was all I had at my disposal.

So far, our plan was working. Rossalyn and I were counting on the chaos caused by the hunt to act as our able assistant and it appeared to be doing its job.

* * *

The next morning, we set off for the castle earlier than perhaps was wise. I warned my friend that we should wait, but she wasn't having it.

"I can't resist taking a peek at what they're all up to," she said. We'd crept along the shore of the loch until we were close enough to watch the commotion as the party mounted their horses and prepared to set off in search of stag. Crouching behind a large tree, Rossalyn was confident we couldn't be seen. I didn't share her belief, but I detected no sign of anyone spotting us, although I did keep thinking the new laird was looking in our direction. We waited a few minutes after they departed in a storm of hoofbeats before going inside, presenting ourselves at the servants' entrance instead of the front. This troubled Rossalyn, but I insisted.

Once admitted, we sought out the housekeeper, thanked her for allowing us to collect the items we named—we stressed how insignificant they were—and told her we'd be out of the way as soon as possible.

"I checked with the laird and he had only one objection. He won't let go of the statue of the horse," she said. "It's a particular favorite of his."

"I hadn't realized," Rossalyn said, "but given that's the case, I wouldn't dream of taking it."

We wound through the back corridors to the main living space of the castle and made our way to the library. Although most of the castle's residents had gone on the hunt, some had stayed behind. We were careful to avoid them. It wasn't all that difficult; none of them were the sort of people likely to be interested in reading. I grabbed the objects the housekeeper had said we could take—the small wooden box and the rock—and sat them next to each other on a long table near the massive stone fireplace. Rossalyn found the books, wrapped them in a piece of waxed canvas, and secured it with twine. She then walked to one of the windows on the back wall, opened it, and gingerly lowered the package to the ground outside.

This was only possible because the library was in the new section of the building, not the old tower house, which had walls six feet thick and windows like slits, useful only to someone shooting an arrow. Rossalyn's husband had constructed two new wings extending from the sides. They were far more civilized than the medieval structure.

That done, I went in search of the housekeeper, asking her to come and see what we proposed to take. "We just want to be certain nothing's out of order," I said. She nodded and accompanied me back to the library, but I could see she was distracted, rattling off orders to nearly every servant we passed on our way in preparation for the return of the hunters.

"We do miss you, milady," she said to Rossalyn while I packed the objects into a basket. They exchanged pleasantries for a few minutes. I hovered close to the window, wanting to be sure no one came for—or noticed—the bundle on the ground below it. Fortunately, all proceeded without incident.

We thanked the housekeeper again. Rossalyn made to leave through the servants' entrance, but the housekeeper insisted she use the main door. After we said our goodbyes, we started on the path toward the village, detouring to collect the parcel of books, which Rossalyn hid beneath her heavy cloak.

When, after what I would have sworn was a seven-hundred-and-sixty-eight-mile walk back to the village—it was a little over two and a half miles—we made a point of strolling along the street in as casual a manner as possible, just in case anyone was looking out their window and noticed us. Once inside our cottage, however, we exploded with emotions: relief and excitement.

"It was rather thrilling," Rossalyn said, "even if we didn't take the covert approach I initially favored."

"It appears to have worked." I felt unexpectedly buoyed by the experience. We were both more than a little giddy. Rain started to fall and the temperature dropped so quickly that I wondered if it was going to snow, even though it ought to have been far too early in the year for that to happen. Regardless, the hunting party would be drenched and frozen. That gave me a sublime sense of satisfaction.

I made a stew of sorts that evening. Mutton would never be my favorite, but it was cheap and plentiful in Cairnfarn. Wine would have improved the flavor, but was far too dear for us. We made do, though, and enjoyed our repast. When we'd finished eating and cleaned the dishes and the floor around the hearth—Rossalyn generally caused a great mess when she helped with cooking; in her hands, even stirring took on the appearance of an act of violence—I suggested that we read something aloud.

Rossalyn threw back her head and let out a long, low moan. "If only we could, but we don't have any books. I can't imagine how we managed to leave them at the castle. I'm sure Ewan has no use for them. Perhaps I should write him a note and ask if he'd return them to me."

I have no doubt that the expression on my face made it clear I was wondering if she'd become unhinged. Her voice was too loud and there was something almost hysterical in her eyes. I didn't know what to say. We'd left the bundle of books on a small table near our front window; it was still there. Rossalyn hadn't yet opened it. I looked at her, then at the bundle, then back at her, unsure what to do.

Just then, someone pounded on the door, with such force I'm

surprised the entire cottage didn't start shaking. My muscles tensed; it felt as if my body were made from lead. Another knock came, and another. I forced myself to move and opened the door to reveal Ewan MacAllister, rage painted over his face, and six angry Highlanders armed to the teeth.

9

1905

Mrs. Pringle looked so ill, I fairly flew down the stairs and into the sitting room, where Jeremy was suspiciously eyeing a plate of biscuits on the table next to him. I explained what had happened and he rushed off to fetch the doctor. That done, I went to the kitchen and asked Effie for a pitcher of cool water and some soft rags. She started to pepper me with seemingly unrelated questions, but as soon as I said her mistress had taken a turn for the worse, she stopped talking and fulfilled my request with remarkable efficiency. I wondered if competency was, perhaps, within her reach.

Back in the bedroom, I soaked one of the rags in the water and gently wiped Mrs. Pringle's face. As the surgery was so nearby, it took only a few minutes for Jeremy to return with both Dr. Cameron and Dr. Harris. My friend and I retreated from the room, to give them privacy while conducting their examination. Mr. Pringle came with us, unsure what to do.

"It's so difficult to know what's right," he said, pacing in front of the sitting room windows as we waited for news. "One ought not interfere with the work of a physician, but one does hate not knowing what's happening. My poor darling Caroline. She's so much younger than I, it never occurred to me that she might face a physical challenge before I did."

"She's in good hands, Pringle," Jeremy said. "Cameron's the best there is. Better than anyone I know on Harley Street in London. He'll have her right as rain in no time, mark my word."

"I do hope so. I couldn't do without her, you know. She's everything to me."

I hadn't expected to hear something like that coming from the vicar. He didn't strike me as a particularly sentimental man, more the stiff-upper-lip sort, with an allowance made for the natural enthusiasm of the Scots. I rang for tea and persuaded him to sit down.

"We'd given up hope of having a child," he said, once I'd poured a cup for him. He was clearly upset, but not so upset that he didn't have the presence of mind to refuse Effie's biscuits. "I didn't know she was . . . that is . . . she hadn't yet gone to the doctor, you see. She'd suspected but wasn't sure, and didn't want to raise my hopes until she could be certain. And then, at the ceilidh, she started feeling unwell. She went outside, thinking perhaps she'd become overheated, but the cool air didn't offer any relief. Her pain increased, so she decided it would be best to go home. I didn't know any of this was going on. I was mediating a friendly argument between two of the villagers about whether raising sheep or Highland cattle is more productive. What a useless fool I am. Caroline wanted to find me, but found she could hardly walk. She made it to the door and asked one of the lads standing nearby to send Dr. Cameron and myself to the vicarage."

"I'm so very sorry," I said.

"Forgive me, I ought not grow maudlin and I ought not force the two of you into the awkward position of listening to me speak about such things."

"There's no need for apologies," Jeremy said. "We'll sit with you as long as you need. It's rather like I'm stepping into your role. I've always wanted to play vicar, you know. Think I'd have made an awfully good one. I'm jovial, can give every appearance of listening carefully, and am reasonably optimistic. Perhaps most important, I've not the slightest qualm about raining down fire and brimstone when necessary."

I couldn't conceive of a more ridiculous idea than that of Jeremy becoming a vicar, but his flight of fancy made Mr. Pringle laugh.

"I shouldn't think the archbishop of Canterbury would agree with your idea of the qualifications necessary to become vicar," he said, "although I do appreciate the sentiment."

Dr. Cameron stepped into the room and we all rose to our feet. "Would you prefer to speak privately?" he asked Mr. Pringle.

"No, no, go right ahead," the vicar said.

The doctor crossed to him and put a reassuring hand on his shoulder. "There's no dangerous complication causing her symptoms. My guess is that her current decline has come on as a result of the disappointment with which she's contending. There's no reason to think she won't make a full recovery."

"That's a great relief, Doctor," Mr. Pringle said, pulling a handkerchief from his pocket and mopping his face with it.

"I've left Dr. Harris sitting with her," Dr. Cameron said. "I'd like her to remain here for a bit, just to keep Mrs. Pringle under observation, if it's all right with you."

"Of course, of course, whatever you think is best."

"There's no reason you can't sit with her as well."

"Marvelous." The vicar turned to us. "Will you forgive me for abandoning you?"

We urged him to go upstairs without delay. Dr. Cameron pulled an envelope from his jacket and handed it to me. "These are the full results of the postmortem. Would you be so kind as to deliver them to your husband?"

"Of course," I said. "Did you find anything that surprised you?"

"As I suspected, the blow to the temple is what caused death, and the stab wounds occurred after that. I can say with confidence that man's own knife inflicted them. Time of death was between midnight and one in the morning. The other injuries to his head came from rocks, which I suspect were thrown at him. None resulted in significant damage, but they might have caused him to lose his balance and fall."

All the color had drained from Jeremy's face; he looked ill.

"Could he have hit his head on a rock when he fell?" I asked.

Dr. Cameron nodded. "Aye. It's almost certain that's the way it happened. I've taken specific measurements and compared them with the boulder you spotted that had blood on it. It's a match. It's likely that knocked him unconscious."

"Anything else of note?"

"Nothing unusual in the contents of his stomach. Perhaps more interesting, though, is that he had no scrapes or bruising on his hands, which suggests his attacker was too far away for him to fight back."

"Unless the gamekeeper was throwing rocks, too," Jeremy said.

"Aye, that's possible," Dr. Cameron said. "An odd sight it must have been, two Highlanders flinging rocks at each other. Very strange indeed. If you or Mr. Hargreaves have any further questions, you know where to find me."

I still needed to speak with Effie, but before I started for the kitchen, she popped back into the sitting room.

"Is it a good time for our wee word, Lady Emily?"

She crossed to me, reached for my hand, pulled me to my feet, and half dragged me to the corridor.

"Apologies," she said. "I'm a rough sort of girl and sometimes forget my own strength. I hope you're not hurt."

"No permanent damage done. What did you want to tell me?"

"It's just that I saw the gamekeeper the night of the ceilidh, outside. I wasnae having the greatest time of my life at the ceilidh, you see, and I decided to get some air and go for a little stroll. The moon was full. Bright as the sun. Which is how I know it was them, the gamekeeper and Maisie Drummond," she said. "They were pressed right up against each other not far from the loch. There's a spot people seek out—couples, that is—it's secluded and all that. I dinnae like that Maisie much. She's the pushy sort, you know, the kind of girl who will always take what she wants, and it seems he was what she wants. Which I suppose means she didnae kill him. It's not kind to say, but that's a bit disappointing, isnae it? Much as I'd like to see the back of her once and for all, hanging might be going too far."

There was an edge to her voice that made me suspect she harbored an affection for the gamekeeper. "I can't imagine he would welcome that sort of behavior. Surely he'd prefer someone more reserved."

"Aye, or someone who would bake something special for him," she said. "Not that I ever did, mind you, but I could have."

I couldn't imagine a worse way for Effie to entice a man than through her baking. "I'm sure he would have enjoyed that."

"You're kind to say so, madam, but he never liked me that way. I willnae pretend it wasnae a disappointment. I've never met another

64

lad so fine as he, even if he was lying about his name. I would've preferred he'd choose anyone instead of Maisie, but facts are facts. I could see he had a deep affection for her."

Her opinion was obviously colored by jealousy. "Do you know what time this was?" I asked. "Or how long they were together?"

"Och, I fled as soon as I saw them," she said. "As for the time, it was early. Before ten o'clock. I couldnae even get that louse Callum Fletcher, let alone someone more appealing, to dance with me, which is why I needed the fresh air."

"Did you see the gamekeeper inside the village hall again after that?"

"Aye, madam. He was dancing with Maisie, but I couldnae tell you exactly when. You know all that I do now, which is as it should be. I've work to do now, if you dinnae mind."

With that, she went back to the kitchen while I retrieved Jeremy from the sitting room. He was silent on the walk back to the castle, still unsettled by the doctor's description of the murder. When we arrived, I steered him to the billiard room, sat him down, and poured him rather a large whisky. Then I went in search of Colin and the boys. I found them in the menagerie, ogling a lion.

"Did you know, Mama, that all the animals here were brought by His Grace's mother's second cousin?" Tom asked. "He was a sea captain and collected creatures wherever he went. His Grace says they kept all the most interesting ones here and sent the rest via train to the zoo in London."

"And the troublesome ones, too," Richard said. "I should've loved to be in the carriage when they took the monkeys. They escaped from their boxes twice."

"They gave away monkeys but decided to keep a lion?" I asked. "I'm not sure a lion is the best choice for Scotland."

Henry pulled a face. "First off, there are still a dozen monkeys here. They only donated the surplus. Second, a lion doesn't belong in a northern climate any more than he belongs in London. He wants to roam the plains of the Serengeti. As, evidently, that's not in the cards for him—although I'm not wholly convinced I can't change His Grace's mind about that—I take a measure of comfort in finding that his cage is more or less large enough for him. Even so, I'd prefer he had the run of the estate."

I crouched down so my face was even with his. "I doubt that anyone in Cairnfarn would be happy with a lion wandering about. It could prove quite dangerous."

"You know, Mama, it might be something to consider," Richard said. "Given the violent nature of the kelpies here, a predator like a lion could prove useful."

"I wonder . . ." Tom paused. I could see he was struggling, most likely because, while he didn't believe a mythical creature had committed murder, he didn't want to contradict his brother.

Colin tousled Richard's hair. "A kelpie didn't kill the gamekeeper," he said. "He fell victim to the most dangerous predator there is: his fellow man. Let's get you boys inside. Nanny will have my hide if you're late for your baths, and I need to speak to your mother."

Once we'd handed them over to Nanny, we retreated to the library.

"Where's Bainbridge?" Colin asked as he closed the door behind us.

"In the billiards room with a large bottle of whisky."

"Perfect," he said. He pulled me into his arms, leaned against the door, and kissed me. "You'd think one would have an easier time finding privacy in a castle."

"A murder being thrown into the mix makes everything harder," I said.

"That's no excuse. I've half a mind to throw you over my shoulder, carry you upstairs, and ravish you, but there are responsibilities we must deal with first. Mind you, no responsibilities can keep a gentleman occupied for a full twenty-four hours a day, so consider yourself on notice."

A delicious warmth coursed through every inch of my body, making it difficult to focus, but I somehow managed and passed over the envelope from Dr. Cameron. Colin read the contents with keen attention.

"Right," he said and ran a hand through his tousled curls. "What are your thoughts?"

"The method was a strange way to have killed someone. First flinging rocks until he fell and was incapacitated. Then bludgeoning him and stabbing him after he was already dead. That suggests an intense level of hatred, which in turn suggests that the best way of finding the killer is by learning more about his victim. Who hated him so deeply, and why?"

"Does anything stand out from what you heard in the village?"

"Callum Fletcher despised the gamekeeper, has a temper, and may have considered him a rival for the affection of Maisie Drummond," I said.

"Not to mention he wanted the man's job," Colin said.

"I don't like him for the murder, though. He's too obvious a suspect."

"Obvious may prove a disappointing solution in detective fiction, but that's not necessarily the case in real life. I made an inventory of the contents of the gamekeeper's cottage, but didn't find much of note aside from a box full of polished stones carved with Viking runes very like the one left on his forehead. They're also similar to the one Bainbridge showed us when we were looking at his First Folio. I tried to speak with Nesbitt, who runs the stables, but have never come across such a stubborn and taciturn man. He told me nothing."

"We should focus on finding out the gamekeeper's actual identity," I said.

"He's been here, what, a year or so?" Colin asked. "Let's start with those closest to him. They may have noticed something odd in his manner, his conversation, his actions."

"Could the police in Edinburgh offer any assistance?" I asked. "We know when, more or less, the true Angus Sinclair disappeared from there. Might they have a report of someone meeting our victim's description from approximately the same time?"

"I shall telegraph them and inquire," Colin said. "According to MacDowell, the butler, the gamekeeper was friends with Maisie Drummond; the housekeeper, Mrs. Mackie; and Sandy, one of the stable boys."

"Effie had some interesting things to say about Maisie." When I told him what I'd learned from her, he rang the bell and asked the footman who appeared in response to fetch her.

When she entered the room, her cheeks were flushed a perfect shade of the palest rose, her blue eyes were open wide, and I'd swear she'd put color on her lips. She looked more than a little crestfallen when she noticed me. Colin and I had positioned ourselves at a long table in the center of the room, one on either side, and put her between us, at the head of the table.

"Have I done something wrong, sir?" Her eyes were pleading, her mouth partly open, her tongue just peeking out between her front teeth. I suspected she'd practiced the expression in front of a mirror. If that were the case, it was not as attractive as she no doubt hoped.

"Not at all, Miss Drummond," Colin said.

"Oh, sir, there's no need to address me so formally." She smiled and fluttered her eyelashes.

Colin did not reply to this inanity. "I understand that you were close to His Grace's gamekeeper."

"Not inappropriately so," she said.

"No one is suggesting otherwise." Colin returned her smile and warmth shone from his dark eyes. If it were possible for a human being to melt into a puddle, she would have done so. That's the power he possesses, one of them, at least. He didn't often deploy it, but when he did, it was irresistible. "You are also close to Callum Fletcher, is that correct?"

"Not close like I was to Angus—er, whatever his name really was."

"How was it different?"

"I've known Callum forever," she said. "So far as I'm concerned, he's like a brother to me. You know: irritating, always around when you dinnae want him there, poking into your business. He's got a wicked temper and thinks me knowing that will inspire me to keep on his good side. He couldnae be more wrong about that."

"You may consider him a brother," I said, "but I can't imagine he thinks of you like a sister. You're a beautiful girl, Maisie."

She turned toward me and gave an expression of surprise, followed by one that suggested she might welcome me as a friend, so long as I continued to compliment her. "I'm sure you, Lady Emily, have loads of experience in this department. When you were young, you must have had countless lads after you."

When I was young? How old did she think I was? I doubted she was beyond eighteen or nineteen, and probably considered anyone older than that ancient. "Did Mr. Fletcher attempt to win your affection?" I asked.

"I guess you could call it that, but his efforts were more than a little disappointing." Now she turned back to Colin. "I'm sure you never tried to woo a lady by giving her thistles."

"The thistle is a noble plant," Colin said, "a symbol dear to Scotland."

"But prickly and horrible. I prefer roses."

"Did the gamekeeper give you roses?" I asked.

"No, although I'm certain His Grace widnae have objected to him taking a few out of the hothouse. I even suggested it. He said it widnae be right, that it was akin to stealing. Men can be so disappointing, can't they? If he was that worried about it, he could've asked His Grace for permission, but he almost fell over dead when I told him as much."

I wasn't quite sure how to respond to this, so ignored it. "We'd like to know all we can about the gamekeeper, and it's clear that he considered you to be one of his closest"—I paused, just for a moment, and smiled at her knowingly before continuing—"one of his closest friends."

"That's clear, is it?" Maisie asked. She sat up taller in her chair.

"Abundantly so," I said, noting her posture. She wanted to be considered close to him; I could exploit that. "Everyone in the village agrees. What can you tell us about him?"

"There's so much I hardly know where to start. I suppose he invented the tale about being born in Cairnfarn, but anyone could see he wasnae cut out to be a farmer." She leaned closer to me, as if I were her confidante, and lowered her voice ever so slightly. "Anyone looking at him could've told you that. I do believe that he came here from Edinburgh. He found life there unsatisfactory."

"How so?" I asked.

She returned to speaking at a normal volume. "He never went into detail, but I got the impression that it had to do with a lady." Now she looked at Colin. "City ladies can be something of a burden. They're very needy. Very haughty. Not down-to-earth and game for a laugh, like us Cairnfarn girls."

"He got into trouble with one of these ladies?" Colin asked.

"He never said anything specific," Maisie said, "but I can't imagine anything else would've driven him from the city. Why else would a successful man flee?"

"Did he mention any friends from his time there?" I asked.

"There was someone called Jimmy, but I dinnae know his surname. He talked about him once in a while. They were great mates."

"Had they lost touch?" Colin asked.

"Oh, I shouldnae think so, sir. They were ever so close, although he never came to visit."

"What were his hobbies?" I asked.

"Hobbies?" Maisie pulled a face. "He liked wood carving, but didnae have much time for it. This is a large estate. There are constantly poachers to be warned off, trails to be kept in shape, traps to check, and who knows what else. The man hardly had a moment to himself. It's why we had so little time together."

"What did the two of you like to do when you did have time?" Colin asked.

"I'm a simple girl, sir, content to go for a little walk, maybe with a picnic lunch. We always danced when there was a ceilidh. He was a very fine dancer." A single tear made its way down her cheek.

Colin handed her his handkerchief. "We were to be married, you know. We hadnae told a single soul yet, because I'd have to give up my position as soon as we did. It was a very great secret."

"I'm very sorry, Miss Drummond," Colin said.

"When did he propose?" I asked.

"You're a bit of a busybody, aren't you?" Maisie said, grinning. Her mood certainly was changeable. "I shouldnae talk like that, I know, but I feel like you and I, we could be friends if we'd met in different circumstances. We appreciate the same sort of things." She gave Colin a pointed look; he shifted uncomfortably in his seat. "It was a perfect day, just a few weeks ago. We'd arranged things so we both had the afternoon off. He had Cook put together a picnic with all my favorite foods. When he collected me, he brought a huge bouquet tied with a bright blue ribbon. We walked to a secluded spot in the woods near the river and ate there. Then we went to the loch, where he rowed us around for an hour or so before he stopped the boat in the dead center of the water, knelt down, and proposed. Most girls never get anything half that good. When Mr. Pringle proposed to his wife, he quoted some dreadful poem. I cannae imagine anything more boring."

"It must have been a lovely day," I said.

"The loveliest of my entire life." Her voice trembled. "I may not know his true name, but I do know he didnae deserve to die the way he did, but I suspect you already know that. I cannae picture anyone overpowering him. He was so strong, so—if you'll forgive me for saying it—so virile. A girl isnae supposed to use words like that, but I cannae think of any better way to describe him." She was shaking and her face was ashen. I might not give credence to much of what she had told us, but I could see her grief was sincere.

"Did he have any enemies?" Colin asked.

"He was generally congenial, too much sometimes."

"How so?" I asked.

"Well . . ." She paused and looked down at her hands, which were folded in her lap. "It's not that he didnae have opinions, but it was as if he didnae want to ruffle any feathers or stir up controversy. Sometimes that made me wonder if he was hiding something, that he worried someone might figure it out if he pressed his views too strongly."

"That's very interesting, Miss Drummond," Colin said. "You're an observant girl. Is there anything else we should know about your late fiancé?"

"He was an honorable man, Mr. Hargreaves," she said, "always keen to do the right thing, even when it wasnae what he wanted. That's all I can tell you."

We thanked her and told her she could return to her duties. She gave me a smug smile and bobbed a curtsy to Colin. Her account of the gamekeeper's proposal fell somewhere between a sensational novel and a young girl's fantasy. It was possible he had proposed in a less flamboyant manner, but it was equally possible Maisie had made it all up. She'd stressed that they'd told no one, which conveniently made it impossible to confirm her story. Nothing about her inspired trust.

10

Tansy

1676

"You are trying my patience," Ewan said. He didn't look much like his father. He was shorter and squatter and had mean eyes set too close together. His hair was dark, badly cut, messy, and always oily. His clothing, however, was in perfect order, from his long kilt to his beaver sporran to the skene-dhu he'd stuck in his checkered hose. "You abused my kindness today. I didn't allow you to enter the castle to steal from me."

"Steal from you?" Rossalyn's eyes flew open wide. "I would never do such a thing, milord, particularly when you were so generous allowing me to collect the little things I'd forgotten when I moved to this cottage."

"Someone was seen dropping a bundle out of the library window," he said. "Did you think I would be so foolish as not to have you watched? Especially when I saw you watching me from behind a tree when I was preparing to leave for the hunt?"

She laughed softly, the sound like tinkling bells. "Oh, Ewan, how could I resist watching you all set off? It's a sight to behold, the MacAllister men gathered together. I always loved the hunt, you know. I felt a great deal of pride seeing you all, as I know your father would have."

"Don't mention my father." He pushed his way into the cottage, followed by his men. They were drenched from the rain. "What did you take that I did not authorize?"

"Nothing, Ewan," she said. "I swear to you."

"You're an untrustworthy cow. I don't believe a word you say." He nodded at the small table where the parcel of books was still sitting, unwrapped, and pushed one of his men toward it. "Open it."

My heart was racing. A series of horrific images cycled through my mind. Watching my hand being cut off. Rotting in a prison. Walking to a scaffold. The man obeyed the order, a trail of water dripping from his soaked kilt. He tugged roughly at the canvas, spilling the contents onto the floor.

There were no books.

Instead, I saw the last sub-satisfactory batch of biscuits I'd made, two tallow candles tied together with twine, a bunch of dried herbs, and a loaf of coarse bread.

"If I thought you'd want it, I would have left it," Rossalyn said. "I'd brought it for you as a way of thanking you for letting me return for my things. You know full well I don't have much at my disposal. I've very little money and own nothing of value. I cobbled together what I could, but after being back in the castle and seeing all the fine objects there, I was too embarrassed to leave you my pathetic little gifts."

"So why drop them out the window?" he asked.

"Because if anyone noticed me carrying the bundle, they'd have asked what it was and I would've been obliged to give it to you. I'd already determined that was a silly idea and felt fortunate no one had spotted it on our way into the library."

"I don't believe you," Ewan said.

"I can't make you," she said. Her voice was calm, sweet, even. "You'll believe what you want. You're welcome to search the place. I've nothing to hide."

I'd closed the door behind the men when they came in and watched all this unfold standing as far away from them as I could, my back pressed hard against the wall. What was Rossalyn doing? She must have hidden the books, but where? Dizziness consumed me. My head pounded. My heart raced. My breath came rough and ragged. I wished to be calm like she was, but that was impossible. The stakes were higher for me.

The men searched every inch of the cottage, behaving like the brutes they were. They swept our dishes from their shelves, breaking them. They flung our clothing out of the cupboards and onto the floor. They pulled our chairs away from the table and knocked them over. Finally, they searched me, as if I could hide books in my skirts. Their hands were rough. They pinched and squeezed and sneered.

Eventually, there was nowhere else to look. Ewan grabbed Rossalyn by the arms and pulled her close to him.

She shrieked and tears coursed down her cheeks. "You're hurting me. I'll be bruised tomorrow."

"You never could stand the slightest discomfort, could you?" He pushed her onto the floor and stood over her, glowering. "I don't know what you've done, but I know it was wrong. You've made a grave mistake, thinking you can trick me. I'll let you keep the objects you took today, because I am an honest and generous man. I have no interest in claiming something that belongs to another. Don't rest easy, for when I discover what you stole, I will punish you. You can count on that." He stormed out, his ruffians trailing in his wake.

I latched the door behind them, then went to each of our windows and checked that the shutters were fastened as well. We then started to clean up the mess they'd left. Rossalyn's veneer of calm had vanished; she was shaking so hard, she broke the only two plates that remained intact, dropping them when she tried to return them to their shelf. I wasn't happy we'd need to allocate some of our limited funds to buying new ones from the village potter. I ordered her to sit down and poured her a glass of whisky from a bottle Cora had given us.

"What was all that?" I asked. "Where are the books?"

She half smiled. "I knew he'd come looking for them, but I also knew he wouldn't be sure what it was he was seeking. Ewan didn't attend our wedding, you know, so he didn't know what my father had given me. When you went to buy the mutton for our stew, I hid them in the hollow tree near the stream behind the cottage."

I pulled on my cloak, lit a lantern, and went outside. I walked up and down the street, wanting to be sure the men were well and truly gone. Then I walked around the cottage three times, in case they were lurking in the shadows. Only once I was confident I was alone did I go to the stream and find the tree. There, inside the trunk, wrapped in waxed canvas, was our precious bundle.

I took it into the house and slammed it onto the table. "You should have told me what you'd done," I said, "instead of leaving me to be terrorized by those louts. Why were you acting unhinged earlier and pretending we hadn't taken them?"

"As I told you, I knew they'd come," she said, "and I knew that before they knocked on the door, they'd listen at the windows. I wasn't sure they'd be able to hear anything, but just in case, I said what they needed to overhear in order to believe us."

"They don't believe us."

"That doesn't matter. I didn't tell you what I was doing because I couldn't be certain how you'd react when they came. I don't know how great your capacity for deception is, Tansy. You might have given something away without meaning to. I had to keep you in the dark. As it is, they found nothing. I'm sure they'll return, likely more than once, but before long, Ewan will tire of harassing us and leave us alone."

"We can't keep the books in the open," I said. I was angry with her. Angry that she hadn't confided in me. Angry that she raised doubts about my capacity for deception and made it sound like a bad characteristic. Angry that I was stuck here, living with her in a small cottage, not an equal but an unpaid servant.

"You're right, of course. We'll have to find a suitable and safe place for them. Perhaps in your mattress?"

"They'll cut open the mattresses when they return," I said.

"We'll have to make sure that never happens."

"And how, Rossalyn, are we to do that?"

"I have my ideas. Suffice it to say, I can handle it on my own."

If I was angry before, now I was infuriated. She was playing easy with our safety, with our freedom. "You should have asked Ewan to let you take the books in the first place," I said. "He agreed easily enough to let you have what you claimed you wanted."

"Except for the horse statue. He denied that just to be cruel. As for the rest, he only let me take them because they were obviously pitiful little objects of no value. He wouldn't care about the books, but he'd know they were worth something. It would have made him take notice and I wasn't willing to risk losing them forever."

"You may lose more than that forever now," I said. "He's taken notice."

"Not of the books."

"Rossalyn—" I stopped myself. Took a deep breath. Tried to rein in my ire, which had gone from gentle simmer to full boil. "You're accustomed to a comfortable life, a life that has made you feel safe and secure. I was forced to learn that it can all vanish in an instant, the day I was kidnapped in Tunis, ripped away from my home, my family, from everything I held dear. Now I'm in Scotland with no hope of ever seeing the people I love again."

"I freed you, Tansy," Rossalyn said. "You're not a slave any longer. You can leave if you want, but it would break my heart."

At that moment, all I wanted to do was slap her. "Two things. First, how could I leave? I have no money, no resources, no one willing to help. My letters to my family go unanswered. How would I ever be able to make the journey back to Tunis? Do you have any idea what such a thing would cost? Second, how dare you try to make me feel bad about any of this? I'd break your heart if I returned to my home? Your heart? Your heart?" My voice was rising. "What about my heart? It broke years ago."

She looked down at the floor. "I—I never thought about it that way. I suppose it seemed to me that you were happy here. That you like me. I consider you a friend, Tansy, and did even when you were my servant. I've always been good to you."

"My name is Tasnim, not Tansy. My previous owner couldn't pronounce Tasnim, so he changed it," I said. "Did you never once stop and consider what my life is like? Can you imagine how it feels to not even be called by your own name? Yes, you've been good to me. Is that supposed to keep me content? If bandits came to the cottage tonight, took you away, forced you to travel thousands of miles, and then sold you into slavery, would a kind mistress make up for everything you'd lost?"

"I'm sorry." Her voice was low. "I've been thoughtless. I assumed . . . I don't know what I assumed. I suppose the truth is I never gave it much thought."

"Very few people do," I said, "but they should."

She pressed the palm of her hand against her forehead. "And now I've no way to pay for you to return home. I've been selfish and won't ask you to forgive me."

"This isn't about you and forgiveness, Rossalyn. We're here now, stuck together, all each other has," I said. "I learned a long time ago to make the best of things and shall continue to do that. What other choice do I have? What I will not do, however, is sit back quietly and let you put us both in danger. Your antics with the books were always a bad idea. Yes, it would be sad to lose possession of them, but in the end, they are only things. Objects. We are human beings. Human beings that can be sold as possessions if we fall into the wrong hands. Short of that, we could suffer serious consequences if the laird finds a way to prove we stole from him."

"I do appreciate what you're saying," Rossalyn said, "but, Tansy, we aren't in North Africa. We're in Scotland. People here don't get kidnapped and sold into slavery. Ladies don't get executed for stealing. Nonetheless, I promise you, I shall be more careful."

"Ladies might not get executed for stealing here, but I don't doubt that Moors do," I said. "I'm not the same as you. I wish you would try to understand that." I put the books on the table near the fireplace. A wood crucifix hung above.

"We can't leave them where they might be seen; I thought we both agreed on that."

"If we're going to keep them, we'll have to brazen it out," I said.

"If anyone notices them, we'll say they were in your room at the castle and that I packed them the day we left. No one can prove otherwise. If Ewan comes back and insists they weren't here tonight, we'll tell him we'd hidden them in a cave near the loch because we were afraid someone in the village would steal them, but that once we realized no one in Cairnfarn had any interest in such things, we knew we'd been foolish."

"Yes." She was relaxed now; all the tension had disappeared from her face. There were no more lines on her forehead, no more fear in her eyes. She smiled. "And it's right good fun, too. I like your ideas much better than mine, Tansy, and I swear I will take into account everything you've said. I'm sorry for all you've suffered, sorry that I was so blind to it all. Someday, if our fortunes change, I will send you back to Tunis and you'll see your family again."

She wanted to be my savior. That's what happens when you're used to having a measure of power. You take what you want. You fix what you want. I needed a savior, but in that moment I realized it could only be one person: myself.

11

1905

On the surface, Effie's admission that she had witnessed Maisie and the gamekeeper in a compromising position appeared to bolster Maisie's claim that they were engaged, but Effie was half in love with the man herself. Jealousy would have primed her to expect to see them in a passionate embrace. Regardless, I rejected the idea that he had proposed to Maisie. If he'd wanted to marry her, surely he would have informed his employer of his intentions. He wouldn't have wanted to do anything that might jeopardize his position, something being seen trifling with a maid would certainly do. Colin and I decided to query Jeremy about it. He was still in the billiard room, but his spirits had improved since I left him there. I credited the rapidly emptying decanter of whisky.

"The gamekeeper? Engaged to Maisie?" He snorted. "She's a sweet girl and pretty as anything, but I can assure you their friendship was rather uneven. He was too polite to put her off entirely, which I told him was a mistake more times than I can count. It only encouraged her. He tolerated her, but had no interest in cultivating a closer connection."

"She claims to have spent a great deal of time with him," I said.

"She'd descend upon him at his cottage whenever she could, preferably when he was alone," Jeremy said, rolling first a red ball across the felted table, then a green one. "That's why I know about it. He came to me, concerned that I might think he was entangled in an inappropriate relationship. Thought it might threaten his job."

"So there was no friendship between them?" Colin asked.

Jeremy tilted his head and pressed his hands on the wooden edge of the table. "I wouldn't say that, not exactly. He felt a bit sorry for her. She was so cloying and desperate with him. Most blokes would've been put off entirely—and he was, in terms of considering her as a romantic prospect—but he did offer her friendship. Told her to consider him like an older brother, someone who would look out for her and help if she got into trouble. I've no doubt it hurt her. Now that he's dead, she probably thinks she can lessen her humiliation by claiming they were engaged."

"Did anyone else know he'd rebuffed her?" Colin asked.

"Not so far as I know," Jeremy said.

"Effie told me she saw them together the night of the ceilidh, together in a way that suggests he did not think of her like a sister."

"I don't believe that for a minute," Jeremy said.

"Then how do you explain what she saw?" Colin asked. "Or do you think she's lying?"

"Lying?" Jeremy considered the question for a moment. "No, I don't think she's lying. Not that I'd put it past her in general, only not in this precise circumstance. Word is she was rather fond of the man herself. If she stumbled upon him with Maisie, she'd assume the worst."

"So what did she see?" I asked.

"How should I know? Maisie can be a handful. Perhaps she was pretending to be upset and in need of consolation. No decent bloke would've have walked away from her at a time like that."

"Might Miss Drummond have manufactured the circumstances?" Colin asked.

"I wouldn't put it past her," Jeremy said.

"If your gamekeeper was so upstanding, surely he wouldn't have gone to a secluded location alone with her," I said. "Should Effie have told the vicar or anyone else what she saw, he could easily have found himself in a situation where he had to marry the girl."

"Effie and Miss Drummond were both taken with him," Colin said. "Is there anyone else we should know about? He sounds a terrifically popular man."

Jeremy heaved out a breath. "Look, Hargreaves, I can't claim to keep track of everything that goes on at this estate, particularly when it comes to the personal lives of my servants. He only confided in me to protect his position—he would've done anything to avoid losing it. He wasn't who he claimed to be, but I do believe he'd found happiness here in Cairnfarn. That does not, however, mean I was privy to the details of his life or his relationships or any rumors concerning him. I considered myself close to him, but only in that way we men are. You understand. I'd have a wee dram with him while we talked about stalking and fishing, but that's all rather impersonal, isn't it? I'm English. I speak about things of substance as little as possible. I wish I could be of more help, but you'll find I'm as useless as ever." His expression was pained.

"I understand how frustrating it is to feel that one can't do anything to help," I said, "but you're not useless. You've confirmed that Maisie was telling tales. That may prove significant. Go easy on yourself, will you?"

He poured more whisky into his glass and then lifted an empty one toward Colin. "Do you fancy some, Hargreaves? And maybe a game of billiards?"

"I never object to a good single malt," Colin said. "Emily, are you happy to go to the stables without me?" We'd planned to talk to the stable boy Sandy, whom the butler had identified as a friend of the gamekeeper's, but I could tell by the look my husband shot me that he thought he should stay behind with Jeremy.

"I'd never want to be the sort of wife who stood between her husband and his whisky."

The stables were a quarter-of-a-mile walk from the castle, set in the direction away from the loch, where the grounds were more open, a series of lush meadows brimming with heather. A large barn stood between two round pens. In one of them, a burly man was exercising a horse. He ignored me when I approached, not responding even when I called out to him, so I went into the building, where I found two boys. They were sitting, bent over a game of some sort, but before I could see what it was, they spotted me and snapped to attention.

"Did you want to ride, madam?" the shorter one asked. He had light brown hair that would've gone golden if it ever saw much sun and a riot of freckles over his nose and cheeks. "We were just, er . . ."

The taller boy stepped forward. "We're allowed a break now and again, madam. His Grace doesnae mind."

"I'm certain he doesn't." Jeremy was not the sort to run a tight ship. If I hadn't already known that, it would've become apparent when the man outside ignored me. "I'm looking for Sandy."

"That's me," the shorter boy said. "How can I be of service?"

"Let's go for a little walk, shall we?" His colleague looked disappointed. I wondered if that was because he'd be left behind to work or because he suspected we'd be discussing the murder. Neither of the boys could have been more than ten years old, and I suspected the gamekeeper's death was the most exciting thing that had ever happened in the course of their short lives.

When we left the barn, I spotted a narrow trail leading into the woods at the edge of a meadow. We walked toward it while I peppered him with a variety of innocuous questions, mainly about horses.

"You know quite a lot about them, don't you, madam?" he asked.

"I've always been a keen rider," I said. "My own horse, Bucephalus, is the finest on earth."

"Bucephalus. That's a funny name."

"Have you heard of Alexander the Great?"

"No, madam, I cannae say I have."

"He was arguably the best general ever to have lived. He conquered most of the known world before he died at the age of thirty-two. His horse was called Bucephalus."

"Och, does that mean you'll be wanting to conquer the world?"

This made me laugh. "No, I can't say it does."

"Aye, that's good, then," he said, "because I dinnae ken if a lass, even a fine one like you, could do such a thing. Can you even lift a sword above your head?"

"You'll find, Sandy, that these days lifting a sword is less essential than other qualities when it comes to leadership. Still, though, I don't know either if a lady could conquer our world the way things stand today."

"Och, that's just the kind of thing the gamekeeper used to say to me. He did like to haver, didnae he?"

"Haver?" I asked.

"Whitter on," Sandy said. "He was always one for doing that, talking on and on."

"I wish I'd had a chance to get to know him," I said. "We met at the ceilidh, but only briefly. I understand you two were quite close."

"Aye, he was good to me. Treated me like a son. My own father was in the army and killed in the Second Boer War, which left me all alone in the world. My mother died when I was born."

"I'm very sorry."

"Thank you," he said, "but I'm used to it now. Or at least I was for a long time. I started to go soft again what with the gamekeeper being so kind. Now it's back to life as it used to be." His voice quavered and he wiped his eyes with the back of his hand. My heart ached for him. He was too young to have had so much grief in his life. My own boys were nearly the same age, and I couldn't bear the thought of them suffering as he had. Sandy deserved better.

"My husband and I are investigators," I said, "and we've promised the duke that we'll do everything we can to identify whoever killed your friend. I've found that the best way to embark on such a project is to learn whatever I can about the victim of the crime. That's where I need your help. I'm told you knew him as well as anyone."

"You're an investigator?" He stopped walking and looked at me. "Och, maybe ladies can conquer the world."

I smiled. "Perhaps. For the moment, though, I'll be satisfied with getting to know what the gamekeeper was like."

Sandy chewed on his bottom lip, looked up at the sky, and crinkled his forehead. "He liked to make things out of wood. Carved me a box to store me treasures in." He spoke slowly, thoughtfully. "He didnae like rabbit, not to eat, that is. Even with mustard sauce, which has always been a favorite of mine. He knew that, so sometimes he made it for me. Usually we ate in the servants' hall, but every once in a while, he'd take me back to the cottage and cook supper just for the two of us and he'd tell me about all kinds of things."

"Like his time in Edinburgh?"

"That was never very interesting," Sandy said. "Sounds like a right mess, that place."

"How so?"

"Well . . . all that schooling couldnae have been much fun, although he didnae mention it much. I heard about it from Maisie. She likes to talk, that one. Nonsense, mostly. As for the gamekeeper, he believed a man might need a fresh start now and again. We talked about that a lot. That's what he had when he left Cairnfarn for the city, and he got another when he came back. Said that a man should never squander the opportunity to begin again."

"Did any friends from Edinburgh come to visit him?"

"Nae. He'd left them all behind and that made some of them *feargach,* er, angry. New lives can do that, he said, but you cannae take everyone from the past with you."

"Did he particularly miss anyone he left behind?" I asked.

"Maybe his mate Jimmy, but I cannae rightly say. He told me stories about the trouble the two of them got up to when they were lads. I would've missed him if it were me."

"What sort of trouble?"

"Oh, the usual kind. Taking slices of pie from the larder when they shouldnae have. That's how it started, he said. I never was quite sure what he meant by that."

This gave me my first insight into the gamekeeper's time in

Edinburgh, before he took on the identity of Angus Sinclair. If he'd embarked on a life of petty crime, no wonder he craved a new beginning. "Did he like to give advice?" I asked.

"Well, the not squandering opportunity bit was important to him. Talked about that nearly every time I saw him. He wanted to be sure I remembered it."

"I understand Maisie was fond of him."

He rolled his eyes. "Aye, but he wasn't of her. She was a right pain, that one. Always trying to barge in when the two of us was up to something. He'd be about to take me out to walk the traplines and there she'd be, crying and whingeing and carrying on. The other girls who visited him weren't such dunderheids."

I raised an eyebrow. "Who were the others?"

"Well, Mrs. Mackie, of course. The housekeeper. They were thick as thieves. She's a good one. Takes care of all of us. And there was Cook. She'd bring him little treats, that sort of thing. The maids all thought he was a fine specimen, but figured out right quick that he didnae want to bother with them. I didnae pay much attention to anyone but Maisie. She was the only one who gave me trouble. Mrs. Mackie would never keep a lad from checking the estate's traps."

"You can't remember anyone else?"

He shrugged. "Nae, but I can't see how it matters all that much. He wasnae the sort to marry. He told me that more times than I can count."

"So he wasn't walking out with anyone?"

"Och, he walked all the time. It was his job, you know." He grinned. "But I know as what you're getting at. There wasnae anyone particular. Mrs. Pringle, the vicar's wife, she'd call round, always with ideas of bonnie lasses from the village who would make him a good wife, but he was having none of it. He made her laugh, the way he talked about her suggestions. I figure he didnae have much interest in a marriage like hers. Who'd want a girl making cow's eyes at you all day? He liked his life the way it was. Always said I should find a way to like mine and that the best way to start was by being happy with what you have."

"A wise man," I said. We'd reached an enormous yew next to a stand of towering trees. "Are you happy with what you have, Sandy?"

"Aye, madam, I am, although I do wish I still had my friend, whatever his name. Life will be poorer without him."

I walked Sandy back to the stables and then went into the castle to speak with Mrs. Mackie, whom I found in the armory hall, upbraiding two young maids for having inadequately dusted the contents of the room.

"Do you see this?" She was pointing at the hilts of an array of swords crossed one over the other hanging on the wall. "Dust, all over the hilts. I'm not an unreasonable woman. I dinnae expect you to pull out a ladder and do the spears high up above every day. Once a week is enough for that, but I will not tolerate you skipping something at eye level. Start again, and do it right this time or I'll be telling His Grace your work is unsatisfactory." The girls scurried to do as she said.

"Forgive me for intruding, Mrs. Mackie," I said. "I was hoping we might have a quiet word?"

She looked at the watch pinned to her bodice and nodded. "I've time enough for a cup of tea. Will you come to my room?" I followed her belowstairs, along a narrow corridor, up a half flight of steps, and into her private space. We entered a pleasant sitting room with sage green walls and a fireplace. A door opposite the hearth must

have led to her bedroom. The furniture was serviceable but not particularly comfortable. Two framed sketches of Highland landscapes
stood on the mantel and there was a half-finished piece of embroi-
dery on the small table next to an upholstered chair.

I watched as she stirred the embers in a small iron stove in the
corner of the room. She put a kettle on top of it and then measured
tea into a clay pot. I couldn't make out how old she was, but assumed
she was well into middle age; her position would require significant
experience. Her chin was narrow and her cheeks plump, which gave
her a rather sheeplike appearance. Fortunately, her voice sounded
nothing like a bleat. She artfully arranged some shortbread biscuits
on a plate and set them on the table beside me.

"Now, then, you'll be wanting to speak about the gamekeeper,"
she said as the kettle started to whistle. She poured the boiling water
into the teapot. "He was a good man, although not one a person
could ever get to know all the way. I dinnae hold that against him.
He may not have been the real Angus Sinclair, but I do believe
he lived in Edinburgh and had a difficult time there. That sort of
experience can make a person hold things back. I'm not saying he
wasnae reliable. I dinnae ken that I've ever met someone more gov-
erned by duty. He never left a task unfinished and never shied away
from hard work."

"Do you know what made things difficult for him in Edinburgh?" I asked, then sipped the tea she'd poured for me.

"He never let slip a word about it." She stirred two lumps of
sugar into her cup. "My impression was that he'd suffered some
great loss, traumatic enough that he didnae want to talk about it.
I've no idea what it stemmed from and I never pressed him on the
subject. Most of the time he was right cheerful, but every now and
then a cloud of darkness would pass through him. He'd pull away

from everyone during those times and retreat right into himself. He was never crabbit or ornery or particularly out of sorts, just sad. It made a person want to take care of him."

"Did he present a character or letter of reference when he came to Cairnfarn?"

"He did not, which was highly irregular. Of course, His Grace had no reason to doubt he was who he claimed. He remembered him and had known the family. We Highlanders are close-knit. Everyone was pleased to welcome his return. I'd have sworn on my mother's grave it was Angus. That hair is unmistakable!" She shook her head. "I never suspected for a minute he was putting one over on the lot of us."

"Whoever he was, you were close to him. I'm hoping you might be able to tell me something that could shed light on his true identity."

"He never revealed a thing," she said. "I can promise you that."

"I imagine he would've been careful not to, but anything you remember would be helpful. The more I know, the easier it will be to determine why someone wanted him dead."

"Hindsight being what it is, I can already tell you that I should've suspected something. He never once talked about all that fancy schooling he supposedly had, except to say in passing that he'd had it." She paused, closed her eyes, and nodded her head slowly. "Thinking on it, I'm not sure he even did that. He'd told His Grace, of course, but he never mentioned it specifically to me."

"Had the real Angus Sinclair kept in touch with anyone from Cairnfarn after he left?"

"No," she said. "There wasnae a letter, not a word. It's hard on a young boy to lose both his parents so suddenly. I was working as a housemaid at the time and was in no position to exert any influence on him. Truth is, we all thought he'd come back before a week had gone. Do you know what did become of him?"

"Only that he was engaged to marry Dr. Harris. She might be able to tell you more."

Mrs. Mackie smiled, and every inch of her face crinkled. "That I can see. Even as a wee lad, Angus wanted more from life. He was the sort who'd take to a woman doctor. They'd be kindred souls, both insisting on a better station than the one into which they'd been born."

"Did the gamekeeper get along well with the rest of the staff?"

"Aye, more or less. We all like some people more than others. He took issue with Nesbitt, who runs the stables. He's a crabbit one. You'll never get a kind word from him, if you're lucky enough to even get a word at all. Good with horses, though, and His Grace says that's all that matters. His Grace is a fine sportsman and knows what is what. Which means we all tolerate Nesbitt. The gamekeeper kept his criticisms mostly to himself. He never gave anyone cause to dislike him."

This proved to be the general consensus among the household staff. Those who'd known the real Angus as a boy were shocked to learn the gamekeeper was an imposter, but most weren't troubled by the revelation. More than one said they'd never blame anyone for coming up with a reason to make Cairnfarn his home. Only a few showed signs of worrying about what had become of the child who ran away from the village. The rest were content to believe that he was living the life he wanted, and if that meant he'd run away again, this time to escape marrying Dr. Harris, that was understandable. They couldn't comprehend why anyone would want such an educated wife. I didn't feel I was getting closer to knowing enough about the gamekeeper to understand why someone would want him dead and hoped the police might be able to offer insight into the man's true identity.

If I was even half considering relying on the police for anything, that meant I was flailing. I had to focus, stay on task. They could tell us facts, perhaps, but I needed more than that. I needed to understand the man. It was my best chance to find his killer.

12

Tansy
1676

Sometimes, the things that are critically important to one person are meaningless to nearly everyone else. That's how it turned out with the books. All that tension, all that stress, all that fear amounted to nothing. Ewan and his men didn't return to the cottage. They'd found better ways to amuse themselves: the witch trials taking place in Balieth, at least a two-day ride from MacAllister land. The villagers were gossiping about it, but more quietly than usual. No one wanted to run the risk of being overheard saying something that could be twisted into evidence of their own relationship with Satan. Seven of the residents of Balieth had already been burned, with more waiting, locked up in a house guarded by twenty men.

As weeks passed, I began to accept that maybe, just maybe, I wasn't about to once again be torn away from the life I knew. Which is not to say that I didn't startle every time I heard someone coming up the path to our door.

Rossalyn started making an effort to be more sensitive to my plight. For three days, she remembered to call me Tasnim, but then slipped back into using Tansy. She may have failed there, but she did start asking me questions about my family and wanted to know everything about Tunis. I described for her the embroidered damask silk of my favorite robes, the intricate wooden screens on our windows, the rich layers of spice in our food, the sublime beauty of our music. She gave me paper and pencils and asked me to draw pictures of it all for her. So I did. I sketched the deep creases of my father's face, my mother's wide-set dark eyes, my little brothers playing together. I drew the columns of the great Al-Zaytuna Mosque, taken from the ruins of the ancient city of Carthage, destroyed by the Romans more than a thousand years ago. I sang while I sketched, melodies I remembered my mother singing when I was a little girl.

"It's so wonderful," Rossalyn said, examining the pictures. "I've never seen anything like it. Isn't it like magic, how the world is filled with places that are all so different? I thought Cairnfarn was otherworldly when I first arrived here. It was like nothing I'd ever seen. The castle seemed primitive and rough compared to what I was used to in Inverness, but the longer I lived in it, the more I appreciated its beauty."

"And the servants."

She sighed. "Yes, the servants. My mother only had two. In the beginning, I couldn't see the castle as anything but a fortress, a haven, a place of protection. Duncan always made me feel safe. It was part of the reason I fell in love with him. Together, we made those stone walls a home, a place of warmth and comfort. And now I live in a drafty cottage with no servants."

"What am I, then?" I asked.

"My friend, I hope. You're my equal here, Tansy," she said. "If you want employment, you'll have to seek it elsewhere. I don't have the funds to pay you." I could tell from her tone that she was trying to be lighthearted and tease me, so I decided to take her words in the spirit they'd been given.

"If I find employment, perhaps I'll earn enough to hire you as my servant."

"If you find employment, we'll hoard your wages until we've saved enough for you to return to Tunis."

"If you find employment as well, we'd have enough that we both could go."

Her face brightened. "Would you really want me to come?"

It was an inane question; we'd never be able to save enough money even for one passage. "Of course. My mother would adore you." My mother would be horrified by her, not because she was a Christian, but because she would consider Rossalyn's education inadequate. She'd take her into the fold, though, and see to it that the deficiencies were corrected. She'd hire tutors. Teach her to write poetry. Train her to be a good wife.

No, Rossalyn wouldn't like Tunis. She was too used to getting her own way, doing as she pleased.

We'd been in the village for more than two months. Cora had become a regular fixture in our household. Her father raised sheep; she spun their wool and weaved it into the crisscrossing colorful patterns Highlanders loved. She took us out with her to collect plants to use for dyes. Wandering, she called it. We gathered lichen from the rocks that ringed the loch and formed the mountains. Some of it turned cloth crimson, some brown, and some purple. Berries called *braoileag*—bilberries—produced a shade of blue; heather made a lovely dark green. Alder bark made brown, willow a pale shade of peach.

Before I had started wandering with Cora, I'd never given much thought to the plaids worn by the Highlanders. The men, in their long, bulky kilts with one end of the fabric draped over their shoulders, had looked somewhat ridiculous to me when I first saw them. As I grew accustomed to the Scottish weather, however, I began to better appreciate their choice of clothing. Fine wool—and there was none finer than Cora's—was soft and warm, not scratchy like most. I liked to watch her select from the skeins she'd dyed as she invented patterns. She never wove the same one twice. Her colors may have been limited by the plants we found in the area, but she could alter the appearance by changing the order in which she used them or the width of the stripes.

Most women in the village made their own cloth for their families' daily wear, but when they wanted something special, they got it from Cora. No one else had her eye for design, and people were willing to pay dearly for it. For reasons not entirely explicable to me, this meant she was the most popular maiden among the young bachelors. I would've thought a man would want a wife who could run a household, bear and educate children, but in Cairnfarn, having a potentially lucrative occupation was more important. I wondered if I'd find things the same in Tunis, had I not grown up in the comfortable circumstances enjoyed by my family.

Cora may have had the attention of every man in the village, but she had no interest in any of them. "I'd rather stay home with my father," she said when she came to call one day. It was raining. Not drops, but a deluge, as if an angry god had turned over a bucket so enormous it could cover the sky and drench the entire planet. We were sitting in front of the fire. She had a treadle spinning wheel at home, but never went anywhere without her *dealgan,* a drop spindle without a whorl that she could use even when she was walking. "I don't see what use any man is."

"Your father won't be able to farm forever," Rossalyn said, "and a husband would at least provide you with a house."

"I can earn enough on my own to do that."

"Even in Cairnfarn?" Rossalyn asked.

"Nae, I'd need to sell my goods a bit farther afield," Cora said, "but that's not an impossible thing. Look at the two of you, living here all alone, no man to be found. That's what I want, and I'll do whatever I must to have it. My version of heaven, it is."

A version of heaven made possible only because the small sum of Duncan's will had settled upon his widow. Even with that, we had to scrimp and save and make hard decisions about things I'd long taken for granted. A person can generate enthusiasm about eating mutton only so many days in a row. I didn't know how much income Cora's weaving brought, but she'd need a fair amount to run a household on her own.

"I was thinking about approaching the laird and asking if he'd give me a cottage in exchange for supplying wool to the castle," she continued. "Do you think that's something that would interest himself?"

"I haven't the slightest idea," Rossalyn said. "You could always come live here."

"Thank you, but there's not nearly enough room," Cora said.

I felt a stab of insecurity. Perhaps Rossalyn would prefer to live with Cora rather than me. Where would that leave me?

"I can't see how it would hurt to inquire if the laird would be willing to give you a cottage," I said. Yes, I was being selfish, but I also wanted to encourage our friend to live the life she wanted, not one that was expected of her or foisted upon her. She inspired me. If she was capable of doing such a thing, maybe I could, too. Adopt a trade and earn enough money to someday make my way home. I looked at Rossalyn and felt an unpleasant tugging in my gut. If I ever managed to do that, it would mean leaving her alone in Cairnfarn. I didn't owe her my whole life, but the idea of abandoning her didn't sit right with me. Still, that didn't mean that I couldn't seek employment. Even if I stayed in the village, having extra money would help us both. Difficult decisions about the rest could come later.

And so I tried to find a position, but no one was interested in hiring me. I couldn't decide if this was due to my being a Moor or having served Rossalyn at the castle in a role that didn't look like useful work to the villagers. Had I been employed as a scullery maid, I would've had more useful experience and more options. As it was, I was limited. I knew nothing about farming, but was willing to take on any sort of unskilled labor. No one wanted me. I offered my services to shopkeepers, to the local herbalist, and to the church. I thought, if nothing else, the priest might agree to take me on to help with housecleaning. It was all to no avail. I could provide nothing anyone wanted. Then I started to wonder if the mere fact of my being an outsider was becoming dangerous. I'd noticed fewer women speaking to me on the street or at the market since the witch trials in Balieth had begun. Cora and Rossalyn both insisted no one was suspicious of me, but neither could offer any evidence to support their position. I started having difficulty sleeping. I worried all the time.

Ewan refused to give Cora a cottage. That is, she refused to take it when he explained what he would require in return; it was more than just plaids. She came to me when she left the castle, her eyes rimmed red.

"I don't know why I thought it would be any different," she said, sniffing. I passed her a handkerchief. "Men are all the same. He was affronted that I said no to him. Can you imagine? Him, affronted? Was not I the one who ought to be?"

Of course she was. What I would give to live in a world where that mattered.

13

1905

Colin and I had no opportunity to speak privately until late in the evening. Jeremy had insisted the boys dine with us, a highly unusual request, which scandalized both Mrs. Mackie and Nanny. The talk at the table was dominated by theories about the murders (primarily coming from Richard, who was still convinced a kelpie was responsible) and strategies for returning the animals in the menagerie to their native habitats (exclusively coming from Henry, who blanched whenever someone mentioned Mr. Sinclair's death). As always, Tom, the perfect little gentleman, did his best to participate in all conversation. Jeremy's great-aunts, Miss Adeline and Miss Josephine, weren't there. The Greats, as he'd always called them, had trays sent to their rooms, as usual.

When at last we retired—Jeremy had installed us in the suite formerly occupied by his uncle's dearest friend—we were emotionally exhausted and physically agitated. Colin was tugging at his cravat even before we reached the door and by the time we were inside, had already begun to unfasten his stiff evening shirt. He flung the cravat on the floor, pulled off his jacket and shirt, and tossed them across the back of a chair.

"Would you like a bath?" he asked. "I can ring for water."

"I've no energy to do anything else tonight, and I'm sure the servants wouldn't mind skipping lugging it all the way up here."

"That's the trouble with castles. Very few modern conveniences." He leaned against the wall. His naked chest was inordinately distracting.

There was a knock on the door. Colin pulled it open and revealed a tall footman holding an envelope. "From Miss Adeline and Miss Josephine for Lady Emily, sir." He gave a little bow and disappeared back into the corridor.

I opened the message. "They request that I come to their sitting room."

"Now?" Colin asked.

"Now." I held the note out to him. "They've drawn a little map so I can find my way."

When Jeremy's father had installed his aunts at Cairnfarn, they'd taken over the old medieval section of the building. They rarely left their wing, preferring each other's company to anyone else's. We hadn't caught a glimpse of them since our arrival. Exhausted though I was, what else could I do but go see them, now that they'd summoned me? I made my way to a narrow stone staircase that curved along the side tower of the old structure. Another footman—an extremely handsome footman, at least six feet tall, with broad shoulders, copper hair, and flashing dark eyes—greeted me at the top holding a flaming torch.

"There are no gaslights in this section of the house, madam.

Miss Adeline and Miss Josephine insist on authentic period details whenever possible," he said. "If you'll come this way, please."

I kept close to him so I could see in the dark passageway. The stone floor was rough and uneven. When we reached the fifth door, he knocked. A maid, dressed in Bainbridge tartan, answered and admitted me to the room.

"Oh, Emily, dear, what a treat to see you," Miss Adeline said. "Do take a seat. She'll find our salon most comfortable, won't she, Josephine?"

Her sister nodded amiably. Both ladies had to be in their eighties, but their faces were incongruent with their age, at least at first glance. Close up, in brighter light, one might have noticed thinning skin and wrinkles, but only if one was bent on searching for flaws. Who would be, though, when the ladies' eyes were bright, their cheeks were pink, and their smiles were as bewitching as they'd been in their youth?

The room was a riot of color. Large tapestries hung from the walls, and the wooden chairs—Gothic in style, with tall, straight backs—had cushions that matched the colors of the gaudy Bainbridge tartan. A soft Axminster carpet covered the stone floor and thick crimson velvet curtains hung over the small windows. Given the number of flammable objects around, I was glad to see oil lamps on the tables instead of open flames. A long hearth heated the room, which was surprisingly snug and cozy.

"Pour the girl a whisky, and then leave us in peace," Miss Josephine said. "We've much to discuss." The maid did as ordered. When she shut the door behind her, the sisters looked at each other, slowly counted aloud to sixty, and then laughed.

Theirs wasn't the laugh of elderly ladies. It was girlish, gleeful, and full of life.

"We always count," Miss Adeline said. "A minute is generally long enough for servants to tire of trying to listen. Astonishing that anyone would care what us old biddies have to say, isn't it, Josephine?"

"I don't agree in the least," she said. "We're endlessly diverting, Adeline. Always have been. Now, let's talk about you, Emily. We've seen your husband from the window. Shockingly good-looking. You'd best be careful we don't steal him from you."

"We are something of connoisseurs when it comes to the masculine form. It's why we insist on approving all potential footmen who come to Cairnfarn," Miss Adeline said. "As a result, we're abundantly qualified to state authoritatively that your Mr. Hargreaves puts all other gentlemen to shame."

"But that's not why we've summoned you," Miss Josephine said. "Our dear great-nephew has proved unsatisfying when it comes to filling us in on the murder in the village. It's as if he's a small boy again, playing in his Highland dress and doing nothing useful."

"My dear sister, he is the most useless man in England. It's part of the reason we admire him so."

"Quite, quite, but it can be inconvenient at times. Times like now." Miss Josephine pointed at my glass. "Finish that whisky so I can pour you more and we'll sit back and hear the whole story."

I took a deep breath and swallowed the rest in a single gulp, surely a bad idea for one as tired as I was, but it was obvious sipping wouldn't be acceptable to the Greats.

"That's more like it," Miss Adeline said. She picked up the decanter that was sitting on the table between her and her sister and tipped more of the golden liquid into my glass.

"We'll let you take this one more slowly," Miss Josephine said.

Miss Adeline winked at me. The two ladies had been born so

close together they were more like twins than ordinary siblings and this was more evident than ever to me now. It wasn't simply that their hair was the same color—rich brown when they were young, shining silver today—or their similar features. It was the way they moved. Their gestures. Their manner of speech.

"Now, tell us everything," she said.

The whisky coursed through me, spreading its pleasant warmth. For the moment, it perked me up instead of putting me to sleep. Further, it loosened my tongue. I gave them the broad strokes of what had happened; they demanded more details. I went deeper; they wanted still more. Only when I'd described every last bit, down to the gory intricacies of the wounds on the gamekeeper's body, were they satisfied.

"We don't shy away from violence," Miss Josephine said. "It's part of life, after all. There's no point pretending it doesn't exist."

"So much pretending is required by Society," Miss Adeline said. "It's tedious in the extreme."

"You've escaped from it here," I said. "Do you ever miss London?"

"Heavens, no," Miss Josephine said, "but we're not interested in discussing that. Surely you'd rather question us about the victim. We did know him, after all."

"How well?" I asked.

"As Josephine explained, we're connoisseurs of the male form. He was a prime example. Well-built. A good head of hair. Pleasant eyes. We both gave up shooting years ago but decided to take it back up after Jeremy hired him."

"He would take us out for a drive or two. Adeline proved to still be a fair shot and got more than a few birds, but I think he knew we weren't all that interested in the sport. We'd go back to his cottage afterward for tea. The man was incapable of brewing a decent cup, but it was quite fun, sitting with him and listening to his stories."

"He listened to ours, too," Miss Adeline said. "When you reach our age, you'll find very few people bother with more than a passing interest in what you have to say. It's rather discouraging."

"Another reason to flee Society," Miss Josephine said. "The gamekeeper, however, encouraged us."

"We suppose that was partly due to him keeping his own cards close to his chest," her sister said. They spoke so rapidly, one after the other, that it was almost as if one person were doing all the talking. "Better to pay attention to us than to draw it to himself. Of course we didn't suspect that at the time."

"Once we learned he was posing as someone else, we couldn't help but wonder if that's why he was so attentive," Miss Josephine said. "Although—" She stopped and looked at her sister.

"You're quite right," Miss Adeline said, nodding. "He wasn't feigning interest. It's obvious when anyone does that. I can state unequivocally that he liked us and our stories about the old days."

"He was fascinated that we left it all behind and holed up here at the castle. Not that we had much choice."

"Aside from that, it's similar to his own story. Fleeing Edinburgh—if that's where he actually came from—and hunkering down in Cairnfarn. It gave him a certain sympathy to us."

"Quite." Miss Adeline turned back to me. "He was a man of great passion. I could tell that the moment I met him. It oozed from his soul. I don't simply mean in matters of a romantic nature, although I've no doubt that his emotions ran deep. It was broader, however. He was passionate about his work. Passionate about the estate. Passionate about Cook's scones. Simple currant scones. To watch him eat one was to see Michelangelo appreciate a work of Leonardo."

"Did they appreciate each other's work?" Miss Josephine asked. "I've never given the matter any thought before now. You've raised something fascinating to consider. Are there any records pertaining to this?"

"We shall have to find out," her sister said. "Emily, have you any connections in the art world who might be able to offer guidance on the matter?"

"I shall see what I can do."

"You know it doesn't quite work, Adeline," Miss Josephine said. "The Michelangelo–Leonardo comparison. They were both artists. Our friend was a gamekeeper and Cook, well, a cook. They didn't share a profession. Even so, I'd like to know more about the artists' relationship with each other. Do please see what you can learn, Emily."

"I shall, I promise," I said. I needed to get them back on track. "Was the gamekeeper involved with anyone romantically?"

"He was dedicated to avoiding any entanglement with Maisie Drummond," Miss Josephine said.

"She claims they were engaged," I said. The sisters laughed, long and hard.

"Poor, dear Maisie," Miss Adeline said. "She does have a frightfully active imagination."

"She's a decent girl," Miss Josephine said. "Or rather, she would be if she'd stop trying to manipulate everyone around her."

"What is the aim of her manipulation?" I asked.

"Maisie has never been content with her lot in life," Miss Adeline said. "She believes she's above domestic service. Don't think I'm criticizing her. I admire the ambition, but it's not realistic for her to believe there's a better life waiting for her somewhere else. When the new gamekeeper arrived, she thought he might be her way out."

"A foolish notion," Miss Josephine said. "The fact that he'd returned here shouldn't have given her reason to believe he'd decide to leave again."

"Quite," Miss Adeline said. "Furthermore, now we know he hadn't actually returned, only pretended to. If I were to adopt a new identity and hide myself away in the middle of the Highlands, I'd be doing it to escape something."

"Or someone," Miss Josephine said.

"Quite," Miss Adeline said. "Either way, I shouldn't leave again, unless it became unavoidable."

"Which could only mean the something or someone discovered where I was," Miss Josephine finished for her. "I understand it's Dr. Harris who alerted you to his being an imposter. That's rather interesting, I think. We had her round for tea just before you arrived at Cairnfarn. She herself had only been here a day or two. She never mentioned once that she'd been engaged to the real Angus Sinclair. What's her reason for wanting to keep it a secret?"

"A secret from us, at least," Miss Adeline said. "She admitted to Dr. Cameron that part of the reason she applied for the position he'd advertised was to be in the village where her fiancé—"

Miss Josephine interrupted. "Former fiancé."

"Where her former fiancé was born. Surely when a man has thrown you over—"

"Abandoned you without explanation," Miss Josephine said.

"You wouldn't want to seek out a place from his past," Miss Adeline finished.

"How did you come to know all this?" I asked. Dr. Harris had only just told Dr. Cameron, yet the Greats already heard about it?

Thoughts were racing through my mind in a catastrophically disorganized fashion, fueled by the whisky. I put my half-full glass down on the table.

"No, no, Emily," Miss Josephine said. "Do not abandon your libation. Steel yourself and drink it. As for the gossip, we hear everything that goes on in the village."

"Our spies are everywhere." They giggled.

"Don't look so shocked, Emily," Miss Adeline continued. "We don't have spies. There's no need for them in a small village. Word gets out. It always does."

"No one's precisely sure how," Miss Josephine said.

Miss Adeline nodded. "It's a mystery."

"A mystery that can be relied upon."

"What else have you heard about Dr. Harris?" I asked.

"She's been keeping as much to herself as she can," Miss Adeline said. "Which means much of what we hear comes from nothing but baseless speculation."

"It's rather disappointing," Miss Josephine said, "but she won't be able to stay so private for long. Not in Cairnfarn. Everyone here is intimately involved in everyone else's business."

"Yet no one admits to knowing much about the gamekeeper," I said.

"Not to you," Miss Adeline said. "You're a foreigner. English."

"And a newcomer," Miss Josephine said. "Not to be trusted." Despite her admonishment, I'd left my glass on the table. She tipped more whisky into it and rather forcefully shoved it back at me.

I didn't pick it up. "As you asked, I spared no details when telling you about the murder. I need you to do the same for me about the gamekeeper and Dr. Harris. You've led me to believe that nothing stays private in the village. I want to hear everything."

14

Tansy

1676

Ewan's demands of Cora, should she desire a cottage from him, came as no surprise to me, but I'd been owned by a someone who wanted me for nothing but tending to his pleasure. It was repulsive, but sadly not unusual. I hadn't always understood that. Cora's outraged shock reminded me of how I'd felt when I first realized what that odious man required of me. It was a nightmare from which I feared I would never wake up. I hated him with every fiber of my being. I dreamed of violent ways to kill him, but that stopped when I realized that death brings with it a kind of relief, so instead I imagined torturing him. Mutilating him. Scratching his face. Scarring him.

I'd never been vindictive before. I didn't like it. It made me even more miserable than I already was. It hardened me, made me aware of a darker side of the world, one I'd rather have never seen. As the months passed, I started to become numb. It was that or go mad. The nightmare ended only because he tired of me. That was his way, apparently. He went through girls at a shocking rate, selling them when the novelty was gone. I wished I'd known that in the beginning. It might have given me some hope when I feared I would drown in the seemingly endless hell in which he kept me.

I was glad Cora was in a better position than I'd found myself in. She could say no, and she did. Ewan MacAllister let her say it. Didn't force himself on her. Horrible though he was, he could've been worse.

When Rossalyn listened to Cora's story, she was shocked in that way that only an innocent person can be shocked. There was a purity to her. She'd been thrown out of her home, which was unpleasant and inconvenient, but she hadn't been abused.

"I never liked him," she said, taking Cora's hand and squeezing it hard. "Never. I tried to get along with him for Duncan's sake, but I could never manage more than a superficial civility. Now I know why. I must have known, somehow, that he had this evil in him."

I let her believe what she wanted to believe. She had no concept of evil.

So Cora didn't move into a cottage. She stayed in her parents' house and saved the money she earned from her weaving. Someday, she hoped, she would amass enough to pay the rent on a home of her own. She was naïve to think Ewan would accept money alone as payment, but she didn't need to be told that now. I had no doubts that his evil ran deeper than we'd seen, but I couldn't prove it.

We didn't see Cora as often after that. At least I didn't. She was busy with her work, but I felt like something had changed. She wasn't as carefree. She started mumbling to herself. She didn't invite me to wander with her so often, but she took frequent walks with Rossalyn. It all made me feel unsettled, like I was waiting for something awful to happen. And then, I met Finella Logan.

15

1905

The combination of exhaustion and whisky is not a good one, particularly when it's exasperated by the rapid conversation of the Greats. It was clear they kept abreast of all village gossip, which I realized could prove useful, but at the same time, getting them to stay focused was no simple matter. I prodded them again, asking about Dr. Harris and the gamekeeper.

Miss Adeline sighed. "There's only so much to tell. As we've already said, Dr. Harris has maintained her privacy up to this point."

"More or less," Miss Josephine said. "There has been some talk."

"About the cat, of course," Miss Adeline said.

"The cat?" I asked.

Miss Josephine nodded. "She brought it with her from Edinburgh. It fled the very day she arrived here."

"Showed up the next morning at the croft Angus's parents

worked before they died. The real Angus, that is," Miss Adeline said. "That tells you something."

"It certainly does," Miss Josephine said.

I had not the slightest clue what they meant. "What, precisely, does that tell us?" I asked.

"The cat knew there was a connection between the doctor and the real Angus."

"It's a rather fine-looking cat," Miss Adeline said. "A gray British shorthair. Lovely face. Didn't Irene MacDuff, the herbalist, tell you about it?"

I decided it was best to ignore all discussion of the cat. "She was away from the village when Jeremy and I called on her after the murder."

"She was one of the few people who didn't go to the ceilidh," Miss Josephine said. "Refused point-blank and told Dr. Cameron that she wanted nothing to do with Dr. Harris."

"Do many of the villagers seek care from her rather than the doctor?" I asked.

"No, not for medical complaints," Miss Adeline said. "They know it's better to trust a man of science. They get potions from her. Tonics that will make someone fall in love with you, turn your enemy into a toad, that sort of thing. I don't think anyone puts much stock in what she does, but they think it's a good bit of fun."

"I do wish one could turn one's enemies into toads," Miss Josephine said, tapping her long, tapered fingers against the side of her whisky glass. "It would be devilish good fun."

"Tell me more about the gamekeeper," I said.

"Everyone liked him," Miss Adeline said. "I never heard anyone speak cross words against him. Not in a serious way. There were little arguments here and there, but that's only natural."

"Who argued with him?" I asked.

"Callum Fletcher," Miss Josephine said, "but he told you that himself. He's a tricky one. Don't let his gruff ways take you in. He's all heart inside."

Jeremy must have told them what Mr. Fletcher had said to us. "I'm sure your nephew made it clear that I wasn't taken in."

"Jeremy hasn't spoken to us since he returned home," Miss Adeline said. "Our sources are speedier and far more reliable than he is."

"Who are your sources?" I asked, "and what else do they tell you about the gamekeeper?"

"The entire village is our source," Miss Josephine said. "Give us some time to find out more. We'll reconvene over dinner tomorrow night. Jeremy never objects to us coming to dine."

"He's always encouraging us to leave our little lair," Miss Adeline said. Both sisters giggled.

"I'll tell Cook to serve something that doesn't trouble a nervous stomach," Miss Josephine said.

"Jeremy has a nervous stomach?" I asked. I'd never seen any indication of that before.

"Heavens, no," Miss Adeline said. "He's in the rudest of good health. You, however, may have started feeling a bit unwell by then, what with all this talk of murder and having to probe into the entire village's dark secrets. It takes a toll, I'm sure."

"I don't like to recommend strange concoctions," Miss Josephine said, "but it's quite possible Irene would have something to settle your stomach."

"I'm sure there's no need for me to—"

Miss Adeline stopped me. "She'll talk to you if you consult her about any sort of ailment. It would be well worth your while."

"Unless you'd prefer she shuts up like a clam," Miss Josephine said. "It is a clam, not an oyster, isn't it, Adeline?"

"A clam, indeed," her sister said. "Yes, yes, Emily, you're already starting to look rather peaked. A consultation with Irene is definitely in order."

With that, they ordered me to bed and rang for the footman, who once again lit my way through the corridor with a flickering torch.

"If you'll forgive my impertinence, madam, I wouldn't consult with that Irene MacDuff. She's not right in the head. Most everyone views her as harmless, but I see it differently. Mark my words: you should never let a potion she's made pass your lips. Nothing but regret could come from it."

"How did you know—"

"It's like the ladies said, madam, in Cairnfarn, we all hear everything."

When I returned to our rooms, I found Colin—wearing nothing but a pair of silk pajama trousers—sprawled on a settee reading *Where Angels Fear to Tread* by E. M. Forster. He stood up when I came through the doorway.

"This bloke has a remarkable voice for a young man," he said, holding up the book. "This novel will be the start of a brilliant career. How were the Greats?"

"Exhausting. Overwhelming. Confusing. Intoxicating." I dropped onto the settee and pulled him down next to me. "The last, literally."

"Plying you with whisky, were they?"

I ran through all they'd told me, as succinctly as possible, and then described what happened with the footman.

"So what will you do?" Colin asked. "Consult with this would-be witch?"

"The Greats weren't trying to convince me she's a witch," I said.

"It's been suggested to me by at least three different people," he said. "Bainbridge's valet told me directly because he thought Richard might want to meet her to discuss folklore. Dr. Cameron skirted around the issue at the ceilidh, and the cook warned me that I should look after you if you decide to consult her."

"When did you speak to the cook?" I asked.

"She knocked on the door about five minutes before you returned."

"I'm not sure I like this place," I said. "There's no privacy whatsoever."

"Not much, that's for sure," Colin said, "but I think we're safe in this room so long as we stop answering the door. It's part of the reason Bainbridge put us here. There's no connection to the servants' passageways, and the walls are extra thick."

"Thicker than in the rest of the wing?" I asked.

"Yes. Apparently his uncle's dear friend who lived here with him was rather paranoid about being overheard."

"Wise man," I said. I let my head drop onto Colin's shoulder. "I suppose I might as well go see the witch tomorrow."

After climbing the stairs to the nursery the next morning to check in on the boys—who all seemed in good spirits, even Henry—I called on Irene MacDuff. She lived in a small cottage on the outskirts of the village. Its limewashed walls were in need of a fresh coat, but it was situated in the midst of one of the prettiest gardens I've ever had the pleasure of seeing. The layout was linear and precise, although that wasn't immediately discernible through the leafy greens and widespread blossoms of the plants. I recognized the ones in the large beds lining the path. They were all poisonous: hemlock, foxglove, deadly nightshade, and more. A slight chill ran through me as I walked past them, so I hurried forward and knocked on the door. The woman who pulled it open was wiry and tall, in her late thirties. Silver had started to streak her dark hair, which she wore pulled back in a tight bun at the nape of her neck. Enormous blue eyes dominated her face. Her lips were well-formed, a perfect Cupid's bow, but it didn't look as if she smiled often. Deep lines between her eyebrows told me she was more prone to glaring.

"Och, you," she said. "I wondered when you'd come." I started to introduce myself, but she waved me quiet. "I know who you are. I'm Irene and you can call me that. You might as well come inside. I'll brew you a tisane. You don't need to pretend to want something. Miss Adeline and Miss Josephine aren't always right about me."

I followed her into the house. It was only a single room with a ladder in one corner that went up to what I presumed was a sleeping loft. The space was consumed by an enormous table placed in the center. Heaps of dried plants, numerous mortars and pestles, and a variety of instruments necessary for her work covered its surface. Bunches of herbs hung from the ceiling beams. Long, narrow tables lined the walls, with wooden shelves hung above them, crammed full of jars carefully labeled in a calligraphic hand. That handwriting was the only thing inside that wasn't absolutely chaotic. It was the sort of place unlikely to inspire confidence in Irene's efforts.

"I can lay my hands on anything I need in an instant," she said, as if reading my mind, "and see no point in wasting time sorting and organizing. Anyone who doesnae approve of my methods can go elsewhere."

"Dr. Cameron, perhaps?" I asked.

"You get straight to it, dinnae you?" She pulled down several jars from a shelf, put them on the large table, opened them one at a time, and shook a bit from each into strainers she fitted into two roughly hewn pottery mugs. "Dr. Cameron poses no threat to me. Our work may intersect on occasion, but I've never considered myself in competition with him. That's more a comment on the way the villagers here think than on how things ought to be. I've no interest in changing what people believe. They'll always do what they're convinced is best, no matter how much evidence to the contrary you show them."

"I didn't come here to talk about Dr. Cameron," I said. "I was hoping you could tell me about the man you knew as Angus Sinclair."

She hung a heavy iron kettle on a hook over the fire. "It didnae come as a shock to learn that he wasnae who he claimed. The man was a liar through and through. It was obvious from the beginning."

"How so?" I asked.

"The way he moved, the way he spoke. There was always a nervousness about him. He picked at the skin on his thumbs. He never rested easy. Whenever he came into a room, he stood where he could watch the door, like he was waiting for someone to come after him."

"Was he looking out for someone from the village?"

"There widnae be much point looking out for anyone else, would there?" The kettle was boiling. She wrapped a heavy rag around the handle and poured the steaming water into the mugs on the table. "Cairnfarn isnae a place strangers visit."

"Mr. Sinclair was a stranger," I said.

"He was posing as a native villager, which makes it a bit different. All lies, of course, but it gave him what appeared to be an acceptable reason for coming. Maybe he thought someone would follow him here, but he widnae have had to keep his guard up against that all the time. A newcomer would be noticed in an instant. There's no hiding in Cairnfarn."

"Was there anyone in the village who disliked him?"

"The vicar never took to him," she said. "Not that he ever made a scene about it. He was welcoming enough at the beginning, but the gamekeeper wasn't a churchgoer. That always puts off religious sorts. I periodically saw them with each other, sitting on a bench on the green talking. I always assumed Mr. Pringle was trying to bring him back into the fold."

"Back into the fold?" I asked. "You presume he was there to start?"

"There was something about him that stank of vicarage. I'd stake my claim on him being the son of a priest who fled his family and the church. It's the only thing that could explain his enmity. Most people these days dinnae get so heated over religion."

"You're sure that's what they were discussing?"

She shrugged. "What else do you talk to a vicar about? Mr. Pringle isn't the sort of man with broad interests."

"Their discussions were heated?"

"Indeed they were." She removed the strainers and passed one of the mugs to me. I couldn't quite determine what the brew smelled of. There was mint, that much was clear, but as for the rest, I couldn't be sure. Again, it was as if she could read my mind. "It's peppermint, which you've already identified, along with rosemary, sage, and heather. It will stimulate your mind and improve your ability to concentrate. Helpful, I think, for a murder investigation."

I took a tentative sip. It didn't taste bad, but it didn't taste good. Her tone had shifted, ever so slightly. It wasn't quite friendly, but it had lost its edge. I decided to adapt my methods accordingly. Villagers, I kept being told, like to gossip. It was time to test the theory. "I'm sure you've heard that Maisie Drummond claims she and the gamekeeper were engaged."

"Aye, we've all heard about it. That news spread faster than word of the actual murder. Utter rot, of course. He was a fine specimen of a man and not the sort to shy away from female attention. He would've been better suited to city life. That sort of man . . . he's half animal. Magnetic and oozing charm. Irresistible to the feeble-minded. But there's a limited supply of options to be found in a place as small as Cairnfarn."

"Did you have any interest in him?"

"None at all," Irene said, "but that wasnae because of anything specific to him. I've no interest in finding a man. What would it gain me? I'd rather live here alone and do what I want, unfettered by the ever-changing demands of someone else. I'm in a position shared by few women—especially in a village like this—but I've never much cared what other people do or what they think. I'm happy for them to call me a witch and laugh behind my back. Let them have their entertainment where they find it."

"They shouldn't laugh behind your back," I said.

"It's what people do when they dinnae understand someone. I notice you dinnae ask about me being a witch?"

"I've never believed in witches."

She narrowed her eyes. "That's a strange position, Lady Emily. I suspect you like to exist in a world where you dinnae have to think about them. They need not be evil, you know. It's more a question of finding a connection—a deep connection—with the natural world. Our ancestors had that. Today, most people have walked away from the old wisdom. Others choose not to."

"What, exactly, makes someone a witch?"

She laughed. "A question few have ever satisfactorily answered, although they've certainly tried over the centuries. Many women were burned in the process. Scotland was notorious for it. There was even a trial in Cairnfarn. However, that should be a conversation for another day. Murder is more pressing."

I didn't object to her changing the subject. I'd no doubt her views on the natural world and ancient wisdom would prove fascinating, but the only thing that mattered now was discovering who had killed Mr. Sinclair. "Do you think he was involved in a relationship with someone other than Maisie?" I asked.

"I'm certain he was—he fed on attention and affection and widnae want to live without either—but I cannae prove it," she said. "There were a lot of comings and goings at his cottage, which is more private than most places here."

"Yet not private enough that you didn't notice comings and goings."

"I make it my business to notice things."

"From what I can tell, that's not unusual in Cairnfarn."

She laughed. "Aye, that's true enough. He struck me as a satisfied man and I dinnae think that was only because he enjoyed his work, if you understand my meaning. I cannae tell you who was putting the spring in his step, but someone was."

"There were no rumors about it?"

"Nae," she said. "Which goes to show how careful he was being about it. As soon as the gossip started, he would've had to marry the girl, and he was a smart enough man to know that."

"Can you be sure it wasn't Maisie he was seeing?" I asked. "I'm not suggesting he wanted to marry her, but he could've been trifling with her. That would require discretion on both their parts.

It also would explain why, now, she's telling everyone they were engaged."

"I widnae put it past her, that's for sure," Irene said. "You have a bit of a devious mind, dinnae you? I like that in a friend. Come again tomorrow and in the meantime I'll find out what else there is to learn about Angus and Maisie."

16

Tansy
1676

Finella Logan must have been a year or two older than I. There was a worldliness about her, despite the fact that she'd never traveled more than two miles beyond Cairnfarn. It was her confidence that made her appear sophisticated. She wasn't especially smart, but neither was she stupid nor willfully ignorant. There was something deep in the background with her, something animal. A sort of cunning. She would always make sure to look after herself, no matter what the cost. It was a skill I wished I'd learned earlier in life. It might have kept me safe in Tunis.

She had a changeable nature. One minute she was smiling sunshine, the next a cold wind blowing across the loch. It kept everyone around her on their toes, never sure what to expect. Nothing about it should have been endearing; it was a terrible quality. Yet, nonetheless, the warmth of that smiling sunshine was like a tonic we all craved. Her smile had a greater impact because it wasn't always there. She knew just how far to push, how long she could be sullen before losing her sway over those around her. It was an art, an art she had mastered.

She had also mastered the art of knowing what people needed. This, without exception, stemmed from their vulnerabilities, and rarely was the same thing they'd admit to wanting. She understood the difference between want and need: how to identify it and how to use it. Need gave her the opportunity for immense power.

I was drawn to her almost from the moment I got to know her. Don't we all like that friend who's just a little bit dangerous? Who pushes us—gently, gently, then with a firm shove—to move beyond where we're comfortable? That's the friend who makes us feel alive. Who convinces us that we're growing. Who makes us believe we can be a better version of ourselves.

Unless we come to realize the version she's pushing isn't better at all. That's it's a version she's imposed. A version we shouldn't want anything to do with. Not if we were sensible. But who wants to be sensible? There's no joy to be found in that.

I didn't meet Finella until we'd been in the cottage for several months. Not in any meaningful way, that is. She did drudge work in the castle, so I'd seen her before we moved to the village, but we'd never spoken anything more than perfunctory niceties in passing. Then, one rainy morning—as usual—I encountered her on my way back from buying—as usual—some mutton. She was standing in the street, soaking wet, nothing over her dress to keep her warm.

"Are you all right?" I asked. "You'll freeze out here. Come, we can both squeeze under my cloak."

"My mother's dead," she said. "Why should I care if I freeze? I've nothing to live for."

"Let's get you inside." I pulled her toward me, wrapped my half-soaked cloak around us as best I could, and steered her back to our cottage. She didn't say a word for nearly a quarter of an hour, which is a long time to remain silent. Far longer than is comfortable. Rossalyn brewed a pot of tea, put a cup in her hands, and told her she would slap her if she didn't drink it.

So Finella drank it, and Rossalyn sat down across from her in the chair I usually occupied in front of the fireplace. I stood behind her.

"I'm sorry," Finella said. "I dinnae know what to do with myself. It's all too much. She'd been ill for years. Ill in the way that's just bad enough to be inconvenient, but not so bad that anyone begins to worry. I took for granted she'd always be there. I half believed there was nothing wrong with her. In the end, there was no warning, no visible change. She must have taken a turn for the worse, but I wasn't there to notice. I work in the castle, you know." She paused and looked at us both.

"Of course," Rossalyn said, "I remember you very well. You're the only member of the household who could get a wine stain out of pale wool."

"You knew that was me?" This was the first time I saw that stunning smile. Finella wasn't noticeably attractive. Her features were not worthy of comment, her hair was dull and messy. But when she smiled, all her ordinariness vanished, replaced by an almost divine radiance.

"Were my compliments never passed on to you?" Rossalyn asked.

"The housekeeper mentioned something, but I assumed she was just being kind. I never thought you'd take any notice."

"Only a fool doesn't notice and commend good work."

Rossalyn had always been masterful with her staff. She cultivated loyalty by noticing them, which sounds ridiculous; but I learned in my years as a slave—more so with my second master than my first—that servants are generally treated more or less like furniture. They are useful, they serve a purpose, but there's no reason to engage with them more than necessary. I was guilty of this myself with the kitchen workers in my parents' house. I didn't take the time to speak to them, to get to know them, to thank them for their work. As individuals, they were wholly separate from my daily life. I was grateful for the food that appeared at my table but rarely, if ever, gave thought to its preparation. I took for granted that it would be done. Rossalyn never made this mistake. She knew the names of everyone in her household, knew the tasks to which they'd been assigned. When she saw them, she asked after their families, noticed if they seemed upset, and made a point of praising them for a job well done.

Yet she hadn't complimented Finella in person? That struck me as uncharacteristic. True, the laundry was the most unpleasant place on the castle grounds, but I wouldn't have thought that would keep her away.

"I'm glad I was able to satisfy you, madam," she said.

"We'll have no talk like that," Rossalyn said. "I'm not your mistress any longer, Finella. Here, you and I can be friends, and Tansy, too, of course. Come to us when you can. I know the pain that comes from losing a parent. There are times you'll need quiet companionship and times you'll want to weep. You can do either here."

"That's a very kind offer, but I'm sure I couldnae"

"You can and you will." Rossalyn's voice was firm. "If nothing else, come to us on Sundays and we can walk to the kirk together."

Finella smiled again. "That, I can do."

And she did. From that day, we were friends, Finella and I. Rossalyn liked her well enough, but didn't get on with her the way I did.

It felt as if we instantly understood each other. We could finish each other's sentences. Make one another laugh with nothing more than a gesture or a facial expression. We spent as much time as we could together, gossiping about the villagers and poking fun at them, and she always came to Sunday services with Rossalyn and me. Finella was the only person I'd met in Scotland who asked me why I attended. The only person who'd wondered how it made me feel.

"It's not your religion, is it?" she asked, one week when we were walking back to the cottage. "So why do you go?"

I shrugged. "It's been expected of me for so long I hardly think about it anymore."

"Do you still pray to your own god?"

"I do. Five times a day."

"Och, that's commitment," she said. "Your god doesnae care that you go to our kirk?"

"I believe there is only one God, Allah. He knows I worship him alone."

"What's it like for you, going to the kirk?" she asked. "You dinnae have to answer if it's painful. I know you're from very far away and I know you were a slave. Does the kirk make you think of everything you've lost? I'm sure it would for me if I were in your situation. Religion is such a profound thing. To have what you believe wrenched away from you . . . it must be a pain like no other."

"I've never thought about it that way," I said. My stomach clenched. "Now that I do, yes, it makes me unhappy."

"Then you shouldnae go," she said. "Rossalyn cannae make you."

"She's never tried to. In the beginning, it was always assumed I'd go, and then it became a habit."

"It's wrong of her not to consider how it makes you feel." Finella frowned and thunder crossed her face. "Maybe when she was living at the castle it was different. You were more like a companion than a servant. A lady-in-waiting of sorts. It would be expected that you accompany her wherever she went. It's not like that now. She no longer outranks you. She has no control over you. You dinnae have to do what she says."

"She doesn't order me around." I turned around to look for Rossalyn, who had stayed behind to speak to the priest. She was still near the church door. Even listening to the way Finella was talking made me feel disloyal. I guess I liked Rossalyn more than I realized. But there was truth in Finella's words.

"I dinnae mean to stir up any trouble." She gripped my arm, hard, and pulled me around so I was looking at her directly in the face. "Please believe that. Rossalyn is kindness itself. That's why I'm saying all this. She wouldnae want to do anything that would cause you to suffer. Have a quiet word with her. Tell her how you feel. She'll never pressure you to go to the kirk again."

On all counts, Finella was right. Rossalyn sat, subdued, when, four days later, I got up the nerve to speak to her about it.

"I had no idea," she said. "I assumed . . . but that was foolish. I believe strongly in my faith. I wanted to share that with you. I gave no thought to your own ideas on the matter. I won't lie and pretend that it doesn't worry me. I know, without doubt, that my faith and my God are the true ones. It pains me to think that you might never reside in heaven, Tansy. I want you there. Yet I also know that faith must reside in one's heart, and if it's not in yours—"

"I have faith," I said, standing up very straight. "It's different from yours, but my beliefs are no less strong. Forcing yours on me would be no better than mine being forced on you. This is something upon which we will never be able to agree. All we can do is accept our differences."

"I will pray for you, though."

"And I, you."

She reached for my hand; I gave it to her. From that day, never again did I voluntarily set foot in a Christian church. It was a small victory, but a victory nonetheless.

It was also the first step in a slow march toward the world around us both falling apart.

17

1905

When I left Irene's cottage, I headed back toward the village, hoping to speak with Dr. Harris, but she and Dr. Cameron were out on a call, so instead, I returned to the castle, where I found Colin and Jeremy in the sitting room with a young man. The chamber was in one of the newer wings of the building, which meant it felt more like a Georgian mansion than a Scottish castle. The walls were plastered and hung with gold silk, and the furniture would have fit in neatly at Versailles in the days of Louis XIV. An enormous portrait of Uncle Albion dominated the space over the Carrara marble mantel. In it, he was depicted in the manner of the Sun King, complete with a long curly wig, shoes with diamond buckles, an elaborately embroidered coat, lacy cuffs, and knee breeches.

All three men leapt to their feet when I entered the room. Jeremy introduced the newcomer as Ian Kircaldy, the detective sent from Inverness, and we all sat down. For an instant, at least. Jeremy rose again almost at once. He was dressed in a kilt and a handsome tweed jacket, perfectly embodying a Scottish laird. I could see he was unsettled, nervous even; he was relentlessly tapping his left foot.

"Well, there it is," he said. "I'm no expert in these matters, so you won't need me anymore. I'll leave you to it. Anything you require, of course, just ask." He all but raced out of the room.

"It's to be expected," Mr. Kircaldy said, watching him go. He was a young man, not yet thirty, dressed with obvious care despite a slight shabbiness to his clothes, visible in the fraying cuffs of his well-starched shirt. "The aristocracy is always uncomfortable around the police. I'm accustomed to it. It's a pleasure to meet you, Lady Emily. Your husband has explained to me that you assist in his investigations. That's altogether unusual, but if he doesn't object, I shan't either."

I smiled but said nothing. Being almost enlightened doesn't deserve a compliment.

"I've heard back from the police in Edinburgh," Colin said. "There was a report there of a man called Daniel Gordon going missing around the same time that Dr. Harris's fiancé disappeared. Both men had similar builds, fire red hair, and brown eyes. Years earlier, Gordon was a known criminal in Glasgow and had a long history of skirting the law. Most of the time he was involved in petty theft, but during a robbery there seven years ago, his associate, a James Rutherford, shot and killed a gentleman in the house they were burgling. He believed the place was empty and was startled when the owner appeared. His wife was also at home. She was killed as well."

"No doubt they didn't want a witness left who could testify," Mr. Kircaldy said.

"The victims were shot with two different types of guns, which suggests two different killers. The police suspected Gordon was the one with Rutherford, but they couldn't track him down. It was as if he'd vanished," Colin said. "So far as anyone can tell, he never again showed his face in Glasgow. It's possible he fled to Edinburgh."

"James Rutherford," I said. "Both Sandy and Maisie have mentioned a Jimmy as a close friend of the gamekeeper's, and he spoke frequently to the boy about second chances and fresh starts."

"A mate called Jimmy would be one coincidence too many if your gamekeeper isn't Gordon," Mr. Kircaldy said.

"Given that they were close friends, if the gamekeeper was there the night of the killings, he might have felt guilty about not shouldering any responsibility for what he'd done," I said. "Was Mr. Rutherford hanged for his crimes?"

"Yes," Colin said.

"A pity, really," Mr. Kircaldy said. "He would've made an excellent suspect for our murder. I'd like to examine the location where the crime occurred and go to Dr. Cameron's surgery. I've brought a camera to photograph the body. My colleagues in Glasgow will recognize Gordon, if that's who it is. Will you assist me, Hargreaves?"

He made such a point of not looking at me as he spoke that it was clear he preferred I remain behind. Ten years earlier, this would have offended me, but I cared less about such things than I had in my youth. Now I was happy to be left to my own devices. I'd already seen the body and the crime scene. There was nothing further I could learn from looking at them again. Far better to take the time to contemplate what we'd learned about the gamekeeper and apply it to what else we knew about the man. To start, I wanted to find Jeremy.

The butler told me he'd gone outside and directed me to a path leading away from the loch. The weather had started to turn. Dark clouds were gathering overhead and a moist, chill wind promised rain. I was already wearing sturdy boots and a smart tweed suit, so had only to pull on a mackintosh and grab an umbrella before setting off in search of my friend. I caught up with him in short order; he hadn't made much progress on his walk, having stopped less than a quarter of a mile from the castle, where I found him sitting on a rock beneath a towering tree.

"What now, Em?" he asked, rising when he saw me.

"We're fairly confident we've discovered the gamekeeper's true identity." I told him what we knew.

"Brilliant," he said. "I was entirely taken in by a charlatan and hired him—a known criminal—to work on my estate. Even worse, I liked the man. Almost considered him a friend."

"You couldn't have known," I said. "I'd like to hear what the vicar has to say about all this. Irene MacDuff told me she saw him embroiled in more than one heated discussion with Mr. Gordon. I believe he's more likely to speak freely to you than me. He obviously trusts and admires you. I could talk to his wife while you handle him."

"He likes me well enough, I suppose, and I never have been able to refuse you anything, have I?" He sighed and threw his hands in the air. "I'll do whatever you want."

When we reached the vicarage, Effie flung open the door before we'd knocked.

"I expected you'd be coming, didnae I?" She was grinning. "Come in now, Your Grace, I've got your special cake ready. Well, that is to say, not quite ready, but it should only need another hour or so in the oven. I put it in just before luncheon."

I can't claim to know much about baking, but couldn't envision a scenario in which a cake of any sort would require so long to cook. It must already be burnt beyond recognition. This theory was confirmed when we stepped into the house. An acrid smell permeated every inch of the space.

"Oh, well, then, maybe I've left it in too long," Effie said. "You dinnae notice, do you, when you're inside with it the whole time? You just get used to the smell. I'm more sorry than I can say, Your Grace. I know you must be disappointed. And now I'll have to find more ginger somewhere. It was a stroke of luck that one of the neighbors had a bit."

"Don't trouble yourself, Effie," Jeremy said, "just go about your work as usual. Is Mr. Pringle home?"

"He's at the kirk, Your Grace. Doing what, I couldnae tell you, but I suppose a vicar belongs there, doesnae he? I can run and fetch him if you'd like."

"There's no need for that," Jeremy said. "I can—" He stopped talking when he saw Mrs. Pringle enter the room.

"I thought I heard voices," she said. She was dressed in a simple tea gown, beautifully cut, fashioned from a creamy fabric with just a hint of rose in it. Her face was pale and her eyes puffy, but she looked determined and well composed. "How good of you to call, Your Grace, Lady Emily. May I offer you some refreshment? Tea, if nothing else. Effie, do make a pot, will you?" She was making an heroic effort to be cheerful, but I understood all too well the pain she must be feeling.

"Tea would be lovely, Mrs. Pringle," I said. "Jeremy, why don't you go see Mr. Pringle? Leave us ladies some time to visit without interfering gentlemen. I'll see you back at the castle later."

When he'd gone, Mrs. Pringle and I sat on an oak-framed settee upholstered in worn green velvet that was turned toward a large bay window overlooking the garden. "It's good to see you up and about," I said. "You gave us all quite a scare yesterday."

"I'm afraid I was overcome with emotion," she said. "Physically, I'm as well as can be expected, or at least shall be in practically no time, but . . ."

I took her hand. "Forgive me for being so forward, but I do understand what you're facing. I've been through the same experience. It takes far longer for the mind to heal than the body in such cases."

She breathed out a sigh, "It's a relief to hear you say that. It's not the sort of thing one discusses, of course, yet . . ." Her voice trailed off and tears glazed her eyes.

"Sometimes we'd be better off if we didn't bottle so much up inside. I'm truly sorry for your loss."

She squeezed my hand. "Thank you. I do appreciate it."

Effie appeared with tea and surprisingly good-looking shortbread biscuits. She scooted a beautifully carved wooden box to the side of the table in front of the settee to make room for the tray. "We're out of homemade, so I had to open a tin, Mrs. Pringle. I hope that's all right."

"It's quite all right. We won't need anything else, Effie. You take all the time you need to sort out the smoke in the kitchen." There was nothing scolding or unkind in her tone, but she spoke with a firmness that not even scatterbrained Effie could ignore. She paused only to turn around and give a half curtsy when she got to the door. "She's a good girl, although something of a shambles. I'm used to her, which is worth something, and I'd hate to see her left without a position."

"Could you, in good faith, give her a character?" I asked, my lips twitching as I tried to keep myself from smiling.

"Lady Emily, you are a cheeky one, aren't you? A little levity is just what I need. Thank you for that. Everything's been so awful. First the baby, then the poor gamekeeper. I never dreamed something like that could happen in Cairnfarn. And to someone like him!"

"Did you know him well?"

"My position as vicar's wife requires that I form acquaintances with everyone in the village and at the castle. Hamish, my husband, quite relies on me to keep up on the lives of his flock. I've never considered it a burden and, in fact, have always enjoyed my work, far more than I imagined I would. There's so much my husband's good at—no one gives a better sermon or can offer a more succinct explanation of Scripture—but sometimes people have a need for simple comfort and encouragement rather than a profound discussion of spiritual matters."

"And you're more suited to that than he?" I asked.

"Modesty forbids me from answering that question."

"What can you tell me about the gamekeeper?"

"He was different from the other men in Cairnfarn, was educated and cultured. Relatively speaking, that is, which, to be fair, isn't a high bar. He liked to carve wood"—she gestured to the box on the table—"and made that for Hamish and me. His talent was quite impressive. More importantly, though, he was a kind man. Generous, both with his worldly goods and his time. The children in the village adored him."

"Did he plan to marry?" I asked.

"Is that a polite way to ask me what I think of Maisie Drummond's claims about their engagement? Maisie is a dear, sweet girl. She can come on rather strong, and as a result is not to everyone's liking, but she's harmless. The gamekeeper handled her deftly. I don't mean to suggest that she has loose morals, but if she'd been bent on winning the heart of someone with lower ethical standards,

I would have feared for her virtue. She was in far safer hands with a man of his character."

"Did he have any enemies?"

"Heavens, no," she said. "A gamekeeper can, of course, draw the ire of any number of people. Poachers, first and foremost. He was firm but fair. If he caught boys with a rabbit, he'd let them off with a stern talking-to. Mind you, the boys would come out of it terrified, but not in trouble with the law. Once he was finished with them, he'd send them to my husband for spiritual instruction. A grown man caught poaching, however, would face very different consequences. He might have been a gamekeeper, but he was very concerned with justice, which isn't surprising given his previous profession."

"As a solicitor?" I asked.

"Of course," she said. "What else could I mean?"

"We've discovered that he wasn't who he claimed. It's likely his name was Daniel Gordon, a thief well known to the police in Glasgow."

She closed her eyes and blew out a long breath. "That explains so very much." She shuddered from her toes to the top of her head, opened her eyes, and picked up the teapot. "This calls for another cup." She poured for both of us, added milk to mine and sugar to hers, then passed me the plate of biscuits.

"While I don't have personal knowledge of his circumstances before he came to Cairnfarn, I do feel I was a good enough friend to him to have noticed things about him that others might have missed," she said. "He was keenly focused on living a good life, by which I mean a moral one. So focused on it, in fact, that it prompted me to wonder what in his past had catalyzed it, for few men naturally come to such a position. Guilt is a powerful motivator. Do you know why he chose to come here?"

"I don't," I said, "but there may be a connection with the disappearance of the true Angus Sinclair, who was living in Edinburgh and working as a solicitor."

"Was? Does that mean he's not anymore?" Her face went pale.

"He disappeared, close to the time when the man claiming to be him turned up in Cairnfarn. It's unlikely to be a coincidence."

"Oh dear," she said. She'd pulled a lacy, embroidered handkerchief from her sleeve and started tugging at it. "That's rather dreadful. You don't think"—she gulped—"you don't think the gamekeeper harmed Mr. Sinclair?"

"The police have never found a body that fits his description," I said, "so I really don't know."

"I cannot imagine—let alone believe there are—any circumstances in which he would have willfully and deliberately harmed a fellow man. I never saw even the slightest hint of violence lurking in him. Quite the contrary, in fact. He was almost too kind. Sometimes he'd go easy on the village boys when, really, strict discipline was required."

"You're the vicar's wife," I said. "I wouldn't expect any of the villagers to reveal lurking propensity to violence in front of you."

"You're right, Lady Emily," she said. "I was so very young when I married Mr. Pringle, it never occurred to me that people might start to look at me differently once we were wed. I grew up in Cairnfarn and have never lived anywhere else. My parents were farmers, and I can't claim to have enjoyed the life. I wanted something more, but I didn't possess the means to broaden my horizons. I'd always known the vicar was a good man, but as I considered my options in life, I started to look at him differently. I noticed things about him. That he was well read. That he'd traveled beyond Britain. That he had a taste for fine food and wine. These were all uncommon among the menfolk of Cairnfarn."

I was shocked that she'd never lived anywhere else. She appeared more sophisticated than the average villager; her voice, alone, suggested as much. She hardly sounded Scottish. "So he made for a more appealing choice?" I asked.

"Indeed," she said, "although I wasn't sure that he would have any fondness for me. I'm much younger. He must've considered me little more than a child, at least until the first time we danced together at a ceilidh. I was eighteen years old and had decided to be bold. I asked him to stand up with me instead of waiting and hoping he'd notice me watching him. From then, it was easy. Men aren't so very complicated. I listened to him. Showed interest in his passions. Made him believe I'd never met a more fascinating person."

"And he fell in love with you?"

"Yes, and, much to my surprise, I fell in love with him, too," she said. "It was more of a friendship at first, but then I suppose that's entirely normal. I'd never believed one can be swept away the moment one meets a man. As Hamish and I shared more experiences, we grew to care for each other; and before long, I couldn't imagine being the wife of any other man."

"I'm glad you found happiness."

She sighed and placed a hand on her abdomen. "And now I've gone and ruined it."

"No," I said, "you mustn't blame yourself."

"We'd long ago given up on having a child," she said. "It had been so many years it seemed impossible. And then . . ." She sighed again. "There's no use being melancholy. It won't change anything. Change only moves forward; it can't alter the past. That's something the gamekeeper used to say. Have you any idea who might have killed him?"

"Not yet," I said. "I understand from young Sandy that you were keen on finding him a bride."

She flushed, ever so slightly. "I couldn't resist. He was a fine-looking man, kind and sensitive. Just the sort who would make a good husband. Although I must admit it wasn't those qualities that spurred my interest—it was an urge to keep him safe from poor Maisie."

"Safe?" It was an odd choice of word.

"I worried that she might trap him," she said. "There are ways, you know, scandalous though it is to speak of such things. Even the most moral man can succumb to temptation."

"Do you really believe Maisie would have done such a thing?"

"Marriage is a sacred bond. Not to be entered into lightly, as we are aware from our own vows. I don't know that Maisie would have stooped so low, but I couldn't stand by and watch anyone—man or woman—tricked into a lifetime commitment." She gave a little laugh. "Now I sound like a sanctimonious lout. I promise you, I'm not so bad."

"Did the gamekeeper want a wife?" I asked.

"No, he was quite adamant on the point," she said. "It's part of what made it so easy to suggest potential candidates. It was a bit of fun, really, nothing more. I'd never before been interested in playing matchmaker and doubt I'd have been so inclined to interfere if I'd thought there was any chance of my influencing his opinion on the subject."

"Did you notice anything odd during the ceilidh?" I asked. "Was anyone out of sorts or behaving in an unusual manner?"

"No, it was perfectly ordinary, everything just as usual."

"Mr. Pringle mentioned that someone poured whisky into the punch."

"That, Lady Emily, is not something I'd consider entirely out of the normal way of things," she said. "Hamish isn't the most observant man. By the second hour of a ceilidh, someone has always poured more alcohol into the punch. Generally, however, it's rum, which I bring from the vicarage, so he doesn't notice as the flavor stays broadly the same. He doesn't think it should be strong, but I don't entirely agree. While I've never been particularly fond of spirits, I find rum less disagreeable than most and I must admit that it can prove quite valuable as a social lubricant. Because my husband does not share my opinion, I go light on the rum and then leave the bottle where any interested party can find it and amend the punch accordingly. This time, however, I was short of rum and had none left to bring. As a result, there was only whisky to add to the punch."

"Forgive me for having to ask this," I said. "When did you leave the ceilidh?"

"I know that I returned to the vicarage a bit before eleven. I heard the clock strike as I was climbing the stairs to the bedroom." Tears pooled in her eyes.

I hated having to question her, all the more so now that I knew she'd reached home at least an hour before the murder. "I'm more sorry than I can say."

"The Lord never gives us a burden we can't bear," she said, "although it doesn't always feel that way, does it? There is one thing about the ceilidh that I've only just remembered. What a fool I am not to have thought of it sooner. When I first started feeling unwell, perhaps an hour or so before I had to go home, I went outside, hoping fresh air would improve the situation. I saw the gamekeeper standing away from the village hall with a man I didn't recognize. They were arguing."

"You're sure it was a man?" I asked. "I saw him arguing with Dr. Harris."

"No, no, it definitely wasn't her. I didn't recognize the man, but he had shockingly pale hair, almost silver in the moonlight, and he was dressed most strangely. He wasn't wearing a kilt, but knee breeches instead. Thinking on it, he must be Norwegian."

"Why do you think he was Norwegian?" I asked.

"His clothing. I don't know the name for traditional Norwegian dress, but that's what it looked like to me. There was his hair as well. Only a Scandinavian would be so blond. It's that heritage where I got mine." She closed her eyes and swayed. The motion was so sudden it seemed contrived. "Forgive me, Lady Emily, but I'm starting to feel unwell again. Will you forgive me if I retire to my room?"

18

Tansy

1676

"Finella Logan? I dinnae like her and I dinnae trust her," Cora said. "Never have, never will. She's had shifty eyes since she was a child." We were out wandering in the mountains, picking up plants to be used as dyes for her wool. For the first time in weeks, Cora had invited me and not Rossalyn.

"She doesn't seem so bad to me." I scraped some lichen off a rock and dropped it into the basket looped over my arm. "Most of us improve from what we were as children, shifty eyes or not."

"Believe what you want, Tasnim. I won't try to change your mind."

She was the only person who'd consistently called me by my correct name since I was taken from Tunis. This endeared her to me and made me hesitate to argue with her. Even so, I wouldn't let her think ill of Finella. "If you got to know her now—"

"Nothing could induce me to do that," she said. "I know this place and I know these people. I've lived here all my life. There's not a soul in the village who can pretend to be someone they're not around me. Finella is always up to something. Always, I promise you that. She likes playing with people. Manipulating them."

"To what end?" I asked. "She's not in a position of power. What can she hope to accomplish?"

"It amuses her." Cora brushed dirt from her heavy wool skirt. "Sometimes, people with no power are the most dangerous of all. Look what she did with you and the kirk."

"She didn't do anything except point out that Rossalyn wouldn't want me to be forced to attend services that are part of a religion I don't—"

"Yes, it's all very innocent, isn't it? Dinnae be naïve, Tasnim. Do you think the rest of village agrees with Rossalyn? That you should be welcome to worship any god you like? I take no issue with it, but this is a primitive place. We're not what I'd call an enlightened group of people. It's not wise to give brutish Highlanders an excuse to persecute you. You told me how concerned you were when Rossalyn wanted to sneak into the castle and remove possessions she'd left there. Skipping Sunday services is at least as dangerous, especially with all the talk of witches in Balieth."

I should never have breathed a word about Rossalyn taking things from the castle. That was the trouble with being so far from one's home. We all need a confidante, someone we can trust absolutely. I'd always known Rossalyn couldn't be that. Not because she wasn't kind or a good person but because she didn't understand what the world was like for me. She wanted to (on occasion) and tried to (on occasion), but it would never matter deeply enough to her for it to be a priority. As long as things were agreeable on the surface, she wouldn't prod for more. I was content with that and kept myself on guard with her.

From the beginning, however, Cora was different. Her experience might be limited, but she understood people and noticed the things that made them unique. She was interested and curious. She wanted to know every detail about how I came to be in Cairnfarn. What the weather was like the day I was snatched from the market in Tunis. The conditions on the ship that brought me to Scotland. The name of my first, and most awful, master. She always said she didn't mean to pry, that she wasn't asking questions so that she could be entertained or deliciously horrified by the answers. She cared. She wanted to understand me all the way, she'd explained, and that wasn't possible without learning my entire history.

As a result, I'd started to trust her more than I had anyone since my kidnapping. Now I started to recognize how vulnerable that made me. The day I'd told her about Rossalyn's aborted plan, I'd had the sense to pull back before I went too far. I'd told Cora that I'd managed to persuade Rossalyn that we shouldn't take anything without first asking for permission and I never breathed a word about how the books came to be in our possession. If she'd asked about it, I would have told her the story we'd invented after Ewan had come to the cottage: that they'd always been in her bedchamber in the castle. Stupidly, I hadn't exercised caution when confiding in her about Rossalyn's initial thoughts.

That was because I wanted to be close to someone. A real friend. Not a former employer who liked me, more or less. When we seek such a person, we become careless. We share things that ought to be kept secret, because we know doing so will form a bond between us. I couldn't keep everyone at arm's length forever unless I wanted to go mad, but suddenly I doubted the wisdom of confiding in Cora. If she gossiped about Finella, she'd gossip about me. I needed to be more careful. So I pulled away, ever so slightly, never realizing that doing so would only make me all the more vulnerable.

I didn't know that, then.

I didn't know the evil that was lurking in the shadows.

I didn't know that some things can't be stopped.

I didn't know how bad it would get.

We never realize, do we, until it's too late?

19

1905

I sought out my husband when I returned to the castle from the vicarage. He was in the library, bent over the First Folio.

"The water damage isn't extensive and is largely limited to the back of the volume. It's as if someone left it on damp ground," Colin said, "but I cannot imagine how that could've occurred. I found this marking a page in *Macbeth*." He held up a piece of faded saffron-colored ribbon.

"Which page?" I asked.

"The one that includes *By the pricking of my thumbs, / Something wicked this way comes.*"

"Ah, the witches." I took the ribbon from him and felt a jolt through my body. The silk was old and delicate, yet somehow imbued with energy. I put it back in the book and recounted for him my conversation with Mrs. Pringle.

"Do you believe there's any veracity to what she told you?" he asked.

"Not the bit about the potentially dodgy Norwegian," I said. "Everything about that was suspect, from the way she conveniently remembered it to the details she used to describe him. She insisted that only a Scandinavian could have hair that color, but it's the same shade as hers. She's not the only Scot with Viking heritage. It's clear she was trying to keep suspicion from falling on one of the villagers. I get the sense she likes to mother them, which I suppose isn't altogether unusual for a vicar's wife."

"A vicar's wife should care about the truth," Colin said, frowning. "If she doesn't, why not? She knows more than she's admitting."

The door opened. Jeremy came into the room and flung himself onto one of the leather-covered chairs arranged in front of the fireplace. "Detecting is surprisingly draining. I'd no idea. If I had, I'd never have agreed to speak to Pringle for you, Em."

"How did he respond when you told him the gamekeeper wasn't who he claimed?" I asked.

He filled two glasses of whisky, one for him and one for Colin, but only after first pouring a glass of port for me. "First off, he didn't seem surprised in the least, which prompted me to do my best impersonation of a detective and ask why. I felt a strong need for a pipe and a deerstalker hat. Isn't that what that Holmes bloke has? At any rate, Pringle denied knowing anything specific, but admitted that they met each other frequently to discuss *troubling things in the man's past.*"

"What sort of things?" Colin asked.

"He wouldn't say. Apparently a bloke can tell a vicar pretty much whatever he wants and be confident that not a word of the conversation will ever be shared with anyone, even a duke. I tell you, this title is bloody well useless."

"Very like its bearer," Colin said.

"Thank you, Hargreaves. It warms my heart to hear you say that. I do work hard to earn such lofty accolades. And apologies, to you, Em, for my beastly language. My sense of decorum is nonexistent." He drained his glass and put it down on the small table next to his chair. "I did my best to press Pringle regarding the gamekeeper, but he wouldn't budge an inch. Told me nothing of any use and now I come home to find that detective harassing my servants. It's too much to be borne. London would be more peaceful."

"I shouldn't worry about Kircaldy," Colin said. "He's more interested in the fresh batch of scones your cook prepared than in figuring out who killed Sinclair. He won't do more than go through the motions. I've just about convinced him that he should leave it all to us, which will be better for everyone."

"That's a relief," Jeremy said. "There was one other thing with Pringle. He mentioned that Callum Fletcher left the ceilidh earlier than he admitted when Emily and I spoke to him. When Pringle heard about his wife and went rushing home, he saw Fletcher coming out of the woods on the path that leads to the loch."

"Why didn't he tell us that before?" I asked.

"He claimed he only just remembered."

"It's possible that's true," Colin said. "Given the nature of his wife's medical emergency, his memories of the evening may not be wholly reliable."

"Interesting that Mrs. Pringle suddenly remembers seeing a stranger while her husband simultaneously recalls seeing the village's most cantankerous resident," I said. We told Jeremy about the mysterious Norwegian.

"Oh." He stood up, refilled both his and Colin's whisky. "She should've known better. That's just Old Harald. Auld Harald, I should say. He's a Viking ghost, so it's unlikely he had anything to do with the murder. Possible, I suppose. Perhaps we should consult Richard on the subject. He's rather keen on that sort of thing. Knows an appalling amount about it."

"A ghost." I raised an eyebrow. "Surely you don't believe that."

"Not for an instant, Em," Jeremy said, "although I've always thought it makes for a splendid story. There's something appealing about the idea of a giant Viking tromping around Cairnfarn, watching over us all."

"If there were a Viking tromping around, he wouldn't be watching over the place, he'd be looking for a fight," Colin said.

"I'm not going to let you get me caught up in details, Hargreaves. In my mind, a Viking would be my ally. My hair, after all, is vaguely blond. Perhaps when I die I could return and haunt Cairnfarn. That would be jolly good fun."

"I doubt you'd make a frightening ghost," I said.

"I'd never try," he said. "I'd prove that spirits can be as useless as a living man."

I ignored this and turned to Colin. "I can accept that Mr. Pringle might not have been thinking clearly, given his wife's situation."

"Which also will have influenced her memory of the night," he said. "Even so, I think it's likely that what you speculated earlier is correct: she's afraid one of the villagers will be accused of the murder and thinks inventing a mysterious Norwegian will protect that person."

"No, I can't agree," Jeremy said. "If that were the case, she wouldn't have described him the way she did. Everyone recognizes Auld Harald."

"Let's suppose, then, that she's telling the truth," I said. "Might someone in the village have deliberately altered his appearance to conjure up the image of the local ghost?"

"It would ensure that no one would take it seriously when a witness—like Mrs. Pringle—reported what she saw," Jeremy said.

"Only if we're to believe that the residents of Cairnfarn think Auld Harald is anything but a good story," Colin said. "I'm incredulous on that count."

"As am I," I said. "No adult would—"

"Oh, Em, you're wrong," Jeremy said. "Auld Harald is as real to the people of Cairnfarn as the fairies are."

"Fairies?" Colin's eyebrows shot nearly to his hairline. "You're not strengthening your position, Bainbridge."

"This is Scotland, man. You cannae deny the existence of fairies!"

"Please, don't attempt to adopt a brogue," I said. "At best you'll offend every Scotsman on the estate; at worst you'll bring down the wrath of the fairies."

"So you do believe they're real," Jeremy said.

"No, I don't." I crossed my arms. "Nor do I believe the villagers think Auld Harald is."

"There's no use arguing," Colin said. "We shall accept that it is possible someone dressed as a Norwegian—or a Viking—in an attempt to hide his identity while murdering the gamekeeper. We also cannot reject the notion that Mrs. Pringle is lying to protect someone."

"Her husband?" I asked. "She's devoted to him."

"There's no chance the vicar murdered someone," Jeremy said. "It's inconceivable. Pringle doesn't have it in him. And even if he did, what would motivate him to act in such a barbaric manner?"

"We know he and the gamekeeper shared private conversations

that Mr. Pringle believes should be kept confidential," I said. "What if Mr. Pringle learned something about the man's past that he couldn't tolerate? Something that so affronted him he knew his only course of action was to mete out justice on his own? Dr. Cameron says that the first injuries likely occurred when rocks were thrown at the victim. The vicar might have initially kept his distance because he knew he wasn't capable of overpowering him."

"Come, now, Em, you can't believe old Pringle would do anything of the sort," Jeremy said.

"I admit it seems unlikely," I said. "Which leaves us with the notion that Mrs. Pringle is protecting someone else. Who?"

The next day, Colin received a telegram from Mr. Kircaldy, confirming that the police in Glasgow had identified the photographs of the body as Daniel Gordon. At last we knew our victim's name. I set off to see Irene MacDuff, who'd promised she'd try to uncover more information about the relationship, such as it was, between Maisie and the gamekeeper. She didn't answer when I knocked on the door, so I walked through the front garden and around the house, where I found her crouched down, gathering mushrooms that were growing at the base of a tree.

"I didnae expect you to take so long getting here, Lady Emily," she said, not looking up as I approached. "I've news for you." She said nothing further until she'd collected all the mushrooms. Then, at last, she stood up and handed me her basket. "Walk with me."

We followed a path through the rest of her neatly planted beds to the back fence, where she opened a blue gate and stepped through. The path, which was straight and true in her garden, now started to wind, taking us through a meadow until it skirted the forest. There, it crossed a narrow stone bridge over a stream and began to make its way up a towering mountain. Twice I asked Irene questions, and twice she told me to be patient.

The path gave way to what looked like a meandering sheep trail that shot steeply toward the summit of the peak. I pride myself on keeping in fit condition, but found the going extremely rough. Physically, it was challenging; I wished for hobnailed boots and a divided skirt. Jagged rocks poked up from the ground and a wicked wind whipped around us, blowing the hat from my head. I watched it bounce along the side of the mountain until it disappeared over a terrifying precipice. Moments after that my hair—unruly even in the best of times—started to fall, the pins securing it no match for the wind.

"Tie it back with this," Irene said, handing me a bright blue ribbon from her jacket pocket. "It will keep it out of your face. The summit isnae as far away as it looks. You're more than capable of making it."

The sun came out—briefly—and, for an instant, I almost believed it was a sign she was correct. My lungs thought differently, however, and I had to sit on a rock and catch my breath before I could continue. But continue I did, despite moments of panic where I despaired I would ever make it home or anywhere else. After what felt like a most unwelcome eternity, I took the hand Irene offered and, together, we scrambled onto the rocky top of the peak. The view was magnificent. I could see the river winding its way toward the loch and counted at least three streams. Trees that looked like toy soldiers dotted the valley all the way across to where more mountains rose on the other side. Irene murmured something in Gaelic that sounded like a prayer.

"It's spectacular," I said. "Thank you for bringing me here."

"Och, it was necessary," she said and sat on a boulder. "I've had a wee word with Nesbitt. He knows better than anyone what goes on at the castle."

"Nesbitt?" I asked, sitting on a rock across from her. "The man who runs the stables?"

"Aye. He said your husband talked to him. Took great pride in having told him nothing. He's not the sort who likes outsiders."

"When I encountered him, he didn't strike me as the sort who likes to speak, period."

"That's true enough," she said, "but he's known me since I was a wee lass. I make him a tisane that helps with his rheumatism, so he knows better than to stay silent when I come around. Told him I wouldnae give it to him until he'd confessed everything he knows."

"And what does he know?"

"Why dinnae you ask him yourself?" She motioned behind us. I turned my head and saw the groom, who scurried up a scree field on the other side of the summit from the path and stood in front of me. He was a sturdy man, short and broad, with a dark, disheveled beard better suited to the previous century than the present. He wore a pair of tweed breeches, hill boots, and a jacket covered with pockets of various sizes. He crossed his arms and glowered at me.

"I didnae want to speak to you, but Irene here told me I must, so I'll get on with it. I was at the ceilidh, but only for a moment or two, to have some of Mrs. Pringle's famous punch," he said. His voice was like gravel. "It was a scandal, that. Wholly bastardized by someone pouring most of a bottle of fine whisky into it. Whisky and rum dinnae go together, so it was ruining them both, wasnae it? I knew full well which boys in the village did it—they're always the ones giving trouble—so I dragged them outside and threatened them with a thrashing if they ever did something so stupid again."

"That seems like something of an overreaction," I said.

156

Nesbitt shrugged. "Depends how you feel about wasting perfectly good whisky. When I knew they were scared enough to behave for a little while, I started back for the castle, taking the path that goes along the loch. I saw two things. The first was the poor, soon-to-be-murdered man and Maisie Drummond, that cheeky wench, together in a secluded spot, verra close together, if you catch my meaning."

"We've learned his name was Daniel Gordon," I said.

Nesbitt nodded. "On the edge of the clearing, there was Effie, the maid at the vicarage, watching them. Effie didnae stay long. She'd an expression of longing on her face. Hurt, too, she looked. Another one of Gordon's victims."

"Victims?" I asked.

"Aye, it might not be the kindest of descriptions, but it's a fitting one," he said. "The girls in the village couldnae get enough of the man. Not that it was his fault. He didnae go out of his way to encourage them, but he didnae do anything to put them off, either. Cairnfarn is a small place. When someone new and fine looking appears, he will be noticed. Gordon didnae want to hurt anyone's feelings, so was often too kind."

"What was the second thing you saw?" I asked.

"Now you must understand, Lady Emily, that Maisie Drummond is no particular friend of mine," he said. "Even so, she's harmless as a midge."

"Would we describe them as harmless?" I asked. I'd encountered enough swarms of the tiny insects that plagued Scotland to consider them differently. Their bites might be small, but the itching they caused could drive one mad.

"Och, they're annoying as anything, but dinnae cause serious harm," he said. "They do a bang-up job keeping outsiders away from the Highlands, so I'm happy to share the place with them. Better a few midges than loads of Englishmen. So, aye, on balance, Maisie is harmless."

"I'm inclined to agree with you," I said.

"You might consider changing your mind about that after you hear what I have to say, but you shouldnae. I only stayed watching her and Gordon because I knew he didnae want to be caught in her clutches. It was clear—more than clear—that's exactly what she was trying to do. I willnae go into details, but I could see what she was playing at." Nesbitt's cheeks colored. "When things progressed to a point that might have, er, become problematic, Gordon pushed her away. She stumbled and fell. When she got up, she flung herself right at him, again and again, slapping and kicking and doing anything she could to attack him. Now, she's a wee one and couldnae accomplish much, so I didnae step in. I would've if I'd thought Gordon was in danger. The girl was humiliated and lashing out. She wasnae going to cause him any lasting injury."

"How far is this spot from where Mr. Gordon's body was found?" I asked.

"A short walk. You could cover it in a minute or so."

"How did it all turn out?" I asked.

"Gordon let her do her worst for a while and then he took her by the shoulders and sat her on the ground. He crouched down in front of her, said something, then turned around and went back toward the village hall."

"What did he say?"

"I couldnae make out the exact words, but his tone wasnae full of kindness. He'd had enough."

"Did Maisie follow him?" I asked.

"Not at first. I wondered for a minute what I should do. I didnae

want to embarrass her, but I couldnae leave her sitting there all miserable, could I? I walked over, gave her a handkerchief, and told her to
get back inside and demand that Gordon dance with her. He wouldnae cause a scene with so many people around. It would soothe her a
bit and they could both walk away holding their heads high."

"Did she take your advice?"

"That I cannae say. She headed toward the village hall and I
headed home."

"What time did this occur?" I asked.

"I dinnae ken."

"You've no idea?"

"None. I'm not the sort of gent who wears a watch." He laughed,
apparently amused with himself.

"I appreciate you telling me all this," I said.

"I've done so only because Irene said I must. Dinnae think that
means I'll want to be speaking to you again. If you insist that I do,
you'll have to come all the way back up here to meet me. That'll
keep you from giving me any more trouble. You already know all I
have to say, so that should be that."

I crossed my arms, mimicking his pose, and gave him a fierce
look. "Did you consider Mr. Gordon a friend?" I asked.

Mr. Nesbitt looked at me and squinted. "Aye, I suppose I did."

"Then you'll want justice for him," I said. "Because of that,
should you think of anything else that might have bearing on his
murder, you'll tell me. If that means I need to climb this peak again,
I shall. I won't let his killer go unpunished."

He didn't reply, only nodded, but he met my eyes as he did it,
and there was no venom in his expression. Or at least less than there
had been. It felt like progress. Silent, he turned around and scrambled back down the peak.

Irene had sat still and quiet during all of this. "So was that helpful to you?" she asked.

"More than I could've hoped," I said.

"He's right to say you shouldnae get the wrong impression about Maisie. She didnae kill Gordon. I'd bet my life on that."

I didn't reply, not at once. Maisie certainly had motive for wanting him dead and she'd made a great show of lying about their engagement. "I'm not convinced either way. I agree it seems unlikely, but at this point I can't dismiss any possibility. Until I have more evidence, everyone must be considered a suspect."

"Even me?" Irene smiled. "Och, that's a good one. How do you think I did it? Throwing stones at him until he keeled over? And then stabbed him dead with his own knife?"

Knowing how gossip spread in the village, I shouldn't have been surprised to hear her words, but they took me aback me nonetheless. All of a sudden, I felt vulnerable on the top of the peak, sitting so close to the edge, across from a woman who might have killed Mr. Gordon.

"What would your motive be?" I asked, modulating my voice to give the appearance of calm.

"He was a blooming annoying bugger," she said, "although I dinnae ken if that's grounds for murder. Too handsome for his own good, but never gave me any trouble. I cannae say I took to him, but I've known worse in my life. Nae, he didnae deserve what he got."

I looked into her wide blue eyes and believed her. It wasn't rational, it probably wasn't wise, but somehow she'd convinced me. Perhaps she was a witch, after all.

20

Tansy
1676

The less time I spent with Cora, the more life in Cairnfarn took on the appearance of endless drudgery. Wandering with her had been the brightest part of my days; without it, my life grew devoid of pleasure, for nearly all that was left was toil. It took an enormous amount of work for Rossalyn and me to run our little household. She helped, there was no denying that, but she wasn't suited to heavy labor. She couldn't do laundry. Couldn't deal with the ever-encroaching weeds in our garden. Couldn't even bring herself to touch any form of raw meat.

"It's squishy and bloody," she said, watching me butcher a rabbit I'd caught in a snare. "Quite repulsive. I'm not sure I'll be able to eat it."

I ordered her to stay out of sight until I was ready to serve dinner. By then, she was hungry enough that she'd forgot how much she hated seeing how it was prepared. I was glad she ate, but less pleased to have to take on yet another duty on my own. Cooking now became my exclusive domain. I shouldn't complain. Rossalyn washed dishes without moaning, at least she did until the hot water and harsh lye soap chapped the delicate skin on her hands and made it crack.

The sorry state of her skin led me to seek out Finella. Given the type of work she did in the laundry, she'd know how best to treat painful skin. I walked to the castle, relishing the sunlight shining down from the sky. It appeared so rarely that when it did, there was something magical about it, almost like the stars were dropping down on us. It made the loch sparkle and the mountains glow. The trees looked taller, reaching up to the heavens, greedy for more light. It was as if Allah were showering the earth with favors.

I was still more than a little afraid of Ewan MacAllister and didn't want to burst into the castle without specific permission. When I arrived, I went to the servants' entrance and asked for the housekeeper. She greeted me warmly enough, but didn't offer me a cup of tea, only told me I could find Finella in the washhouse.

I'd never before been near the washhouse. The odors emanating from it, even from what seemed like a great distance, were appalling. Every step I took closer made it worse. When I tugged open the door, I covered my nose with a handkerchief, then, almost immediately, put it away again. It made no discernible difference. Huge cauldrons full of steaming water hung over fires. In the corner stood vats reeking of urine, where dirty clothes and linens would be soaked until they were ready for the women to bang them clean with long, wooden beetles. I knew urine was an effective stain remover, but it disgusted me nonetheless. Home in Tunis, we preferred sweetly scented soaps to human waste.

Finella was wringing out clean garments and piling them in a large wicker basket. When she saw me, she motioned for me to wait a moment. As soon as her basket was full, she picked it up, came to me, and we went outside so that she could start spreading the contents to dry on the grass. I asked her about Rossalyn's skin troubles.

"Aye, what you need for that is a good balm," she said, shaking out a gentleman's shirt. "How are your hands?"

"Cracked, but not so bad as hers."

She held my hands up to her face. "Someone has changed out your soap for something too caustic. Ordinary soap shouldnae be causing anyone this much trouble."

"I can't imagine anyone would do that," I said. "Rossalyn isn't accustomed to labor. She and her skin have been pampered from the time she was a babe. The most gentle soap on earth would irritate her if she used it to wash dishes."

"Nae, this is more than that." Finella frowned, then shook her head. "You should consider who might have done such a thing. In the meantime, Agnes Campbell can help you with a balm. Do you know her?"

She was the herbalist in the village who'd had no interest in offering me a job. "I do."

"Tell her I sent you and that you want the special formula she uses for me. Dinnae let her give you anything else. She's an ornery sort, but dinnae let that put you off. If she knows we're friends, she'll be good to you. Give her this." She fished around in the deep pocket of her apron and pulled out a smooth, shining rock with a few lines carved on it. "She'll know what it means."

I thanked her and went to see Agnes. She had possession of a snug little cottage as far away from the church as one could be and still live within the village. Neat rows of plants, which she kept carefully tended, surrounded the building. The limewash on the walls looked fresh, and the windows sparkled. She opened the door before I knocked.

"Finella Logan sent me to you," I said and handed her the rock. Agnes took it and smiled.

"So she did. Come in, then."

The inside of her cottage was even more orderly than the outside. Narrow shelves lined the walls, filled with jars and bottles labeled in precise handwriting. Below them stood long tables that held the tools of her trade. I confess I didn't recognize most of them beyond a set of scales and a mortar and pestle.

"I'm in need of a balm." I explained the condition of Rossalyn's hands. "Finella suggested the formula you use for her."

Agnes frowned. "Did she, now?" She turned away from me and started pulling things off the shelves. "You're certain that's what you want?"

I was momentarily filled with doubt. How should I know what I wanted? "I—I believe so. Finella was firm about it."

"The Logan girl always knows what's best, doesnae she? At least she thinks so. I'll prepare it for you, but it will take until tomorrow morning for me to finish. I'll bring it to your cottage."

"I can collect it if you'd prefer," I said. "I wouldn't want to inconvenience you."

"Nae, that winnae be necessary." She put her back to the shelves and stared at me, narrowing her eyes. There was something vaguely frightening about her. It didn't make sense, not really. She was perfectly ordinary looking. Dark auburn hair pulled into a tight bun. Brown eyes, neither too far apart nor too close together. Straight nose. Well-formed lips. Yet there was more to it. Her eyes seemed to pierce right through you while her mouth looked poised to start speaking words that could wound you. How did I know this? I felt it. Deep in my soul.

"Thank you." The words felt heavy.

"Why are you afraid of me, child?" she asked. "Is it because I wouldnae give you employment?"

"No, of course not," I said. "I realize I have no qualifications. Why would you take me on?"

She narrowed her eyes. Her brow furrowed. There was something cunning in her face. "I widnae take you on because I dinnae ken you and I cannae trust what I dinnae ken. Do you understand? I must be careful lest people accuse me of things I dinnae do. These are dangerous times."

The witch hunts in nearby Balieth were our local proof that Scotland was more vigorous than anywhere else in Europe when it came to hunting down those guilty of practicing magic. People felt strongly that it was necessary to root out such immoral individuals. Did I believe in witches? I'd never given the matter much thought, but I knew better than to ignore the importance of taking precautions against the evil eye. That was superstition, which didn't feel the same as witchcraft. Everyone instinctively understood the difference. Harmless rituals to protect those we love are a far cry from casting spells.

"It behooves you to be careful," I said.

"As it does you, Tansy. Think on that. I'll come to you at the cottage tomorrow."

21

1905

I wasn't fully aware of how much my hike with Irene had sapped my energy until I was about a quarter of a mile away from the castle. All at once, my legs felt like lead and I had a stitch in my side. The fact that I was desperate for water was the only thing keeping me moving forward. Then, like something out of a dream, I saw the boys on the path in front of me, Henry holding a flask in one hand and Cedric's lead in the other. The crocodile was walking patiently behind him.

"Why is that creature out of his enclosure?" I asked.

"You forbade me to go in it," Henry said, "so I lured him out with a chicken Cook gave me. He's always liked his lead and is much happier when he gets out for a walk."

"It's not safe for him to be out," I said. "A crocodile is a dangerous beast."

"I'm perfectly capable of managing him. He never gave any trouble in Egypt, and I had him on his lead every day. There's nothing to worry about. We've brought water for you." Henry lifted the flask toward me. "The Greats told us you'd need it."

"The Greats?" I asked, taking the flask and drinking deeply from it. "You ought not refer to them in so informal a fashion."

"Och, they told us to do just that," Tom said. He was wearing the kit of Highland dress I'd purchased before we left London and was doing the best to sound like a Scotsman. "They sent us out to wait for you. Is it true you were forced to climb the Smithy?"

"The Smithy?"

Tom slipped his hand into mine. "Aye. That's the name of the Munro—in Scotland, that's what they call mountains over three thousand feet—the witch took you to. Its shape looks something like a blacksmith's anvil."

"She's not a witch," Richard said. I took another swig of water. "Miss MacDuff is an herbalist, which is an entirely respectable profession. For centuries these women—it's a traditionally female role—who often serve as healers as well, have suffered from the ignorance of those around them. They've always played a valuable role in their communities, but because not everyone understands the use of medicinal herbs, people often accuse them of practicing magic. Thousands of them were burned as witches at the stake after Mary Queen of Scots made it an offense punishable by death. It wasn't until 1735 that Parliament passed a law forbidding anyone from fobbing accusations of witchcraft at their fellow man."

"Fellow woman," Henry said. "You told us they were primarily women."

"I was employing the word *man* in the generic sense of *human*," Richard said, frustration creeping into his voice. Henry loved to torment his brothers.

"Miss Josephine and Miss Adeline have ordered us to bring you straight to them," Tom said, speaking loudly enough to reasonably expect that he'd distract me from his brothers' arguing. "No bath, no nothing. They insist upon it."

"We're allowed to stay and hear all about the witch," Henry said. "I'm bringing Cedric as well because I don't expect it to be particularly interesting. I've not heard a single reliable account of any spell she's cast."

"That's because she's not a witch," Richard said. "Herbalists—"

I interrupted him and turned to his brother. "Henry, you are to return Cedric to his enclosure at once."

He murmured assent, but was not best pleased and continued to argue with his brother all the way back to the castle (where he entrusted one of the footmen with the task of taking the crocodile to the menagerie), up the steps, and into the Greats' sitting room. They didn't knock on the door. Instead, Henry flung it open with great panache and announced our arrival, as if it weren't already self-evident. The Greats clapped and cheered.

"Oh, marvelous, Emily," Miss Josephine said. "You're covered with dust!"

"And by tomorrow there will be freckles on your nose," Miss Adeline said. "If, that is, you freckle. Do you?"

"No, not really," I said. "My mother always insisted I would, but, so far it's never happened, despite my callous disregard for parasols. I—"

"Stop, stop," Miss Josephine said. "We've no interest in parasols or freckles. Sit. Are you ready for a stiff whisky or do you need tea first?"

The boys were huddled by the door, their faces a mixture of awe and delight. They'd never heard anyone speak the way the Greats did.

"You boys surely prefer whisky to tea," Miss Adeline said. She reached toward the decanter.

"No, no, they shall not have whisky," I said. "It would be best if they returned to the nursery. Nanny will be beside herself—"

"Mama, no!" Henry exclaimed.

"Nanny's not worried in the least," Richard said.

"I could run up and let her know we're quite safe," Tom said.

"They're to stay with us," Miss Josephine said, winking at them. "There's nothing more to be said on the subject. Now, lads, as your mother objects to whisky, we'll give you lemonade instead." Only then did I notice the pitcher on the table. They'd never planned to give the boys spirits.

"Personally, I'd prefer lemonade regardless," Tom said.

"Me as well," Richard said. "Whisky burns." The instant the words were out of his mouth, Henry whacked him on the arm.

"We've been informed that whisky burns," he said. "Papa explained that's why we can't have it until we're older."

"Much older," Richard said.

"Infinitely older," Tom said.

The Greats laughed. "What lovely boys you are," Miss Adeline said and poured them all lemonade. "Now, Emily, tell us all about your time with Irene the witch."

"Irene MacDuff is not a witch," I said.

"She's an herbalist," Richard volunteered.

"Quite, quite, but that makes it all so much less fascinating, doesn't it?" Miss Josephine said.

Richard blushed furiously. "I'm certain there's some truth to what you say, but if people were more open-minded they'd see that the work she does is fascinating in its own right."

"Yes, but a little bit of the magic spices everything up," Miss Adeline said. "The fairies would agree."

Richard beamed. "Oh, they would, ma'am, they would. Have you seen any in the vicinity of the castle?"

"We'll tell you all about it after we're through with your mother," Miss Josephine said. "She's starting to look impatient."

I gave them a concise description of my hike up the Munro, but omitted the details of what Mr. Nesbitt had told me. The boys didn't need further exposure to the murder investigation; they'd already seen and heard too much. I wouldn't even have mentioned Mr. Nesbitt in front of them, but apparently it was already common knowledge in the village that he'd met me at the summit.

"You're leaving out the good bits," Richard said.

"She doesn't want to further upset us," Henry said. "I heard her saying that to Papa."

"That's quite enough," I said. "You know all you need to. Run off now before Nanny starts to despair."

Henry looked to the Greats for encouragement, which I feared they'd give, but they only shook their heads.

"Do as your mother says or she'll decide we're a bad influence and ban you from seeing us," Miss Josephine said.

"Can't be seen corrupting youth," Miss Adeline said. "Like Socrates."

"Who's Socrates?" Tom asked.

"A philosopher who lived in ancient Athens and was executed after being found guilty of corrupting youth," Miss Josephine said.

"They made him drink hemlock," Miss Adeline said.

"A horrible way to die," Miss Josephine said, "although Socrates didn't seem to mind."

"We'll send for you later," Miss Adeline said, "and tell you all about it and the Cairnfarn fairies."

"Or perhaps we'll dine with you in the nursery tonight," Miss Josephine said.

"Oh, yes, let's do that," Miss Adeline said. "I'll speak to Cook about what we'd like to eat."

"Balmoral chicken stuffed with haggis and drizzled with whisky sauce, I think," Miss Josephine said.

"And whim-wham pudding to finish," Miss Adeline said. "The raspberries are perfectly ripe."

They nodded in unison. The boys scuttled off. Henry came back a moment later, ran into the room, kissed me, and ran back out.

"Delightful lads," Miss Josephine said.

"You'll forgive us for prodding them to behave badly," Miss Adeline said.

"Childhood is too short and generally squandered," Miss Josephine said. "We want to ensure theirs is neither. Now, tell us the rest of what you learned at the Munro."

I did as they asked, sparing no detail.

"That Maisie is cheekier than I guessed," Miss Adeline said.

"Let's summon her," Miss Josephine said. She pulled the bell and ordered the footman who responded to fetch her. It was the same footman who'd given me the torch on the night I first called on the Greats. He turned to me before he left the room.

"I warned you against taking any of Irene's tonics, didnae I? She's got her claws in you now." With that, he pulled the door closed behind him.

I was aghast.

"Don't look so concerned, Emily. I don't believe you're under her spell," Miss Adeline said. "You only had one tisane the first time you visited her, and none today, isn't that right?"

"I assure you, I'm not concerned, but that's right, I only had one. How did you know?"

"That's old ground, already covered," Miss Josephine said. "But you should take care. Irene can be a tricky one."

"How so?" I asked. "She seems perfectly straightforward to me."

"Straightforward, is she?" Miss Adeline asked. "Is that how she got you to the top of the Smithy?"

I heard a soft knock on the door. Maisie opened it a crack and looked in. It was a relief to see her. Tired as I was, I'd prefer not to spar with the Greats about how to best describe Irene. They were making my head spin.

"You sent for me, madam?" the maid asked.

"Come in, girl, come in," Miss Josephine said. "We've heard a bit more about your adventures the night of the ceilidh."

"Perhaps you'd like to give us your side of the story before we draw any conclusions," Miss Adeline said.

"Pull that over and sit down," Miss Josephine said, motioning to a straight-backed wooden chair tucked into a corner. It looked hideously uncomfortable.

"The Chair of Truth," Miss Adeline said. "It's been in the castle for ages, cursed by one of the witches burned here in the seventeenth century."

"Witches were burned at Cairnfarn?" I asked. "I thought—"

"There's no need for details at the moment. Bad things occur when a person tries to evade the chair's powers," Miss Josephine said, "so you might as well get on with it, Maisie."

"I told Mr. Hargreaves and Lady Emily everything," the girl said, starting to fidget almost the instant she sat down.

"We both know that's not true," I said. "There was a witness to your altercation with Mr. Gordon. I assume you've heard that was the gamekeeper's true name."

Pale as her complexion was, I shouldn't have thought there was enough color in it to drain from her face, but evidently there was. She looked like a ghost. "Someone saw me?"

"Two people, actually," I said. "We know about both your attempted seduction and the physical attack you mounted against Mr. Gordon following its failure."

Now she turned crimson. "I wasnae trying to seduce—"

Miss Adeline waved her hand. "There's no use in denying it. He was a fine specimen."

"If I were younger, I would've tried to seduce him," Miss Josephine said.

"Not that you would've admitted it then," Miss Adeline said.

"Quite," Miss Josephine said. "One of the pleasures of becoming aged is no longer having to censor what one says."

"Or thinks," Miss Adeline said.

Maisie's eyes looked as if they would pop out of her head. I needed to take back control of the conversation.

"You and Mr. Gordon weren't engaged, were you?" I asked.

Tears started to fall down her cheeks. "No, madam. I shouldnae have told such a dreadful lie, but if I couldnae have him in life I thought I might as well have him in death. Who was it hurting, after all? It made me feel better. Less ill-used."

"You think Mr. Gordon treated you badly?" I asked.

"Aye," she said, sniffing. "I won't try to deny it anymore. I loved the man, like no one has loved any other man. He was everything to me. I loved the way his eyes sparkled when he laughed. The way he smelled of woodsmoke and whisky. The way he'd make you feel like you were the only lass in the world when he talked to you. Of course, then you came to find out he didnae think you were the only lass in the world."

"Was there someone else?" I asked.

Maisie frowned. "That I cannae say. I never saw him with anyone else, but he didnae love me and didnae care that he'd broken my heart. He was a callous one. The truth is, if I'd had a rival for his affection, it might have made it easier. I never really believed it was hopeless until the night of the ceilidh."

"When you fought?" I asked.

"Who saw us?" she asked.

"That's not relevant," I said.

"Of course it is." She swallowed hard. "I have a right to know who's telling tales about me."

"They're not tales if they're true," I said.

"I shouldnae have ever trusted that worthless Callum," she said. "A man promises you he'll help, but he's always got his own ideas."

"How did he break your trust?" I asked.

"He saw what happened and now he's gone and told you."

This was unexpected. "How do you know he saw you?"

"He came to me after Angus, er, Mr. Gordon, left me there on the ground," she said. "Told me he'd take care of it. That he wouldnae stand for anyone treating me that way."

"Was this before or after you spoke to Mr. Nesbitt?" I asked.

"Callum told you that, too?" She shook her head. "I know Nesbitt wouldn't have."

"Nesbitt rarely talks," Miss Josephine said.

"Only when it's strictly necessary," Miss Adeline said.

They both stared at Maisie, their eyes piercing.

"You're saying it was strictly necessary?" she asked. "Aye, I suppose it was, but I didnae need Nesbitt to protect me. I never hurt Mr. Gordon and I certainly didnae kill him."

"By all descriptions you tried to hurt him," I said.

She shook her head. "Not that way. Not seriously. Nesbitt knew as much."

"Why did he believe it was strictly necessary to speak to me?" I asked.

"So that you'd see it wasnae me who murdered Mr. Gordon, even if it was my fault he died."

"How was it your fault?" I asked.

"I all but set Callum on him, but I never thought he'd go that far, did I? How was I to know he would? I was heartbroken. I could hardly think or breathe or see." She placed her palms flat on the seat of the chair, one on either side of her legs, and pushed down on them, hard. "Have any of you been heartbroken? It's agony."

"Agony, indeed," Miss Josephine said. Her sister reached across, took her hand, and squeezed it. My heart tugged. I wondered what the Greats had been like when they were young and—at least Miss Josephine—in love.

"Then you understand," Maisie said. "After Callum left, I wasnae myself. I did what Nesbitt told me because I couldnae think what else there was to do. I calmed myself down and went back to the ceilidh. I asked Mr. Gordon to dance with me. He did. At first I thought maybe there was a wee bit of hope that I could win him over. My heart felt so light. I could breathe. That all changed when I saw something in his face. I cannae name it, but it pierced my heart all over again."

"Can you describe what you saw?" I asked.

"Not really. It was just a funny sort of look that passed over him. Unsettling, at least to me. It was like he was on edge about something."

"He appeared worried?" I asked.

"Not exactly," she said. "It didnae seem bad like that. More like he was waiting for someone. His head snapped around every single time the door to the hall opened."

"So it was a person who wasn't at the ceilidh?" I asked.

"Not necessarily," Maisie said. "Everyone was coming in and out. It gets awful hot in the hall once the dancing starts."

"Have you any idea who he might have been looking for?" I asked.

"I've no justification for saying it, but I'm certain it was a girl," she said. "I never saw him lay eyes on her. Never saw the waiting fade from his face. But my heart knew. Somehow, it knew and it drained all the hope right out of me. I decided then and there that I'd give Mrs. Mackie my notice and find another position. I couldnae bear to be around him once he took up with someone else."

"There's no use tormenting oneself," Miss Josephine said. "You made a wise decision."

"And fortunately one that didn't have to be put into action," Miss Adeline said.

"A silver lining in the cloud of murder," Miss Josephine said.

The sisters looked at each other.

"A fortunate coincidence," Miss Adeline said. In unison, they turned back to Maisie, their eyes colder.

Maisie must have been too disheartened to notice they were all but accusing her of having killed Mr. Gordon. She was slumped in the chair, tears pooling in her eyes.

"I know it's painful to remember, Maisie," I said, "but I need you to tell me what, exactly, Mr. Gordon told you when he rebuffed your advances."

"Rebuffed my advances?"

"Refused to be seduced," Miss Josephine said.

"Och, of course." Maisie blew out a long sigh. "Well, it was a lot of stuff and nonsense. Said he didnae feel about me that way, that it wouldnae be right to take advantage, that a man cannae squander his opportunities. Whittered on about how he loved Cairnfarn and working as His Grace's gamekeeper. Which has nothing to do with me, does it? His Grace would have liked to see us married. I'm sure of that."

I doubted very much that Jeremy held any opinion on the subject. "He said nothing about being involved with someone else?"

"Nae, not a word."

A firm knock sounded on the door. Before either—or both—of the Greats could respond, it opened, and Colin stepped into the room, holding a man's shirt full of holes and dotted with blood.

"How long did you think you could hide this, Miss Drummond?"

22

Tansy

1676

My nerves prickled incessantly the next morning as I waited for Agnes to deliver her salve for Rossalyn's hands. I dropped the kettle when I was trying to make tea. I broke two eggs while gathering them from the henhouse. It didn't make sense; Agnes shouldn't have scared me. She didn't scare me. Unsettled me, yes, but not enough to explain my jumpiness.

Finella called at the cottage on her way to the castle. "I've been so worried about your poor hands, Rossalyn. What a horror! I couldn't sleep last night wondering who switched your soap."

"Switched our soap?" Rossalyn crinkled her nose. "Why would anyone do that?"

"To cause you pain," Finella said. Her face was writ with worry. "Unless it wasn't the soap . . ."

"What else could it be?" Rossalyn asked.

"A spell." Finella paused for three beats, then smiled broadly and laughed. "I'm only teasing. There are no witches in Cairnfarn."

"I can't believe anyone in the village wants to cause Rossalyn pain," I said.

Finella picked up the soap that was sitting next to the basin in which we washed our dishes. "This is not the kind of soap that should be used for ordinary tasks. I've brought you a better one."

"We bought it from a farmer's wife," I said. "She assured me—"

"Mrs. Brown is the one who sells soap," Finella said. "This bar is not one of hers. Someone did switch it out." She removed it and replaced it with another bar from the little bag she was carrying.

"I don't understand." Rossalyn frowned.

"It behooves us all to be on guard these days," Finella said, "especially with everything happening in Balieth. I havenae wanted to mention it, but I've noticed that your friend Cora always calls you Tasnim, Tansy."

"It's my proper name."

"I've misunderstood then," Finella said. "A name carries a great deal of power. I thought you had us all call you Tansy to protect yourself. A powerful witch can cast a spell without you realizing it when she knows your name."

"That's absurd," Rossalyn said. "We all know each other's names. It doesn't mean we can cast spells on whoever we'd like."

"Dismiss my concerns if you want, but I've heard tales of terrible things coming to pass from name spells."

"I've never heard of such a ridiculous thing." Rossalyn pulled her brows together. She was getting angry. "Why are you trying to make us afraid over nothing?"

Finella stood very still, staring at Rossalyn. Once the silence had become unbearable, she spoke. "Heavens, I'd no idea you were so gullible! I was only having a bit of fun." She shined her radiant smile on us. "Everyone's so gloomy around here. Dinnae you get tired of it?"

"So there are no name spells?" I asked.

"Of course not. I invented them." She was still smiling. "I must get off to work now. Forgive me for teasing you."

"I don't like her," Rossalyn said after Finella had gone. "She's cruel."

"She means no harm," I said, "and is right that everyone around here is gloomy. I know her pranks can seem juvenile, but at least she's trying to liven things up." I knew that wasn't her only motive, because before she'd gone, she'd pulled me aside and whispered that I should take care around Cora. Some people, she insisted, could draw power from a name.

Before Rossalyn could reply, Agnes Campbell, without first knocking, opened the door and stepped into the cottage. We rose to greet her, but the herbalist motioned for us to sit back down.

"Let me look around, undisturbed, if you will," she said. "There is something in this house that doesnae seem right."

"You're so very serious, Agnes," Rossalyn said. "It's good of you to be concerned, but rest assured all is well in our humble abode."

"Is it?" she asked, crossing to the window in the rear wall of the cottage. She tugged it open, poked her head out, and reached down. When she pulled her hand back inside, she was holding a round piece of wood dangling from a rough string. She held it up to us. Each side was sanded smooth and displayed a carved, flower-like design. "If all is well, why do you have two of these hanging outside?" She produced an identical object from her pocket.

Rossalyn marched over to her and took one of the discs from her hand. "What are they?"

"They're symbols meant to ward off witches," Agnes said. "I can only assume Tansy felt the need for protection after our conversation yesterday."

"Not at all," I said. "I've never seen those before and have no idea how they came to be here."

"You're quite certain?" she asked.

"Quite," I said.

"And you?" she asked Rossalyn. "Have you seen them before?"

"I haven't," Rossalyn said. "I used to have something similar. My husband gave me a gold pendant with the same design. He worried about witches, you know."

"Aye, I remember that about him well," Agnes said. "Always amused me that such a strong man could carry such fear."

It was as if Rossalyn didn't hear what she'd said. She looked wistful. Tears swam in her eyes. "Ewan didn't let me keep it."

I poked my head out the window, saw a small nail hammered into the casement, and then went to the front door. The nail there was identical. "Who would've done this?" I asked.

"Someone worried about your souls," Agnes said. "We've no witches in this village, but if someone thinks otherwise, we should all be afraid. You, especially, Tansy. You're an outsider. Outsiders always pose danger. At least that's how the ignorant think. If you cannae leave this place, keep to yourself. Draw no attention."

"Perhaps Finella did it," I said. "She'd want to protect us."

"She was only just here," Rossalyn said. "Surely she would've told us if she'd done it."

"You're right. Who, then?"

"You'll find out eventually," Agnes said. She reached into the bag she was carrying and handed Rossalyn a small bundle from it. "This is the balm for your hands. If it doesnae work, let me know and I'll tweak the formula. It's mainly lanolin. You should find it verra soothing." Then she retrieved from her pocket the rock I'd brought to her from Finella.

"What's that?" Rossalyn asked.

"An old Viking stone," Agnes said, giving it to me. "Some say they offer protection."

"Why did Finella have me take it to you?" I asked.

"To prove you're not the outsider I might have thought you were," she said. "We find them, once in a while, in the forest or near the loch. There must have been a Viking settlement here, long ago. They're beautiful little things, aren't they? Different from the large rune stones. We collect them and use them however we see fit."

"Everyone in the village?" I asked.

"Not everyone, no," Agnes said. "Only those who pay attention."

"Who are those that pay attention and how do you see fit to use them?"

Agnes gave a weak smile and shook her head. "I've already told you too much. If you have any trouble, send for me. I'd rather come here than have you come to me." And with that, she left.

"Send for her?" I threw up my hands. "How, exactly, are we meant to do that? We've no servants, so the only way would be for one of us to fetch her, which would involve going to her cottage, which is precisely what she claims not to want."

"She's afraid," Rossalyn said. She was still holding one of the carved discs. "We should hang these back up."

So we did, and when we were done, I walked to the castle and asked Finella about them.

"They weren't on the door when I knocked this morning," she said. "Perhaps Agnes put them there herself, which is worrying."

"How so?" I asked. "They're meant for protection."

"Aye, but whose? Yours or hers? She told you she doesnae want you to return to her cottage. I'd be worried about what she's thinking if I were you. It could be that your soul isnae in nearly as much danger as your body. Those found guilty of witchcraft get burned."

23

1905

When Maisie saw the bloodstained shirt Colin was holding, a strange sound emanated from her lips. It was half hiss, half cry, and hardly sounded human. Her eyes opened wide, then closed. She slumped in the chair and collapsed onto the floor in what appeared to be a dead faint. Miss Adeline, without hesitating, picked up the pitcher of lemonade from the table and poured it over her face. Maisie sputtered, choked, and raised herself up on her elbows.

"Well, I wasn't going to waste the whisky, was I?" Miss Adeline said, looking down at her. Her sister tugged at the bell and the footman entered the room.

"Would you like me to remove her, madam?" he asked.

"No, but the carpet shall require cleaning," Miss Josephine said.

"Our poor Axminister!" Miss Adeline sighed. "Murders catalyze all sorts of problems, don't they?"

"One thing leads to another," Miss Adeline said.

The footman went off to fetch maids and cleaning supplies. Colin ordered Maisie to her feet and held the shirt in front of her.

"Explain," he said. "Immediately."

"I've never seen it before," she said. "Where did you find it?"

"Wrapped in a bundle hidden beneath your mattress," Colin said.

"Och, as if I would put something there," she said. "Someone's gone and done it to make me look guilty. Huvnae I been tortured enough today?"

"I'd argue the only one who's suffered torture was Daniel Gordon." Colin held the shirt in front of her face. "Whose is this? I don't take kindly to lies, Miss Drummond."

"Well it's Callum's, of course, isn't it?" She covered her face with her hands. "I dinnae ken how it came to be covered with blood."

"How do you know it's Mr. Fletcher's?" I asked.

"The stains on the sleeves," she said. "He's the only one in the village who buys that color paint. He uses it sometimes when he does the outside of houses."

"And no one else has access to it?" Colin asked. The bright cobalt blue was certainly distinctive. I remembered seeing it on some of the houses in the village.

"How should I know?" Maisie had regained her confidence. She put her hands on her hips and was starting to sound defiant. "I dinnae work with him, do I? I recognize the color but I dinnae ken where or how he stores his materials."

"Why was the shirt in your room?" I asked.

"I dinnae ken. I've never seen it before."

"This is very serious," Colin said. "I'll be keeping a close eye on you, Miss Drummond, and if I see anything odd in your behavior . . ." He let his voice trail.

Maisie opened her mouth but must have decided against saying anything further. She closed it and stared at the floor, silent, until Colin dismissed her. We then took our leave from the Greats and started for the village in search of Mr. Fletcher, whom we found in Mrs. Glendinning's house, drinking tea with the old woman. He asked to finish his cup before he came outside to speak to us.

"I dinnae like to worry her," he said. "She's enough troubles, some real, some imagined. She doesnae need to hear more about the murder and I cannae think what else the lot of you would want to talk to me about."

Colin showed him the shirt and told him where he'd found it.

"Aye, it's mine," he said. "What of it?"

"It's covered in blood," I said.

"So you're of the mind that I wore it to hack Gordon to death and then gave it to Maisie to hide? I've never claimed to be the smartest man, but I'm nae that stupid."

"You didn't mention to me that you saw her attacking Mr. Gordon," I said.

"You didnae ask. You asked about the ceilidh. That didnae happen at the ceilidh."

I wasn't about to let him get me off track. "What occurred after the attack?"

"Nothing that matters," he said. "I went home early. There's nothing more to tell."

"Miss Drummond thinks you killed Gordon," Colin said. "It seems a reasonable conclusion to draw, given the evidence. You're fond of her. She loved another man, a man who rejected and humiliated her. You witnessed this and decided to exact revenge upon him. Doing so would satisfy your sense of honor. What man would stand by and do nothing? Further, it had the effect of removing him from the situation entirely. Miss Drummond would mourn him, but eventually she'd move on and, perhaps, be more open to your advances."

"It's a pretty story, Mr. Hargreaves, and some of it's dead right, but I dinnae want a woman who doesnae want me. Killing a man, no matter the reason, is no way to win someone's heart. Now will you let me get back to work? It's harder drinking tea with Mrs. Glendinning than you'd think. She's got me here on some pretext or another and I'd like to get through with it. If I'm not quick enough about things, she'll force me to eat her marmalade and I'll do anything to avoid that."

"Including killing a man?" I asked, raising an eyebrow.

"Aye, Lady Emily, there you'd have a murder I could justify and one that no one would hold against me, not for a second."

We let him return to the house.

"I don't think it's him," I said. "If Maisie planted the shirt to cast suspicion on him, she should've put it somewhere other than her own room."

"Perhaps someone else did it, to cast suspicion on her," Colin said.

"Could she have killed Mr. Gordon?" I asked.

"I wouldn't have thought so at first glance, but it's possible. We know Gordon was incapacitated from falling onto a rock before he was actually killed. Once he was unconscious, anyone could've struck the fatal blow to his temple."

"After they argued, she went back into the village hall and danced with him," I said. "She'd been furious, yes, but managed to calm down to a point that no one particularly noticed. When I initially spoke to him, Mr. Fletcher described her as out of sorts, but not as angry. Surely if Mr. Gordon believed there was any chance that she'd get into that state again later in the evening he would've made certain not to be alone with her."

"I agree. Even so, we can't dismiss her as a suspect. She could've waited for him by the loch and attacked him when he was walking back to his cottage."

"Nor can we dismiss Mr. Fletcher," I said. "He had motive and he's certainly capable. He left the ceilidh early and could have lain in wait for Mr. Gordon just as easily."

"Quite." He took my hand. "You look exhausted. Let's get you back to the castle and into the bath. After which, I will—"

A voice called to us from across the street. "Oh, Lady Emily, Mr. Hargreaves, how fortunate I am to have found you." It was Mr. Pringle. "You've saved me a walk to the castle to fetch you. We've invited Dr. Harris to tea and would so love for you both to join us. Are you free?"

"I'm afraid I'm not dressed appropriately," I said. I was still in my dusty tweeds with my straggly, windblown hair pulled back by Irene's ribbon.

"No one cares about that sort of thing in Cairnfarn. Do please come with me now if you're willing and I'll give you a wee dram. That will perk you right up after that hike of yours. Yes, yes, we've heard all about it. The whole village has. My wife will be delighted to see you. She's feeling much brighter today and is desperate for good company."

How could we refuse? We followed him to the vicarage, where Mrs. Pringle opened the door, a broad smile on her face.

"This is marvelous! I'd so hoped you wouldn't be too tired after that dreadful walk up the Smithy. Irene should never have gone along with such an outrageous plan, but I do think she enjoys push-ing people, and Nesbitt can be surprisingly persuasive when he makes an effort. That's the power of silence, I suppose. When one does deign to speak, people pay close attention. Irene never means deliberate harm, of course. It's more like teasing or a prank. Funny to those watching, less so to those involved."

She ushered us into her sitting room, which was full of fresh flowers cut from her garden. I counted six vases.

"How beautiful," I said, admiring a bunch of shockingly blue blooms.

"Meconopsis baileyi," Mr. Pringle said. "Himalayan poppies. I saw them in Nepal years ago, when I was fresh out of university and exploring the world. They're not easy to cultivate, but well worth the effort. I far prefer their blooms to that ghastly poison garden of Miss MacDuff's, but I suppose even deadly plants have some use. In medicine, that is, not as actual poisons."

I wouldn't have taken the vicar to be a man with botanical inter-ests. "Your poppies are extraordinary," I said. He handed me a glass of whisky and then gave one to his wife.

"Sit, sit," he said. "You're bound to be fatigued. What do you think of these ladies tramping up and down Munros, Mr. Har-greaves?" He poured two more glasses, for him and Colin.

"Irene is many things, but not a lady," Mrs. Pringle said. "Don't think for a moment I mean to insult either you or her by saying that, Lady Emily. Irene is a true original and there's noth-ing I admire more in a person. She knows herself and lives her life accordingly."

"Indeed," Mr. Pringle said. "She was always a good lass. Wiser than her years."

His wife laughed. "Quite unlike me. I hardly know myself and am more than content to live my life under your guidance." She squeezed the vicar's hand. "I'd be lost without you."

"What a dear, sweet thing you are." Mr. Pringle raised her hand to his lips. "You're my treasure."

She smiled. "And you're my trove." The vicar's ears turned bright pink.

Dr. Harris arrived soon thereafter. There was a flurry of activity while Effie—all the while lamenting that Jeremy wasn't with us—set up the tea service. There were scones whose tops were as dark as the currents baked into them, salmon sandwiches haphazardly cut in a strange selection of sizes and shapes, a large blob of half-runny cream in a bowl two times too big for it, and a dish of honey.

"I'm afraid there's no jam, Mrs. Pringle. I dropped the only jar we had and it shattered. There's glass everywhere in the kitchen, so I hope you can make do with honey instead. I dinnae ken if it's nice on scones, but worth a try, I think."

"I'm sure it will be lovely," Mrs. Pringle said. "Why don't you clean up the glass so there's no danger of anyone getting cut by it?" Effie did as asked, but not before she knocked over the small jug of milk she'd placed next to the teapot. Mrs. Pringle told her not to bring more; we'd do without milk.

"It's a safer course of action," Mr. Pringle explained once the maid was gone. "Once she starts dropping and knocking things over, she doesn't stop for several hours."

"She does seem rather a handful," Dr. Harris said.

"She's been worse since poor Mr. Gordon died," the vicar said. "I'm afraid she was rather sweet on him."

"It's most unfortunate," Mrs. Pringle said, then turned to the doctor. "I can't tell you how delighted we are to have you in Cairnfarn. I want to hear all about your training—not the gory bits, though, I've no stomach for such things—and what it was like to live in Edinburgh. So far as I'm concerned, it's the most beautiful city in the world."

"It's certainly one of the more enlightened ones," Dr. Harris said. She exuded strength, but there was nothing masculine about her. Tall and thin as a whippet, she moved with grace, but when one looked at her, *competent* was the word that sprang to mind. "I studied at the Edinburgh College of Medicine for Women, one of the few places in Britain available for ladies to train, and am as qualified as any male physician. Not that many of my male colleagues agree."

"Change takes time," I said. "Far more time than any of us would like."

"They're threatened, that's all," Dr. Harris said. "Afraid that we'll prove more competent and take their jobs."

"I can't imagine that will ever happen," Mr. Pringle said. As soon as he'd said the words, he flushed and continued to speak with great rapidity. "Not the bit about you proving more competent, but that ladies will take their jobs. Not many have the means to acquire the education to seek such employment."

"Not many have an interest in devoting their lives to a profession," Mrs. Pringle said.

"Yet you have, Mrs. Pringle," Dr. Harris said.

"I do devote myself to my work, but I've never considered it a profession, merely an offshoot of my marriage." When she smiled, her face glowed. "I wouldn't have chosen it for myself and am not convinced I'm very good at it—"

"No false modesty, my dear," Mr. Pringle said. "You're exceptionally good at it."

"I'm adequate now, but it took me years to learn. Let's not talk about me, though." She beamed at Dr. Harris. "Your life is ever so much more fascinating."

"You won't think that in thirty years when all the young girls in the village are laughing about us two old biddies."

"You think you'll still be here in thirty years?" Mrs. Pringle asked.

"I've no intention of living anywhere else," Dr. Harris said. "When I first arrived in Edinburgh to pursue my studies, I fell utterly in love with the place. Then, when I met Angus, who was already settled there, I thought I'd never leave. We both adored the city. When he disappeared . . . I confess I struggled to find my way. Edinburgh no longer felt like home. It became a place of betrayal."

"Yet you chose to come here, where your fiancé was born," I said.

"Which suggests I no longer feel betrayed, does it not?" She reached for one of the burnt scones, sliced it in half, and spread honey over it. "I knew Angus so well, so completely, that once my grief—for that's what it was, grief, even though I had no evidence that he'd died—abated enough for me to once again think rationally, I realized he would never have abandoned me. I don't know what happened to him. He might have been murdered or kidnapped or injured in some way that caused him to no longer remember anything about his life."

"Surely if he were injured, someone would have found him?" Colin said.

"It's the least likely possibility, but I choose to believe there's a slim chance it's what occurred," Dr. Harris said. "The hopelessly romantic piece of me—a very small piece, I might add—half believes he may turn up in Cairnfarn someday."

"Is that why you took the position here?" I asked.

"No, not really," she said. "I wanted to feel close to him, now that he's gone. He spent a good deal of his childhood here and told me many stories about the place. He loved the mountains and the loch, even if farming had no allure for him. I thought that seeing the spots that mattered to him would enable me to build another connection with the man I loved so dearly."

Mrs. Pringle sighed. "It's heartbreaking. And so romantic."

Dr. Harris had taken one small bite of her scone. It was so overcooked I could hear it snap against her teeth. She returned the rest of it to her plate and pushed it ever so slightly away from her. "I could do without the heartbreak, but I'm pleased with my decision to come here. It's beautiful and soothing and I know I'll be happy to make it my home."

"We're delighted to hear that," Mr. Pringle said. "Stability is an important thing in a small village. People like consistency. They see the same friends and neighbors every day. They know what to expect. Change disrupts all that."

Dr. Harris smiled. "Change like a lady doctor arriving on the scene."

"That they'll get used to," the vicar said. "It's the murder that's more concerning. How do we come to trust each other again? I find it inconceivable that anyone in Cairnfarn would take the life of a friend and neighbor."

"Yet that is precisely what happened," Colin said.

"Now that we know Mr. Gordon wasn't who he claimed, doesn't that open the possibility that someone from his past came here to harm him?" Mrs. Pringle said.

"I want to believe that, my dear," Mr. Pringle said, "but we would have noticed a stranger."

"Not necessarily," she said. "What if he'd arrived bent on his evil purpose and deliberately kept himself hidden? He could have camped in the woods until he was ready to strike. Once his nemesis was dispatched, he slunk back from whence he came."

"It's not impossible," Colin said.

Mrs. Pringle beamed. "Oh, I do hope that's the case! It would be such a relief to know that we haven't been living all this time with a murderer in our midst."

The clock on the wall chimed. Our conversation continued, and several minutes later, another chime sounded, this one quieter and more delicate. Dr. Harris shook her head and pulled from the pocket of her neatly tailored jacket a watch with a striking dark green and white enameled case.

"I try and try to keep it running on time, but I never get it quite right. I presume your clock is accurate, Mr. Pringle?"

"Indeed," the vicar said. "I'm rather a stickler about it. What a lovely piece. Might I take a closer look?"

"Of course." She passed it to him.

"You transfix me at once," the vicar said, reading aloud the inscription on the watch's case. "What does it signify?"

"I'm afraid I've not the slightest idea," Dr. Harris said. "It was left to me by my spinster aunt. I'd always admired it from a distance but never knew it was engraved until it came into my possession, at which point, it was too late to ask her what it meant."

"How desperately romantic it sounds," Mrs. Pringle said. She'd flushed full crimson. "Perhaps it reminded her of an unrequited love."

"I certainly hope not. That would be horribly depressing, wouldn't it?" Dr. Harris shifted in her seat and abruptly changed the subject. "This has been lovely, but looking at the time reminds me I ought to be going. I've loads more unpacking and organizing to do at home and ought to check in with Dr. Cameron in case he has any patients I can help. He told me I shouldn't try to work the first week I'm here, just to focus on getting settled, but I've never much liked idle hands."

"Very wise, Dr. Harris, very wise." The vicar smiled as we said our goodbyes and then he escorted her to the door. When he returned to us in the sitting room, his countenance was clouded, his brow creased. He didn't take his seat. "That watch of hers, Mr. Hargreaves, something isn't right with it."

"How so?" Colin asked.

"I've never seen it before, but it's as familiar to me as my own," he said. "Agnus Sinclair—rather, Daniel Gordon—described it to me in detail more than once. It was the most precious thing he ever owned and it nearly broke his heart when he lost it. It was a gift from his mother to his father on the day they were married. The inscription is a play on a line from *Jane Eyre: you should transfix me at once.* I can't claim to remember the original context. Something Mr. Rochester was saying to Jane, obviously. It was his mother's favorite book, partly because she had a romantic nature and partly because it was the volume she was reading the day she met her future husband. They discussed the story and she mentioned the quote. He responded by saying that, for him, regardless of the circumstances, there was no *should.* She had transfixed him, utterly and completely. I don't know how Dr. Harris came to have the watch, but I can promise you it was not a legacy from a spinster aunt."

24

Tansy
1676

As I lay in bed that night, I mulled over the events of the day. It troubled me that someone had been able to hang the wooden discs on our house without Rossalyn or me noticing. How could we have missed the sound of a hammer driving nails into wood? There had been no time that we'd both been absent from the cottage. Rossalyn swore she hadn't gone outside at all. I started to wonder if she'd hung them herself.

Then I remembered that we had no hammer, and even if we did, she wouldn't have known how to use it. She could be willfully ignorant when she wanted to be. Still, she could have asked someone else to do it for her. If she had, though, why wouldn't she have admitted as much?

Suspicion is a strange thing. It creeps up and tugs at you, subtly at first, then with more open guile, until it consumes you. It might start quite rationally, from the smallest seed, but equally, it can come from nothing at all beyond a feeling. An insecurity. A vulnerability.

I sat up in bed. The room was cold and dark. There was no moon that night. I pulled the blanket up around me. My heart was pounding. Something wasn't right. All I could think about was witches and spells. I held up my right hand, open, mimicking a hamsa amulet, the kind I used to wear to ward off the evil eye. I should make one for myself. Agnes could help me. Somehow, I knew that. She'd know how to get clay and might be able to make paint. Or glaze. Or whatever it was one used to color clay. I knew nothing about it. I knew nothing at all.

I have no memory of falling asleep that night, but I must have, for I did wake up the next morning. I was dreaming. The images were vivid and bright, but made no sense. I didn't recognize anything about them. They weren't human, they weren't animal. The colors were like nothing I'd ever seen before. I didn't have the words to describe them, didn't know their names. Then I was aware that someone was shaking me. It was Rossalyn.

"I've let you sleep as long as I can, but Cora's here, asking for you. Something's wrong, but she won't tell me what until you're there, too." She pulled the blanket off me and the cold air that settled in its place shook the last remnants of sleep from my foggy brain. I wrapped a shawl around my nightdress and followed her into the main room of the cottage.

"I heard about your witch's marks, the daisy wheels," she said, "so I thought I'd show you what I found next to me in bed when I woke this morning." She was standing in front of our fireplace holding a cloth doll, simple in design with cross-stitching to represent eyes and a mouth.

"What is it?" I asked.

Rossalyn covered her face with a trembling hand. "It's a poppet. Witches use them to cast spells." She was unsteady on her feet. I pulled a chair out from the table for her and took the one next to it for myself.

"They represent people they want to harm," Cora said, sitting across the table from me. "I didnae make it, so who did?"

"And how did it get in your bed?" I asked.

"I dinnae know. I slept soundly last night," Cora said. "Nothing disturbed me. It's only my father and me in the croft. No one could have got in because the door was latched."

"What about the windows?" Rossalyn asked.

"The shutters were all closed."

"It's impossible," Rossalyn said. "No one could have got in."

"It looks impossible to us, but it must not be." I frowned. "Someone put the poppet there. I'd say the who matters more than the how. You're quite certain it wasn't already in your bed when you went to sleep?"

"Absolutely certain, Tasnim," Cora said. "I would have noticed."

There was something about the way she pronounced my name that unsettled me. She'd said she didn't make the poppet, but she didn't go on to say that she hadn't put it in her own bed. It was the simplest explanation for what had happened, but why would she have done it?

25

1905

A thick silence settled on the vicarage sitting room as we digested what Mr. Pringle had told us. At last, I spoke. "How could Dr. Harris have come to be in possession of Mr. Gordon's watch?" I didn't expect anyone to answer my question, but felt compelled to say the words aloud. "Did he tell you how he lost it?"

"In the midst of some sort of dreadful fire in Edinburgh at a public house called the Wheatsheaf," the vicar said. "He was one of the few people who managed to escape. I assume the watch went missing in the commotion. Rather, that's what he assumed."

"So you knew, all this time, that he was not who he claimed to be?" I asked.

"Not exactly," Mr. Pringle said, "although thinking on it now, I should've thought it odd that a Highland farmer would own such an expensive watch or that his wife would be an avid reader."

"You never met the Sinclairs, Hamish, so how could you have

known?" Mrs. Pringle asked. "They were dead long before you arrived in the village."

"It should've made me suspicious," the vicar said. "In the course of our conversations it became clear to me that he hadn't worked as a solicitor or been sent to school. He was a bright enough man—liked to read—but I saw no evidence of formal training of any kind. Now, that didn't mean he wasn't Angus Sinclair, only that the story we'd heard about his success as a professional was a fiction."

"When was the fire?" Colin asked.

"I don't know."

"What else did he reveal to you?" Colin asked. "If someone from his past came after him, the more we know, the more likely we are to find the person."

"I'm not at liberty to discuss the confidences he shared with me," Mr. Pringle said. "I don't mean to be difficult, but I wouldn't be able to do my duty if my parishioners had reason not to trust me."

"Gordon is dead," Colin said. "His secrets no longer need protecting. Surely God would prefer you do whatever is possible to bring the man who killed him to justice?"

"You're right, of course," the vicar said. He fidgeted uncomfortably and cleared his throat. "The truth is, there's not much to protect, but it still feels odious to disclose any of it. We mainly discussed theology. Not in the academic sense, mind you, but in a broader, more human way. He was not a believer. Knowing now that he wasn't who he claimed, I'd hazard to guess that his father was involved in the church. He never mentioned anything specific—I suppose he needed to be careful not to, lest he reveal his true identity—but there were little things. He was too familiar with the ins and outs of vicarage life, for example."

Irene had reached the same conclusion. She'd said something about him stank of vicarage.

I left my husband to glean whatever else he could out of the vicar, excusing myself so that I could go confront Dr. Harris about the watch. I snapped open my umbrella and listened to the rhythm of the rain on it as I made my way to her house. She'd claimed she had loads of unpacking to do, but I knew that to be a lie from my previous visit. Had she killed the man pretending to be her fiancé? If she had reason to believe he'd harmed the man she loved before adopting his identity, she certainly had motive.

The warmth of her greeting told me she didn't suspect anything was amiss. She hung up my coat, put my umbrella in a stand, and insisted that I sit by the fire.

"I'm convinced the damp here is worse than anywhere else in the world," she said. "It goes straight into one's bones. Yet, some-how, that makes me like the place more, which I realize is wholly insensible. Even the short walk from the vicarage freezes a person, so I expect you're in need of something warming after escaping from there. What can I get you? Tea? Whisky?"

"*Escaping* is an interesting way to describe it." I looked around her neat sitting room. "I didn't believe it when you said you still had boxes to unpack and figured you'd wanted to flee for another reason."

"Mrs. Pringle is just so very earnest, isn't she? I like her, I do, but she can be a lot to bear."

"She's been through a terrible ordeal, losing the baby," I said.

"That's true, and I don't mean to be unsympathetic. It's just"— she sighed—"she's so clearly disappointed by her life and instead of admitting it, she pretends she's delighted."

"She appears to adore her husband, so that must be some con-solation."

"You're correct about that," she said, "but I find it so very hard to believe, don't you? He's intolerably boring. She's doing an admirable job of trying to convince herself to adore him, but can it really take? Look at me. Here little more than a week and already firmly embroiled in village gossip. No, it's worse than that. I'm starting it! Perhaps we should have tea, not whisky, so as to complete the image of village busybodies."

"Tea would be lovely."

While she went to the kitchen to brew it, I looked around. Three photographs in ornate frames stood on the mantel: one showing a large family gathered under an oak tree, one of a group of ladies standing in front of the Edinburgh College of Medicine for Women, and one of a young man I presumed to be Dr. Harris's fiancé. They were the only obviously personal objects in the room. Everything else, from the faded botanical prints hanging on the walls to the empty vases on the tables flanking the settee, seemed generic. There was no bookcase, but there were a few volumes stacked on one of the tables. As they all were on the subject of animal husbandry and farming, I doubted they belonged to Dr. Harris.

"It's a dreadful scene at the moment, I'm afraid," she said, coming in with a tray laden with cups, teapot, milk, and a plate of oat biscuits. "The family who lived here before me received an unexpected legacy that allowed them to move from their croft, but after only a few months in this house they decided they'd prefer to leave the village altogether. I believe they went to Glasgow. They left nearly everything behind, which is quite convenient for me at the moment, but someday I shall have to make it my own."

She was so calm, so unflustered, that I was convinced she had no idea why I'd come. The manner in which she'd rushed off after Mr. Pringle noticed her watch had made me suspicious, but I now doubted she had any concerns about the timepiece linking her to the murder. I waited until she'd poured our tea to broach the subject.

"I do apologize if my bluntness causes offense," I said, "but I'm curious about your watch. You claim it was a gift from your aunt, but I know that cannot be true. It belonged to Daniel Gordon, the man who came here pretending to be your fiancé. Will you tell me how you actually came to have it in your possession?"

She pressed her lips together in a hard line; drew in a deep breath through her nose; and, after holding it longer than I would've thought possible, blew it out hard through her mouth. "As I already told you, after Angus disappeared, I did everything I could to search for him. There had been a fire at his local public house the day after I last saw him, and when I heard the news of the disaster, I feared he'd been one of the souls lost to the flames. Most of the bodies were burned beyond recognition, but Angus always wore a signet ring on his left hand. It was not on any of the corpses, nor among the items recovered by the fire brigade. I went through them all, desperate and terrified that I'd find something of his, but there was nothing. I checked back time and time again, until all the rubble was cleared from the site. The police grew so accustomed to me looking through their boxes of unclaimed objects they hardly paid attention when I was there. After months and months had gone by, the watch was one of the last things left, which convinced me no one would ever come for it. I took it when the officer in charge wasn't looking. I'm not entirely sure why, but . . . part of me has always wanted to believe Angus died in that fire. It would be easier to know, once and for all, what happened. I suppose the watch gives me a physical link to the event and, somehow, I find that consoling."

"It seems a great coincidence that it just happens to have belonged to Daniel Gordon," I said.

"I don't think it's a coincidence at all," she said. "That man had to have known Angus. It's how he learned the story of his life. My guess is that they met at the local, traded stories over a pint, and Gordon decided to murder my fiancé. Steal his life. I shouldn't be surprised to learn he set the fire deliberately to hide what he'd done."

"There were survivors," I said. "Surely someone among them would have noticed if a murder took place immediately before the fire."

"I don't claim to have all the answers, but I've no doubt they're connected through the public house. What else do you know about this man called Daniel Gordon?" I told her what the detective from Inverness had learned.

"He wasn't the sort of man Angus would have befriended ordinarily, although . . ." She sighed. "He did believe in second chances. Fresh starts. Which is precisely what Gordon claimed he was seeking when he arrived in Cairnfarn. I shouldn't be shocked if Angus had encouraged him to leave behind his life of crime and turn over a new leaf."

"Why would Mr. Gordon kill the man who inspired him to do so?" I asked.

"I don't know." Her voice dropped to a whisper. "I wonder if they both wanted fresh starts. Maybe Angus told him about Cairnfarn. Suggested that he come here and pretend to be him. Their hair was the same striking color, and we know that, along with some knowledge of the Sinclair family, was enough for the community to accept him. What if I've been wrong all along? What if Angus did decide to flee? He'd often talked about America. Perhaps the pressure of marrying caught up with him and he decided he couldn't go through with it."

"Did anything in his behavior suggest he didn't want to get married?" I asked.

"No. But how can someone disappear so completely without doing it on purpose?" She clenched her hands together, tight. "Perhaps they traded names and he's living somewhere as Daniel Gordon. There's nothing more awful than having no conclusive answer. I don't know how I'll ever be able to come to terms with losing him when I don't know what happened."

On the walk to her house, I'd considered whether she might have killed the man who'd taken her fiancé's identity. After I arrived, her calm demeanor made it seem unlikely. But now, hearing her suspicions, I wondered if she did blame Mr. Gordon for her unhappiness. The watch connected her physically to him, and she could still be lying about how she came to have it.

"You never mentioned the fire when you originally told me about your fiancé's disappearance. Why not? And why did you lie about how you came to have the watch?"

"I suppose I didn't want you to know about the fire because it might lead you to discover I'm a thief. And a thief could become a murderer. Crime might become a habit, one that can escalate. After I first took the watch, I worried I'd encounter someone who recognized it, so I made up the story about my aunt in order to have something at the ready in case that occurred. I've always felt guilty about what I did. I don't know whether the police ever noticed it went missing. Most likely they didn't. Given what you've told me about this Daniel Gordon, I can't imagine anyone ever came to claim it. It sounds like no one connected to him knew where he was."

I told her the story behind the watch. As she listened, she pulled it out and held it in her hand.

"How absolutely dreadful that I stole it," she said. "I'm thoroughly ashamed. It belongs with someone in the family, or at least someone close to them. I promise you, Lady Emily, I will make it my mission to find an appropriate individual to return it to."

"It's a noble idea and one I hope you will follow through."

"You have nothing else to say on the matter?" she asked.

"At present, I'm more concerned with finding whoever murdered Mr. Gordon."

"And you believe I might be responsible?"

"You've lied to me, which makes it difficult to accept as credible anything you tell me. The fact that you have the watch . . ." I let my voice trail off, wanting to see how she'd respond to uncomfortable silence.

"Do have a biscuit." She held up the plate to me. "The food Mrs. Pringle offered us was inedible."

The next morning, I forsook breakfast in favor of a long, hot bath. My muscles were aching after yesterday's hike. Colin, never one to pass up an opportunity for kedgeree, ate; spoke to Maisie; and then found me, immersed in the tub, steaming water up to my chin, when he'd finished with her.

"I was quite fierce with her," Colin said, leaning against the wall in the antechamber that served as a bathroom. "She presented me with approximately thirty-seven explanations of how the shirt might have got in her room, from one of the dogs bringing it to the stable boys doing it as a prank."

"Were any of them reasonable?"

"No."

"Mr. Fletcher could've done it," I said. "He's sharper than he'd like us to think and knows he's under suspicion. He might believe planting something so obvious would make us think someone else was trying to point a finger at him." I was clean now and the water was starting to get cool, so I rose from the tub. "Hand me a towel, will you?"

He pulled one off a hook, brought it to me, and wrapped it around my shoulders, then held my hand as I stepped onto the tile floor and started to gently rub me dry.

"Were we discussing something important?" he asked. "To do with a murder, perhaps? You've so wholly distracted me there's not a single sensible thought in my head."

"Tell me about the insensible ones." I reached up and ran my hand through his thick curls. He breathed in sharply.

"I'm not sure words would do them justice," he said. "Some things are better served by actions. By touch."

Now it was my turn to breathe in sharply. I leaned closer to him, my damp skin against his shirt. He dropped the towel onto the floor, took my hands in his, and kissed me with such disgraceful thorough- ness I nearly collapsed. He lifted me up, carried me through the sitting room, and had just settled me onto the bed when a knock sounded on the door.

"Ignore it," he said, lowering himself on top of me as I tugged at the studs on his shirt. "If it's Bainbridge, he can wait. Everything can wait."

"Papa!"

It was Henry, He Who Must Not Be Ignored.

I sighed.

"Papa!"

Colin sighed.

"I know you're in there. Is something wrong? I can climb up outside and get in through the window or perhaps it would be better to get one of the footmen to knock down the door . . ."

He continued on in that fashion for long enough to more than justify the moniker I assigned him above. His father stood up, went into the sitting room—closing the bedroom door behind him—and dealt with our unruly child. He returned a few moments later.

"You'd best get dressed," he said. "Someone has broken into the gamekeeper's cottage."

26

Tansy
1676

A sinking feeling churned through my body. I couldn't think of a better explanation for the poppet appearing in Cora's bed than her having placed it there herself. I didn't want to talk to her about it any longer; I just wanted her to leave.

"There's only one thing to do: pretend it never happened," I said. "Whoever did it either has malicious intent or was playing a prank. If it's the latter, we won't satisfy them with a reaction. They'll grow bored waiting and leave us alone. If it's the former, ignoring it will prove that we've nothing to fear."

"It's not a terrible suggestion," Cora said, "but I think, Tasnim, you'd call for more decisive action if you were the one who found something in your bed. How am I to feel safe in my home?"

Rossalyn frowned. "It troubles me, Cora, that what should be your sanctuary has been violated. Take the daisy wheels and hang them in your room. They'll protect you if there is someone with evil intentions out there."

"I dinnae believe in witches," Cora said, "but I do believe in evil. The daisy wheels wilnae do anything to ease my mind. You keep them in case they do yours and in the meantime, let's try to figure out who would want to torment us."

"That's simple enough," Rossalyn said. "Ewan MacAllister. He's always hated me and you rejected him."

"He's the laird," Cora said. "He could torment us openly—and far more easily—in a hundred different ways without facing any consequences."

"No," Rossalyn said. "Ewan is sadistic. He enjoys playing a long game, making his enemies suffer. What sick pleasure would he get by doing something ordinary when instead he could wriggle his way into our heads until we're paralyzed by terror? I always suspected he let me have this cottage so he could keep me close enough to torture."

"That makes our situation all the more precarious," Cora said.

"Does it?" I asked. "If he's responsible, it means we've no witches to worry about."

"Perhaps I jumped to the wrong conclusion," Rossalyn said. "The more I think on it, the less convinced I am that it's Ewan. He's as scared of witchcraft as his father was. This would not be the way he would choose to torment us. He'd be afraid it would open his own soul to an attack from the devil."

Cora looked at Rossalyn with a ferocity that took me by surprise. Even more shocking was that Rossalyn looked back at her with equal intensity. All of a sudden, it was as if clouds were cleared from my eyes. I thought about all the times they'd gone for walks without me, ever since Cora had asked Ewan for a cottage. Rossalyn was unhappy and needed money. Cora wanted a home of her own. If they delivered a witch to the laird, surely he'd take care of them both. I was, relatively speaking, the newcomer, expendable. Is that why Rossalyn had kept me close to her all this time after we'd been forced from the castle? Was I her way back?

Rossalyn picked up her book of plays, flipped through it, and read aloud. *"By the pricking of my thumbs, / Something wicked this way comes.* That's quite enough witchcraft, don't you think?"

27

1905

Colin sat with Henry in our suite's sitting room while I dressed. The sun was hidden behind thick clouds and the air chilly, so I pulled on a tweed suit and my sturdiest boots for the walk to the gamekeeper's cottage. Henry was crushed that we wouldn't allow him to accompany us.

"I'm the one who discovered the broken window," he said. "Cedric was with me—"

"You took the crocodile out again?" I said, coming into the room.

"He needs a daily walk, Mama," Henry said. "I assure you I always handle him safely. Further, he was protecting me. There is a murderer on the loose, you know. I tied Cedric up outside the cottage before I went in through the window, so you might consider him a guard crocodile. It took no small amount of courage to enter to see if the murderer had struck again. And as I exhibited that quality, it's only fair that I—"

"You ought not have gone inside," Colin said. "This is very serious, Henry. You must not be reckless with your safety."

"But you would've gone inside, Papa."

"I've had years of training and experience in dealing with unsavory situations. When you're older, I'll teach you."

"How much older?" Henry asked. I could see his mind weighing whether it would be worth the wait or better to continue on as he wanted.

"Three or four weeks," Colin said. "There are supplies we'll need and they're all at Anglemore Park."

"What sort of supplies?"

"Things you can't even imagine exist. You'll see them soon enough. Run along now, back to the nursery."

He did without protest. It was most suspicious.

"Was he alone at the cottage?" I asked.

"His brothers stayed at the castle after breakfast," Colin said. "Richard in the library, conducting further research on kelpies; Tom with Bainbridge discussing ptarmigan shooting strategies."

The gamekeeper's cottage was about three-quarters of a mile from the castle, past the stables and beyond a group of smaller buildings occupied by retired members of the household staff. It had a thick thatched roof and two small windows flanking the front door, one of which was shattered. It was too far along the wall for whoever had broken it to reach in and unlock the door, but it was also too small for someone to have easily climbed through it into the cottage.

"Difficult, but not impossible," Colin said when I pointed this out. "Henry did, after all."

"Henry is less than half the size of an adult."

"If you approached it one shoulder at a time and had the angle just right, it could be managed."

We took a more conventional approach to entering the house, using the key Jeremy had given us. Henry had crawled out of the window as well. He explained this by saying he didn't want to leave the building unlocked, but I suspect it was because climbing through a window is more fun than using a door.

The interior of the cottage appeared wholly undisturbed. There was no mess, no sign that anyone had been inside. "Whoever did this knew what he was looking for," I said, "and where to find it."

"At first glance it certainly looks the same as it did when I was here the morning after the murder," Colin said. He pulled out a notebook from his jacket and flipped through the pages. "I made an inventory and I recall . . . yes, there it is. *Jane Eyre*. Let's see if it's still on the shelf."

There was a single bookcase in the cottage, tall and narrow, with approximately three dozen volumes on it. The other shelves displayed a rather appalling collection of stuffed birds along with a few small furry creatures whose eyes seemed to follow me no matter where I went in the room. There was also a beautifully carved box. I lifted the smooth lid. Inside was a collection of small, smooth rocks carved with Viking runes.

Colin nodded at me. "Just like the one left on his forehead. I noticed as much when I was here before."

I looked at the spines of the books. "No *Jane Eyre*," I said. I took the notebook from him and checked the remainder of the titles. No other was missing. We scoured every remaining inch of the cottage, finding nothing else incongruous until I looked into the sink by the hand pump.

"Should this be wet?" I asked. "The pump isn't dripping."

"No, the sink shouldn't be wet," Colin said. He picked up the teakettle. "This was empty when I was here before. Now there's water in it."

"Is it warm?" I asked.

"No, but are we to conclude that whoever broke in stopped for a cup of tea?"

"It's beyond strange." I was going through the cupboard and found a half-drunk bottle of rum. "What a pity Mrs. Pringle didn't know he had this. She could've used it for her punch."

We moved into the bedroom, where Colin looked under the mattress while I searched the dresser drawers.

"What's this?" I picked up a little booklet. The cover was made from a thick sheet of cream paper and decorated with six hearts painted in different shades of violet; a smudge of grease had smeared one of them. Inside was a thinner sheet of paper. They were folded together and tied with a bright blue ribbon identical to the one Irene had given me to hold back my hair when my hat blew away on the mountain.

"An old Persian legend about a princess who charmed the man she loved by giving him a cake infused with a magic potion," Colin said. "I saw it when I was here before."

"At the ceilidh, Richard mentioned something that sounds just like this. I think Dr. Cameron had told it at a gathering earlier on the summer solstice." I started to read. "The handwriting is distinctly girlish and not particularly neat."

Colin crossed to me and looked at the paper over my shoulder. "It's not Maisie's," he said. "I saw a half-written letter when I was searching her room."

"I'll speak to Irene and confirm the ribbon is the sort she uses.

She claims to have no romantic interest in him, but this might suggest otherwise." I tilted my head and studied the booklet. "Regardless, this tells us that Mr. Gordon was involved in a relationship, one that he kept secret."

We went through the rest of the objects Colin had catalogued, but nothing else was missing. "It appears our intruder came for *Jane Eyre* and a cup of tea," Colin said. "Given that the novel—now missing—is the source of the quote on Dr. Harris's stolen watch, I think we must draw the conclusion that there's some connection between it and Gordon's death."

"Perhaps there's something specific about Mr. Gordon's copy of the book that could link it to her," I said. "She claims not to have met him until the ceilidh, but what if she's lying, like she did about the watch? They might have known each other in Edinburgh. What if they were the ones who bonded over the quote, not Mr. Gordon's parents?"

"She would've had plenty of time to come here and retrieve the book after you left her house," Colin said. "Let's go back and see if she's got it."

We walked to the village, rain lashing us the entire way. Tweed is a lovely fabric: warm, comforting, attractive. It resists an extraordinary amount of damp and a credible amount of water, but once it's soaked, it's heavy, uncomfortable, and begins to smell like sheep. We were drenched and reeking of ovine by the time we arrived.

When she answered the door, Dr. Harris showed no sign of having been recently out in the rain. She let us in and made no objection when we asked if we could search the house. "Daniel Gordon was my only hope of learning what happened to my fiancé. I'll do anything to help you find his murderer." She paused, pursed her lips, and then looked Colin in the eyes. "Does this mean you think I murdered him?"

"No," Colin said, with a breezy confidence that visibly soothed her but told me he was lying. "I'd like to eliminate you as a suspect and this is the simplest way to accomplish that."

She waited in the sitting room while we systematically scrutinized every square inch of her home. Colin worked on the ground floor while I went upstairs, where there were three decent-sized rooms and a water closet. One room she was using as a study. In it was a desk, bookcases laden with medical references, and a table pushed up against the front windows of the house. The desk contained the usual sort of correspondence, stationery supplies, stamps, household records, and a bank book that showed a healthy balance. I pulled down each of the medical texts, but there was no copy of *Jane Eyre* hidden behind them. On the table was a stack of files containing patient records. The room was quite cold; the fire showed no sign of having been lit recently.

The bedroom was at the back of the house. The wardrobe contained well-made, practical clothing. The tables on either side of the bed each held an oil lamp. There were no books. A row of bottled toiletries stood beneath the dressing table's mirror. Aside from a monogrammed sterling silver dressing set, the space was largely devoid of personal items.

Between this and the study was a third room, smaller than the other two. Here, at last, I found Dr. Harris's books. Books to read, that is, rather than books to study. There were tall bookcases on two of the walls. Large aspidistras with shiny, dark green leaves filled the space in three of the room's corners between them. In the center of the wall opposite the blazing fireplace was an overstuffed leather chair next to the room's single window. Snug and cozy, it would be the perfect place to read, particularly on a rainy day.

Aside from two shelves filled with books that must have been favorites during childhood, there was no obvious organization to her library. The collection was a hodgepodge of fiction and history, with a dozen or so volumes about gardening. Right at eye level, I found a copy of *Jane Eyre* next to a matching edition of *Wuthering Heights*. I pulled it down and opened it, but found nothing remarkable. No inscription, no missing pages, nothing hidden inside.

I took *Jane Eyre* downstairs and handed it to Colin, who was in the kitchen. "Is it the same edition as the one you saw in the cottage?"

"I only saw the spine and can't be sure." He flipped through the pages.

"There's nothing to see," I said. "No way to connect it to Mr. Gordon."

Nonetheless, we asked Dr. Harris if we could keep hold of the book. She didn't argue, nor did she ask why we wanted it.

"You won't believe me, but I've never even read the thing," she said. "That's why I brought it here, so I could. I assumed village life would leave me plenty of time for reading. I'm sure I'm not the only person in Cairnfarn with a copy of it."

"No doubt you aren't," Colin said.

"Maisie Drummond is an avid reader, an avid reader who was in love with Daniel Gordon. From what I've heard, he rebuffed her advances. *Heaven has no rage, like love to hatred turned, / nor hell a fury like a woman scorned.* Perhaps it's her possessions you should be searching."

We gave her no response and took our leave.

I slipped my arm through my husband's. "There's a certain amount of truth in what she said. Love to hatred. It's a powerful thing, and the rage that comes with it is the perfect mirror to the passion of love. It could have given Maisie a strength that surprised even her."

"If there was a relationship between Gordon and Dr. Harris, it could've given her strength as well," Colin said. "I can't believe it's a coincidence that she has his watch."

"I agree, but we know that Maisie had attacked him that evening but caused no physical harm. He returned to the ceilidh without any visible marks on him. No bruises, no cuts. They danced and she thought—just for a moment—that maybe things would be all right. Maybe she could make him love her. Then, she notices he's distracted and she's convinced it's because he's looking for another woman. This sends her into another rage, one fueled not only by jealousy but also by what she views as betrayal."

Colin nodded. "Doubly angry, she leaves the ceilidh and waits for Gordon by the loch. She knows he'd have to pass that way to get home."

"Part of her would still have been hoping that maybe, just maybe, he'd see the error of his ways, take her in his arms, beg her forgiveness, and pledge his undying love. Instead, what happened was even worse than their earlier encounter. He may have refused her more forcefully or he may have brushed her off in a casual manner that infuriated her. Either way, she starts throwing rocks at him. One strikes him hard enough that he stumbles and falls."

"And while he's down, she picks up a larger one and smashes in his temple."

"Were there any books in Maisie's room when you searched it?" I asked.

"Stacks of them, all from the castle's library. No *Jane Eyre*, however."

"It might be there now," I said, "but why? Dr. Harris has a connection to the quote, and hence the book, but we've no reason to think Maisie does. Unless . . . let's suppose Maisie was infuriated and killed Gordon after he rejected her. Or that Mr. Fletcher killed him because of how he'd treated her. If either of them knew about the quote on the watch, they could have planted the book in the cottage and then stolen it in order to draw our attention to the doctor."

Colin looked skeptical. "How would they have known about the watch?"

"Mr. Gordon told the vicar about it. Someone might have overheard. Everyone gossips in Cairnfarn, which tells me they're all eavesdropping whenever they get the chance. It's not inconceivable that Maisie might have heard the story. Both Mr. Fletcher and Irene took notice of their conversations."

"No doubt the villagers are aware that I searched the cottage and made an inventory of the contents," Colin said. "If Maisie or Fletcher knew that the novel was the inspiration for the engraving on the watch, they might have assumed stealing it would make the police take notice. And they would be unlikely to conclude that a day laborer and a servant would have anything to do with it."

"It might have been a sort of insurance for them. The book could've been retrieved any time after you initially searched the cottage, and the window broken only when they needed it to be noticed. We assumed the theft was catalyzed by me confronting Dr. Harris about the watch, but the two things aren't necessarily related."

"A valid point," Colin said. "So where do we go from here?"

"It's time to speak with Maisie again."

28

⸎

Tansy

1676

"I think you're taking this too hard."

I'd gone to Finella's the next evening to confide in her my suspicions about Rossalyn and Cora. She was still living in her mother's cottage, but would soon have to find other lodging. She couldn't afford the rent on her own.

"If you had seen the look they exchanged you'd feel differently," I said. "And it's not just the look. They've been excluding me for some time. There's something going on. I'm certain of it, especially given what Rossalyn read from this book." I'd brought it with me and opened it to *Macbeth*. "*By the pricking of my thumbs, / Something wicked this way comes.*"

We were sitting at her table. I pulled my cloak closer around me. Even with it on I was half frozen. The windows were drafty and there wasn't enough wood for the fire to adequately heat the space, despite its small size. The place was untidy and dirty as well. No doubt she was too exhausted after working all day to come home and clean.

"It's eerie," Finella said. "Is the whole book about witches?"

"No, it's a collection of plays about loads of different things."

"Is that the only line in this particular play that has to do with witches?"

"There's more," I said.

"Read them all to me." Finella sat still, focused and concentrating as I did what she asked. When I finished, she had on her face that unsettling look that usually preceded a smile. That night, the smile didn't come.

"This is very serious. You were right to come to me. That little rock I gave you . . . there are women in Cairnfarn who still have sympathies to the old religion."

"The old religion?" I asked.

"What the Celts practiced before the advent of Christianity."

"They're witches?"

"I wouldnae go that far," Finella said. "It's more about sisterhood and ritual. They dinnae believe in pagan gods, but I suppose . . ."

I waited for her to finish, but she only shook her head.

"What?" I asked. "You're the one holding something back now."

"I dinnae deny that I am," she said, "but it's for your protection. Do you trust me, Tansy?"

"Why wouldn't I?" She'd always been straightforward and honest, even when it was uncomfortable. She didn't shy away from difficulties. She faced them head-on and wasn't bothered if that angered people. The more I thought about it, the more I admired her. She had a strength I'd not seen in many, a strength I envied.

"Will you let me help you?" she asked.

"I'd be grateful if you would."

"I'll need you to get me some items that belong to Rossalyn."

The skin on my neck tingled. "Why?"

Finella smiled. "Dinnae start thinking I'm a witch. I'm not and never would be. I'm devoted to my Lord Jesus Christ. Leave me the book of plays and get for me the crucifix hanging on the wall in your cottage and Rossalyn's wedding ring."

"The crucifix I might be able to get, but she never removes her ring."

"You're smart and capable. You'll find a way. I have infinite faith in you."

"Must it be so many things?" I asked.

"It's the only the way to be certain we get at least one that's infused with her spirit. When you hold an object that belongs to someone, you feel something inexplicable, something that connects you to that person. You told me you have a ribbon that belonged to your mother. Isnae that why you keep it close to your heart?"

"Yes, that's true." The piece of saffron silk was the only thing I still possessed from my old life. Every time I touched it, it brought my mother nearer to me. I knew she'd touched it, tied it in a bow time and time again; and now, when I touched it, it was almost as if I could feel the warmth of her hands.

"When these women hold Rossalyn's objects, they will be able to sense if there is good or evil in her heart. Perhaps that sounds like magic, but it's not," Finella said. "We dinnae understand everything about the world. That's how I think about this sort of thing. We may not comprehend the hows and whys, but we know what we feel. It requires no spell nor anything unholy, only common sense and listening to our hearts."

"What about Cora?" I asked. "I can't readily get anything of hers."

"We'll worry about her later." Her forehead creased. "It might be wise to give me your mother's ribbon, as well. That will reassure the women that you're good and pose no threat to them. These days, with everything happening in Balieth, one cannae be too careful. Harmless old rituals can be mistaken for witchcraft."

"I don't like to part with the ribbon, even for a moment," I said.

"You know I'll take care of it. I understand how precious it is to you and will make sure nothing happens to it. Dinnae decide right now. Take the afternoon and think about it. I'll come see you tonight, late, after Rossalyn's asleep. The women are meeting at midnight in the valley under the full moon. Have her things ready regardless and the ribbon only if you're comfortable with it. I'm honored you trust me enough to have shared all this. It's rare to find the kind of friend you are." She squeezed my hand.

"I feel the same. Friendships—true friendships—are rare treasures."

"I still want to believe you're taking it too hard about Cora and Rossalyn. I'm sure they're fond of you and would never turn on you, but it doesnae hurt to stay on guard. If I were you, that's what I'd do until this is all settled. Just in case I'm wrong."

I left the book of plays, readying an excuse in case Rossalyn noticed its absence, and considered Finella's words as I slowly made my way back to the cottage. She'd sounded so sure when she'd initially dismissed my concerns about Cora and Rossalyn. It wasn't like her to to make anything appear more palatable than it was, but I couldn't deny that she'd felt less certain about the matter by the end of our conversation. Something had changed her thinking. I would stay on guard. I knew there was something wrong in what I'd seen between them.

29

1905

When Colin and I reached the castle, Maisie was nowhere to be found. She'd been sent to the nearest market town that afternoon and hadn't yet returned. I didn't mind having to wait to speak to her; I was soaked through and in desperate need of another bath. This one I had to rush through, as Jeremy had already put dinner back twice to accommodate us. As promised, the Greats had dined in the nursery with the boys, but they'd finished hours ago and joined us at the table, sipping whisky while we ate.

"That gown is simply divine, Emily," Miss Adeline said.

"It's Worth, isn't it?" Miss Josephine asked. "I can always recognize Worth, even though Charles himself departed the world far too long ago."

"It's been ten years now, I believe," Miss Adeline said, "but his sons are doing an admirable job of following in his footsteps."

"Is it silk chiffon?" Miss Josephine asked. "So daring to wear a tea gown to dinner. I heartily approve."

I had, indeed, committed the faux pas of not dressing appropriately for our meal, but I couldn't bear the thought of squeezing myself into a dinner dress. My legs were still aching from the exertion of climbing the Smithy, and I'd been so cold and wet all day that I was afraid I might fall ill.

"I assumed you were making a deliberate attempt start a new trend," Jeremy said. "Tea gowns have much to recommend them— they can appear almost en déshabillé in a most alluring manner— although the female form is better flattered in other types of dress."

"Words that could be spoken only by someone who's never worn a corset," I said.

"Thank heavens for that," he said.

The Greats roared with laughter. "Your mother would be beyond appalled that you'd say such a thing in mixed company, Emily," Miss Adeline said.

"To use the word *corset*!" Miss Josephine said.

"And now you've used it as well, dear sister," Miss Adeline said.

"She'd faint dead away," Miss Josephine said, "Emily's mother, that is."

"Now, she would," Miss Adeline said. "It was different when she was young."

"Is that so?" I asked, sitting up straighter and feeling suddenly more alert. I'd never given much thought to my mother's youth. Everything about her suggested she'd been a dragon since birth.

"She had her wild days," Miss Josephine said. "Don't let her convince you otherwise."

"When this murder business is finished, we'll tell you all about it," Miss Adeline said.

Jeremy's butler stepped into the room. "I'm most sorry to interrupt, Your Grace," he said. "Might I have a private word?" Jeremy dabbed his lips with his napkin and took the man into the corridor. When he returned, his face was a ghastly shade of gray.

"There's been another murder," he said. "Mrs. Mackie, my housekeeper, is dead."

The Greats immediately fell still and silent.

Together, we all went through the green baize door into the servants' part of the castle. The space was eerily quiet, the only sound our footsteps and the muffled sobs of one of the kitchen maids. The butler took us through a maze of corridors until we reached the ironing room. Large counters dotted with irons lined the walls. A hulking machine in the center was long enough to press table linens. The housekeeper's body was sprawled next to it on the floor.

"I swear I didnae do nothing," a red-faced maid said. "I was ironing His Grace's shirts and Mrs. Mackie wanted to check that I wasnae using too much starch. His Grace doesnae like his collars too stiff." She gave a little bow of her head in Jeremy's direction.

"I've no doubt you're doing an excellent job," he said. "What happened then?"

"Well she just went and collapsed, didnae she? We none of us knew what to do."

There were six other maids in the room. They all murmured assent. Jeremy looked at me.

"What now, Em?"

"Send for Dr. Cameron." I had knelt by the body to confirm Mrs. Mackie was dead. "Did she sound or look strange before she fell?"

"She was standing kind of funny, like her legs wouldnae work," the maid said, "but she kept talking for a while. When she hit the floor her breathing started to sound funny. We got her some water, but she couldnae drink it. Next thing we knew she wasnae breathing at all."

Miss Adeline removed a clean sheet from a laundry trolley, unfolded it, and, with Miss Josephine's help, draped it over the body.

Colin frowned. "Where was she before she came here?"

"Well I wouldnae know that, would I?" The maid crossed her arms tight across her chest. "She didnae speak to us about it. We was all about to go eat our supper. It had been delayed twice, so we'd kept working."

While we waited for Dr. Cameron to arrive and examine the corpse, we questioned the rest of the servants in their hall. No one had noticed anything different about Mrs. Mackie's routine that evening, other than the lateness of their meal, which was due to Colin and me arriving back at the castle so late. As she always did, the housekeeper made rounds to ensure everything was in order for the following day. Until she reached the ironing room, nothing happened that was out of the ordinary.

We spoke with the butler, MacDowell, longer than anyone else. Although he did his best to maintain his composure, I could see he was struggling with the loss of his colleague. Beads of sweat covered his forehead and his hands were trembling.

"We've worked together for more than fifteen years," he said. "She was a rare find, Mrs. Mackie. I've never seen her equal. She could organize anything and never tolerated even the slightest nonsense from her staff. A consummate professional."

"Did anyone call on her this afternoon?" Colin asked.

"No, she didnae receive visitors except on her days off," MacDowell said. "That would be Tuesday, sir. Today is Thursday."

"Given that your evening meal was delayed, is it possible Mrs.

Mackie ate or drank something to tide her over in the interim?" Colin asked.

"She did not," MacDowell said.

"You're certain?" I asked. "She might have had a cup of tea in her room."

"She never does that until she's retired for the evening. She wasnae one for taking breaks in the course of her workday other than for luncheon, no matter how late it got. The only time I'm aware of her making an exception to that rule was when she met with you, Lady Emily."

Dr. Cameron entered the room and MacDowell snapped to his feet. Dr. Cameron crossed to the butler. "I questioned those who witnessed Mrs. Mackie's death about the symptoms she exhibited and, from them, I can surmise she won't have suffered at the end. I hope that's some consolation." This couldn't have been true, but the butler would be comforted by the lie.

"It is, indeed, it is." MacDowell looked at Colin. "Is there anything further you require from me?"

"Not at present," my husband said. "I'll let you know if that changes."

Once the butler left the room, Dr. Cameron took a seat at the long table, and placed his hands flat on the surface, smooth from years of use. "I'll know more after I get her back to the surgery, but it does look like poison."

"By all accounts she was moving about normally until she collapsed and hasn't had anything to eat or drink since luncheon," I said.

"Some poisons take a considerable length of time to act. Given the nature of her symptoms, I suspect she ingested hemlock. Depending on the dose given, it can take several hours before its effects become obvious, but not so long that it could have been administered with her lunch."

The Greats, who were sitting next to each other, exchanged a glance. "Hemlock. Like Socrates," Miss Josephine said.

"Whose execution we were only just discussing with the boys," Miss Adeline said.

"You don't suspect someone was listening?" Miss Josephine asked.

"We might have inadvertently planted the idea," Miss Adeline said.

"That seems most unlikely," Jeremy said. "I don't believe the maids serving you would have had the wherewithal to find hemlock, do whatever one needs to do to turn it into a potion, and trick Mrs. Mackie into drinking it between then and now."

"I quite agree," Colin said. "Don't give it another thought."

"It's an odd coincidence," Miss Adeline said.

"I've never believed in coincidence," Miss Josephine said.

"Bainbridge, take your aunts upstairs and give them some brandy," Colin said. "There's no need for them to be further upset." They all looked relieved to go.

"Maisie's not here, but we should speak to Mr. Fletcher," I said. "And Irene as well. I saw hemlock growing in her garden. Dr. Cameron, was there ever talk of her having been involved with Mr. Gordon? Given the propensity for villagers to gossip, I can't imagine anyone's relationships remain private for long."

"I can't say I've heard anything about the two of them, but if anyone in Cairnfarn is a master of the discreet, it's Irene. She's one of the only people here capable of keeping a secret."

After we arranged for the body to be removed to the doctor's surgery for a postmortem, I changed into more practical clothing so that Colin and I could go back to the village.

We asked the butler to arrange for a carriage and decided we'd start at Mr. Fletcher's cottage. When we arrived, his windows were glowing golden, and the interior was neater than I'd expected for a rough bachelor who seemed unconcerned about appearances. He let us in, offered Colin a whisky, looked at me, and hesitated.

"I can give madam one as well if you'd like, sir."

"Thank you," I said, ignoring his attempt to get Colin's permission. "That would be lovely." I'd never much liked whisky, but I preferred its burn to letting a man erroneously conclude my husband had control over what I might drink. He turned to my husband, who smiled magnanimously.

"Should you ever take a wife, Fletcher, choose one who has a mind of her own," he said. "I can promise you, anything else would be intolerable."

Mr. Fletcher didn't look convinced, but he poured a splash of golden liquid into a glass and handed it to me.

"We have a few questions to ask about what occurred when you saw Mrs. Mackie today," Colin said, after we'd settled into sturdy wooden chairs that looked as if their owner had constructed them. They were surprisingly comfortable.

"Mrs. Mackie? I didnae see her today. I was last up at the castle . . . let's see . . . it must've been nearly a week ago, to help Nesbitt repair some fencing near the stables. He's shorthanded these days."

"Did you see her while you were there?" I asked.

"No. I had no reason to go inside."

"How long has it been since you last saw her?" Colin asked.

"Heavens, man, who do you think I am? A fancy gent who can drop in for a spot of tea with a housekeeper? We might recognize each other in the street, but I cannae say I've ever exchanged three words with her. She'd probably take offense at someone as lowly as me speaking to her."

"Where were you working today?" Colin asked.

"I spent the day helping Dermid Tait move his sheep to different pasture. We were up past the Smithy, a place I hear you're well acquainted with Lady Emily."

"How long were you with Mr. Tait?" I asked, not commenting on my hike, but taking note that—naturally—he'd heard all about it.

"We met at his croft just as the sun was rising and returned to the village when it was starting to come down. Sheep are an ornery bunch. They dinnae like taking direction. Why does it matter?"

"Where can we find Tait?" Colin said.

"This time of night he's likely to be in the pub. You didnae answer my question. Why does it matter what I was doing?"

"Mrs. Mackie was murdered tonight," I said. I'd chosen the words carefully, not wanting to let on that we were more interested in his whereabouts during the afternoon, when we believed she'd drunk the hemlock.

His eyes widened and he clasped his hands in his lap. "Well, now, that's a blow," he said. "Not that I feel the loss personally, mind you, but it's a right mess, all this death in Cairnfarn. What happened?"

"Dr. Cameron is conducting the postmortem," Colin said. "We'll know more once it's complete."

"So her head wasnae bashed in like the gamekeeper's?" He pursed his lips. "A different killer, then?"

"That remains to be seen," Colin said.

"When I got back home tonight, I made myself a meal. Well, heated up a meal from what was left from yesterday's stew. Rabbit," Mr. Fletcher said. His tone was decidedly more serious than it had been before. "While it was on the stove I cleaned myself up, just a little, to get rid of most of the smell of sheep, but I wasnae too bothered about it as I wasnae planning to see anyone. I ate, then I washed my dishes and started to work on my spurtles."

"Your spurtles?" I asked.

"Aye, spurtles," he said, rising from his seat and crossing to a small worktable on the other side of the room. "You've probably never cooked in your life, so I suppose it stands to reason that you dinnae ken anything about making porridge. A spurtle's what you stir it with, using your right hand—only your right hand—in a clockwise direction. Move it widdershins and the devil will rain down bad luck on you."

"Widdershins?" I asked.

He rolled his eyes. "Anticlockwise." He picked something up from the table, came back, handed it to me, and sat down again. It was a long, smooth cylinder-shaped piece of perfectly finished wood, the top carved like a thistle. "You can have this one. Give it to your cook in London or wherever you live, but be sure to instruct her in the proper use of the thing or you'll have no end of trouble."

"Thank you," I said. "Did your travels with the sheep this afternoon take you past the gamekeeper's cottage?"

"Nae," Mr. Fletcher said. "I wasnae anywhere near the place. Why?"

"It's been burgled," Colin said.

"Well, I wasnae there today and cannae imagine there's anything in the place worth taking, unless you're in the market for bad taxidermy or boring books."

"When were you last there?" Colin asked.

"More than three weeks ago. I'd seen poachers in the woods and thought it was my duty to alert Gordon. That's the only reason I went to his place. You know I wasnae fond of the man."

He might claim not to have been to the cottage since Mr. Gordon's death, but I wasn't altogether convinced. I couldn't imagine Mr. Fletcher was the sort of man who would take notice of books without a very specific reason.

30

Tansy
1676

When I left Finella's squalid little cottage, I was more unsettled than when I'd arrived. The idea of taking—borrowing—Rossalyn's precious possessions troubled me. Even if it could be done without her noticing, it wasn't right. It was a betrayal of our friendship. If we had a friendship. We lived together, but there was no real intimacy between us. We shared a space because we each needed what the other could provide: I, a home; she, someone to tend to it.

Finella was altogether different. She told me things that some would consider dangerous. She trusted me. She was honest. Most important, I had no doubt that she was genuinely interested in me as a person. Not as a slave. Not as a servant. Not as someone in need of being rescued. It had been so many years since anyone had looked upon me as an individual. I craved it more than I ever could have imagined possible.

I didn't want to go back to the cottage and face Rossalyn, so instead walked through the village and along the shore of the loch, looking up at the mountains across the water. I sat on a boulder, closed my eyes, and imagined I was back in Tunis, that none of this had ever happened. How much happier I would be. I'd be married by now and might even have children. I'd always wanted a large family. As a girl, I'd spent countless hours embroidering linens to take with me when I left my parents' house. My father had bought a large chest made from olive wood and inlaid with mother-of-pearl to store them in. At first, I thought I'd never have enough to fill it, but only two weeks before I was kidnapped, I'd noticed it was almost full. This had made me anxious and excited. More of the former than the latter, for I had no idea who my father would choose as my husband.

Sometimes, after I'd been ripped from my old life, I tried to convince myself that it might not have turned out well if I was still at home. What if I'd been married to a man odious and cruel? I could never take the possibility seriously. My father had too much love for me to make such an unfortunate choice. When I was little, he'd joked that he'd only marry me to a prince. When I misbehaved, he threatened to sell me to Barbary pirates, but that was a jest, too.

Sometimes, now, I wondered if my loving family had been more curse than blessing. If I'd never known such kindness, such care, would I be so unhappy now? Perhaps not, but on balance, I'd rather live with the sharp contrast of joy and pain than have had only the dull monotony of vague discontent.

Sometimes, I wondered if I wouldn't have recognized the joy in my previous life if I'd never experienced the horrors of my current one.

I was considering this when a voice called out to me. It was Cora.

"Tasnim!" She must have been out wandering, as she was carrying a basket laden with plants. She squinted and tilted her head as she came close to me. "You don't look well. Is something wrong?"

I hesitated before replying. The doubts I had about her and Rossalyn were too fresh in my mind to be ignored, but at the same time, I couldn't discount the fact that she had been a good friend to me from the earliest days after we'd arrived in the village. Relationships are never simple, but the complications in this one, if my suspicions were correct, could prove dangerous. Taking Finella's advice, I decided to exercise caution.

"I'm feeling a bit melancholy, that's all," I said.

She sat next to me and put her basket down on the ground. "I cannae imagine how difficult it must be to find yourself so far from your family."

I knew she was trying to be compassionate, but it irritated me. "Not just far away, but far away because someone stole me and sold me. I'm stranded in a country with a culture that's totally foreign, with no hope of ever returning to my home. *Difficult* is something of an understatement."

"I'm sorry. I didnae mean to—" She stopped. "The pain must run deeper than any other could. I wish I could make it go away."

"No one can," I said.

"That's not entirely true," she said. "Someone with enough money could get you back to Tunis."

"Rossalyn had that much money and more before her husband died. She never offered. Given that she's known me longer than anyone else here and claims to be my friend, I can't see there's a possibility that someone with fewer connections is going to offer assistance."

"Is she aware that you want to go back?" Cora asked.

The words inflamed and infuriated me. I jumped up and spun

around so I was facing her. "How could any human being think otherwise? What if it were you, taken away from everything you know? Or Rossalyn? Or your father? Have you ever encountered a person who would accept such a fate with equanimity and calm acceptance?"

"No. No one would. It's obvious when you state it that way."

"Yet none of these people pay the slightest attention to what's been done to me. I'm here, I'm treated decently, and that's supposed to be enough."

She cringed. "Of course it's not enough."

"You say that now, but you're no better than the rest of them." I was being cruel. She had tried to be a friend to me, but I didn't care. Not anymore. "You all want me to act like there's nothing wrong with the situation, as if I had chosen to come to Scotland, because you don't want to be made to feel uncomfortable. How very awful it is to feel uncomfortable. To speak about things that might make it impossible to hold the belief that you're good, ethical people. Ethical people don't own their fellow humans."

"That's why Rossalyn freed you immediately."

"And that releases her from the moral burden? I'm still thousands of miles from my family."

"I'm not arguing that any of it is acceptable," Cora said, "but Rossalyn's action, taken on its own, surely was good. No, it didnae go far enough, but surely it's better not to be a slave, isnae it?"

"How can you ask such a question?" I turned on my heel and stormed off, following the shore of the loch deep into the forest, my rage increasing exponentially with every step I took. I was surrounded by people who cared only for themselves and their comfort. Who thought saying the occasional right word was balm enough to soothe my wounded soul. I hated them. All of them.

By the time twilight turned the sky inky, I knew I needed to get back to the cottage. I was miles from the village. Fear's icy hands started to grip me. It would be dark soon. I had no lantern and couldn't stop thinking about wolves. A full moon was rising, but its light barely filtered through the clouds. I walked more quickly, then started to run. This made me feel more capable, more in control. At least until I tripped on a tree root and sprawled onto the ground.

"What are you doing here?"

A man was standing in front of me. I didn't recognize his voice and I couldn't see his face, but his silhouette was tall and lean. My heart pounded. I started to sweat. I held my breath and tried to focus. How could I best deal with him? If I flung myself at his knees with all my weight, I might take him by surprise and knock him down, which could give me enough time to flee into the woods, off the path. I could climb a tree and stay there, still, until he stopped looking for me. I started to pick myself up, but stayed low to the ground, crouching. I breathed in until my lungs were full to bursting. As I breathed out, I sprung forward and slammed into him. Did he stumble and fall? I didn't know, because everything went black.

31

1905

The sky was nearly dark, but the rain had stopped, the clouds parted, and the moon glowed down from above. As the carriage drove us back toward the village, Colin and I digested what Mr. Fletcher had told us. "I believe he was genuinely surprised Mrs. Mackie is dead," I said, "but mentioning the books in the cottage is suspicious."

"I agree," Colin said. "If Tait confirms his alibi, we'll have to accept that he didn't kill Mrs. Mackie."

The carriage slowed as we reached the Drover, the public house on Cairnfarn's high street. The building was narrow, built between two larger houses. The ground floor contained a long wooden bar and a smattering of tables, only a few of them empty. The first floor, according to a sign hanging precariously on the wall near the stairs, was private, the domain of the landlord, who was standing behind his bar. Colin asked him if Mr. Tait was anywhere to be found. He directed us to a red-faced man with enormous ears who was sitting as far away as possible from the fireplace with the dregs of a pint in front of him.

"I'm most obliged," Colin said. "Could I please have two pints of whatever he's drinking and a half pint of cider?" I raised an eyebrow, but said nothing.

"That would be a heavy, sir," the landlord said. "Are you sure that will that be to your taste?" The scowl on his face made it clear he assumed it would not be.

"McEwan's?" Colin asked.

"Aye."

"Nothing better," Colin said, "save Glenmorangie, of course, but heavy and whisky aren't meant to be compared, are they?"

The landlord smiled. "You're very welcome here, sir." He pulled the pints and then my cider. Colin paid him, gathered the glasses into his hands, and carried them to Mr. Tait's table.

"Callum Fletcher told us we'd find you here," he said, and introduced us. Mr. Tait, who had even less compunction about cleanliness than his friend, smelled strongly of sheep. Colin put the glasses on the table and pushed one toward Mr. Tait. "I hope you won't object to us joining you for a moment?"

Mr. Tait looked at Colin and pointedly ignored me. "I didnae ken you English bring your wives to the pub. What is it you want? I was hoping for a peaceful evening, but I see that's not to be."

"Did you have a difficult day?" Colin asked, taking a swig of his heavy. I sipped my cider, which was surprisingly nice. It was evident it would be best if, at least for the moment, I said as little as possible. Mr. Tait did not appear to be the sort of man who would respond well to being questioned by a lady. Even so, I was glad to be there. People like him needed to see that we ladies won't be limited in what we can do, no matter how uncomfortable it makes them.

"You dinnae ken much about sheep, do you?" Mr. Tait embarked on a detailed description of the troubles he'd faced since that morning, confirming both what Mr. Fletcher had told us about the animals being ornery and that his friend had been with him the entire time.

"Fletcher never left, the entire day?" Colin asked.

"What would I have done if he had?" Mr. Tait asked. "My son's down ill, so he was the only help I had. It's not a job for a single man alone."

What followed was an intricate account of managing sheep: the challenges it posed, the way the environs of Cairnfarn made it even more difficult, and a diatribe against shepherds whose heads were (I quote) *so far removed from God's reality they might as well go live with the fairies.* Such a mindset, apparently, is catastrophically bad for sheep. When he finished, he looked at us—both of us—through narrowed eyes.

"I see now what you're after," he said. "You're the guests His Grace charged with identifying the man what killed the gamekeeper. You willnae find any answers here in the Drover, I'll tell you. Gordon kept to himself. Preferred more refined company, or at least wanted us to think so, because of his fancy schooling."

"Was he close to anyone in the village?" I asked.

"I dinnae ken," Mr. Tait said. "He was fair with the local children and got along with the vicar most of the time, but he never had time for the rest of us. There's not much else to say, especially as we're all about to get free whisky."

He nodded in the direction of the doorway. Dr. Cameron and Dr. Harris had just come through it.

"I'm to order a round for you all, courtesy of Tam Mackintosh," Dr. Cameron said, his voice booming. "Dr. Harris has just delivered his wife of a son. He'll be here as soon as she lets him out of the house and His Grace is coming to join us in a toast."

Depending on how long the labor had taken, it sounded as if Dr. Harris might have a firm alibi for Mrs. Mackie's murder. I picked up my cider, excused myself, and crossed to the doctors.

"What lovely news," I said.

"Sadly tempered by the loss of another, but a birth and a death, hand in hand isn't uncommon," Dr. Cameron said. "They go together nearly all the time." He lowered his voice. "I've finished the postmortem. Hemlock poisoning was the cause of death."

I nodded and turned to Dr. Harris. "What time did you arrive at the Mackintoshes'?"

"I didn't kill Mrs. Mackie," she said.

"Please, Dr. Harris, what time did you arrive?" I asked.

"Her labor started early this morning, but she didn't send for me until noon. It's her first child, so there was no rush. I arrived at their croft before twelve thirty."

"Thank you. I apologize for having to ask."

"I shouldn't let it offend me," she said, "but I'm starting to become rather sensitive about the whole matter. It's quite unpleasant to have people treat you like a potential murderer. So unpleasant it's beginning to make me feel rather murderous, in fact. Perhaps people do become what we assume them to be."

The landlord was making his way around the room with a tray full of glasses of whisky. Soon thereafter, Jeremy and Irene appeared, followed in short order by the vicar and his wife.

"Any news regarding Mrs. Mackie?" he asked.

"Dr. Cameron has confirmed her death was caused by hemlock poisoning," I said.

"Blimey." He shook his head. "I can't think about it anymore tonight. It's time to celebrate the Mackintoshes' new arrival." He removed a glass off the landlord's tray, drained it in a single gulp, then took another.

I pulled Irene to one side and asked her where she'd been that afternoon.

"We all need alibis now, is that it?" she asked. "I was at my cottage, alone. I didnae see anyone until one of the village boys came to tell me the news about Mrs. Mackintosh. We always celebrate new babies at the Drover."

"The piece of ribbon you gave me when we were hiking—do you have more of it?"

"Loads," she said. "I use it for tying packages of my preparations."

"So anyone who's bought something from you might have one?"

"They could. This is what you're interested in? Ribbons?"

"Do you ever use them for anything else? Binding pamphlets, perhaps?" I asked.

She looked at me as if I were daft. "Why would I be making pamphlets?" She spun on her heel and walked away.

Colin and I knew Maisie hadn't penned the story of the princess and her cake that we'd found in the cottage—Colin had seen her handwriting, and it didn't match—but I'd never really believed Irene had, either. Still, I had to inquire. One can never be sure where the key piece of information lurks in a murder investigation. Mr. Gordon was involved in a clandestine relationship. While that might have catalyzed a violent jealousy in Maisie, it also could have led to something else. What if Mr. Gordon had wanted an end to the secrecy? Might his lover have killed him to protect herself? Could Mrs. Mackie have been silenced because she was the only other person who knew about the affair?

I sought out Dr. Cameron and pulled him aside. "Do you recall anyone showing particular interest in the story you told on the summer solstice about the princess and her love cake?"

"I can't say I do," he said. "It wasn't nearly so popular with the audience as kelpies. Highlanders aren't all that fond of the exotic."

I remembered the smudge of grease on the cover of the booklet. "Do you have a recipe for the cake?"

"A recipe? No," he said. "I can tell you the general flavor of the thing, though. It's made from almond flour and has rosewater and cardamom in it. Lime juice, too, and it's decorated with dried rose petals and pistachios sprinkled over the icing. Nothing like your Scottish cake."

The pub was crammed full of people. "Is the grocer here?" I asked.

"Mr. Reid? Yes, he's sitting at the bar, on the third stool from the left."

I thanked him and introduced myself to the man. "I've a rather strange question for you," I said. "Do you recall anyone purchasing unusual ingredients this summer? I'm trying to determine whether any of the villagers attempted to make a Persian cake after hearing Dr. Cameron's story about it at the summer solstice." I listed the items.

"Almond flour, cardamom, and rosewater," he said, his forehead crinkling. "The first two aren't the sort of thing people in Cairnfarn keep in their pantries. Rosewater I dinnae stock. Irene MacDuff makes it, so there's no need. Limes I keep on hand, as I do pistachios. There's only one person who asked about almond flour: Effie Thomson. I'd never heard of it before, so I told her to grind up some of the nuts and mix them with ordinary flour. She's a terrible cook, so I cannae imagine it came out well, but, then, it never sounded any good to me in the first place."

Effie Thomson. The Pringles' scatterbrained and barely competent servant who had been so quick to tell us about Maisie attacking the gamekeeper. I found it difficult to imagine Effie winning Mr. Gordon's affection, but love can be a strange thing. He might have seen something in her we couldn't. I looked around for Mrs. Pringle. She was standing apart from the others, sipping a cup of tea.

"I've never been much for spirits," she explained as I approached her.

"It's good of you to be here," I said. "It's not easy to celebrate the birth of a baby when you've lost one of your own so recently."

She blinked tears from her eyes. "I won't admit it to anyone else, but you're correct. Fortunately, the villagers don't know what happened. We're all terrible gossips, but some things are better kept private."

"I couldn't agree more and am glad you don't have to share that secret."

"The doctors know, of course," she said. "We managed to conceal the truth about what befell me even from Effie. She believes I was ill, but has no idea as to the cause."

"It's Effie whom I want to speak to you about," I said. "Were you aware that she was enamored with Mr. Gordon?"

She smiled. "It was impossible not to notice that."

"Was there any sort of understanding between them?"

"Between Effie and the gamekeeper? Heavens, no." She stepped away to set her now empty teacup on a nearby table. I followed her. "I ought not reject the idea so forcefully, I suppose. It's unkind. Mr. Gordon was very sweet to her, the way he was to everyone. Well, not everyone, but to the girls who found him irresistible. He didn't like to hurt anyone's feelings, but at the same time, he was careful never

246

to encourage them. You can't possibly think she was responsible for his death?"

"The pieces are beginning to fall into place and the details of his murder are becoming clear." I wasn't going to give her—or anyone— insight into what I was thinking. Effie had been with her for years. She hadn't dismissed her, despite the fact that she was terrible at her job, despite the fact that, although her husband adored good food, she was an appalling cook. Given her sympathy for the young woman, I couldn't trust her not to try to hide any evidence that might connect her to the crime.

"They did not have a relationship. I'm certain of that," she said. "If it had been otherwise, Effie would've been shouting it off the rooftops. The fact that she wasn't proves she had not won his affection. The girl couldn't keep a secret if her life depended on it."

"Did you know she tried to bake a Persian love cake after hearing Dr. Cameron's story about one at the ceilidh?"

"Effie? Bake a love cake?" She laughed, just for an instant, then turned serious. "I ought not make light of it if she did. It's just that . . . well, she is a tragically awful cook. It would've proved disastrous."

"To you or me, yes, but perhaps not to the man who adored her."

She smiled and her face glowed. "I very much like the idea of someone adoring Effie. It would be too marvelous, wouldn't it? Everyone should know that kind of happiness. If Effie found it, she would never have murdered the man who'd given it to her. I'm going to fetch another cup of tea. Would you like one?"

I declined and went instead in search of my husband, whom I found sitting with Dr. Harris. I took him outside and told him what I'd learned.

"Effie?" He pulled a face. "I can't picture it. Although her chaotic nature does fit with the chaotic method of the murder."

"I believe she reached the wrong conclusion when she saw Mr. Gordon outside the ceilidh with Maisie," I said, "but she didn't know that. She thought the man she loved had betrayed her and was devastated. She waited for him to start for home and, when he did, she attacked him in a jealous rage. We need to go to the vicarage. I'll persuade Effie to tell me everything."

When we arrived, it took Effie nearly three minutes to answer the door.

"Oh, madam, it is lovely to see you, but I'm afraid the Pringles are out. Mrs. Mackintosh had her baby and they're down at the pub. Not that Mrs. Pringle will be indulging. She's always saying she's not one for spirits, you know, although I do wonder about that sometimes. She makes a fine Glasgow punch, and it's full of rum. I'd say that recipe changed her mind about liquor."

"We've actually come to speak with you, Effie," I said. "May we come in?"

"I dinnae ken why not," she said, ushering me inside. We went to the kitchen and sat at the table there; I thought she would be more comfortable in her own domain.

I declined her offer of tea. "I need to speak with you about Mr. Gordon. I know you had feelings for him and it's come to my attention that he reciprocated them. You baked him a Persian cake, and—"

"Oh, no, madam, I never did any such thing," she said. "I dinnae take to those foreign sorts of food. Sounded right awful to me. Well, not when Dr. Cameron was telling the story about it. I didnae think about it much at the time. But when Mrs. Pringle gave me the list of ingredients she needed for it, it sounded like a right mess to me."

"Mrs. Pringle?" Colin asked.

"Yes, she's the one who wanted to bake it. I offered to help, but she made it on my day off, so I didnae even get to see what the vicar thought of it. Of course he's besotted by her, so I dinnae ken why she even felt the need to do it, but people are strange, aren't they? I asked him the next day if he liked it, but it was as if he haedne the slightest idea what I was saying."

We heard the jingle of keys, the sound of a door closing, and voices in the sitting room. The Pringles were home.

32

Tansy

1676

When I came to, I was in my bed at the cottage, Rossalyn and Agnes hovering over me.

"What you were doing out in the dark with no lantern is beyond me," Rossalyn said. "You're fortunate someone found you."

"Who?" I asked, pushing myself up on my elbows. My head was throbbing.

"Some visitor on his way to the castle," she said. "He saw you stumble and hit your head on a rock when you fell. He couldn't rouse you, so carried you to the village and asked where you belong."

"I'm brewing a tisane that will ease your pain," Agnes said. "You should drink it every few hours until the headache subsides."

"I'm sorry you're hurt, but I'm furious with you, Tansy." Rossalyn was frowning. "You disappear without a word as to where you're going or when you'll be back. I'm left here on my own nearly the entire day, worrying about you. You didn't even return for supper."

And that, I didn't doubt, was what really troubled her. She had no reason to be worried about me, but would not have liked the fact that I hadn't come back to cook for her. Her anger proved a gift: it gave me clarity. I would take the things Finella wanted from her. It would shield us both from harm, but I found I no longer cared so much about protecting her. I needed to look after myself, and, from now on, that would be my priority.

Agnes stayed at my bedside until she was certain I was suffering no shocking ill effects from my fall. I told her I was fine, that a little headache was nothing to cause so much trouble, and thanked her for all she'd done. She left more of her tisane for me, in case the pain got worse, as well as a powder that would help me sleep. As soon as she was gone, I got out of bed.

"You need to take care of yourself," Rossalyn said.

"Truly, I'm not in bad shape. I'm going to make some tea. Would you like a cup?"

"I've been so worried about you that I find myself in dire need of respite. Tea would be lovely."

She didn't press me to stay in bed or offer to make the tea for us both. Instead, she installed herself in one of the chairs by the fire, a plaid shawl wrapped around her. If I hadn't already made my decision, that would have sealed it. I brewed a strong cup of black tea with a splash of milk for myself. To Rossalyn's, I added all of Agnes's sleeping powder.

"It might taste bitter," I said as I handed it to her. There was no point hiding what I'd done. "Worry will make it harder for you to sleep than me. You should have it."

"You're so good to me, Tansy. I don't know what I'd do without you."

A quarter of an hour later, she was fast asleep in her chair. I slipped the gold band off her finger, removed the crucifix from the wall, and slid them into a cloth satchel. I touched my mother's saffron ribbon, which I kept tucked into my bodice, close to my heart. It pained me, but I pulled it out and added it to the bag. Then, I sat waiting until I heard a faint scratching on the door. It was Finella.

"I'll return it all as early as possible in the morning," she said, "and you'll no longer have to worry about any of this."

After she left, I moved Rossalyn to her bed, then slipped into mine. I didn't think I'd be able to sleep, but I was wrong. I fell into a deep, dreamless slumber, only to be awakened by harsh knocking. It seemed as if no time had passed, but the sky was rose colored and dotted with golden clouds.

"Rossalyn MacAllister, present yourself at once!" The voice, loud and booming, was unfamiliar. Rossalyn didn't stir, so I rose, pulled a shawl around my shoulders, and opened the door. There stood six men, none of whom I recognized. I assumed they were from the castle. The one in front leered at me. "Are you a witch, too, or only just a thief?"

33

1905

The Pringles had come home? That put a wrinkle in things. Colin and I stepped into the corridor so we could speak without Effie hearing.

"Mrs. Pringle was the one involved with Gordon," he said.

"Effie asking the vicar about the cake might have alerted him to his wife's infidelity," I said, "but it wouldn't have revealed to him the identity of her paramour."

"We're jumping ahead of ourselves," Colin said. "We can't be sure Effie is correct about any of this and we have no idea what Pringle knew."

"He always seemed so very affable and devoted to his wife."

"Which would make him feel her betrayal all the more keenly."

"It makes sense of the method, doesn't it?" I asked. "He wouldn't have had the strength to easily defeat Mr. Gordon. Rocks were the only weapon he had readily at hand."

"It's believable Gordon wouldn't have rushed to defend himself against the vicar," Colin said.

"Mr. Pringle may not have intended to kill him," I said.

"That wouldn't surprise me in the least."

"How best to approach them?" I asked.

"Carefully," Colin said. "We've no firm proof about the affair. We'll have to tease it all out of them."

"The poor woman." I sighed. "She's already heartbroken over losing her child. Now, to learn that her husband killed the man she loved . . . it's too much to bear."

"I suspect the child was Gordon's," Colin said, "which makes me somewhat less sympathetic to her plight. We'd best get on with it."

We ducked into the kitchen, where Colin told Effie in no uncertain terms that she was not to leave the room, no matter what happened. When we entered the sitting room, we found the Pringles next to each other on the settee. The vicar rose to his feet.

"Mr. Hargreaves, Caroline told me what your wife suspects, but I can assure you that Effie was not involved in any relationship—appropriate or inappropriate—with Mr. Gordon. She—"

"We know she wasn't," Colin said. "As you are both well aware, someone else was."

"It's Dr. Harris," the vicar said. "I'm convinced there's more between them than seems possible given the short time she's been in Cairnfarn. Might she have known him in Edinburgh?"

"That hardly seems likely," Mrs. Pringle said, "and, at any rate, I don't know how it's relevant. What matters is what happened here, in the village. Have you had any luck tracking down the Norwegian man I saw?"

Mr. Pringle sat down and took her hand. "It's very touching

of you to want to protect our flock, Caroline, but I think we both know there was no Norwegian here the night of the ceilidh. Your motives could not be purer, but we must pursue justice, no matter how difficult it may be to face. Someone—one of our friends and neighbors—is responsible for the death of Mr. Gordon."

"I simply refuse to believe that," Mrs. Pringle said. "It must have been an accident. No one here would deliberately take a life."

"Your heart won't allow you to believe anything else, will it?" her husband asked, squeezing her hand. "You are a dear, sweet thing."

"I do wish you'd stop referring to me like that," she snapped. "I'm not a thing, sweet or otherwise, and I never have been."

"I most humbly apologize," he said. "I had no idea my calling you that troubled you. If I had I would never—"

They went back and forth for some time, her criticizing and him apologizing. I stopped listening because a carved wooden box on the table in front of the settee caught my eye. I remembered seeing it before. Now, I lifted its lid. Inside were about a dozen small polished rocks with Viking runes carved on them.

"It's all become clear to me," I said, interrupting the ongoing discussion between husband and wife, "so there's no point continuing this charade. Mr. Pringle, how long have you known about your wife's involvement with Mr. Gordon?"

Mrs. Pringle leapt to her feet and stepped toward me. "Lady Emily, how could you even suggest that I would—"

The vicar reached for his wife's hand, but she pulled it away. "I've known since the beginning," he said. "I've always adored you, Caroline, but I'm not enough of a fool to have ever believed you'd be able to return my affection in kind. You're so much younger than I and so full of passion, a passion I could never inspire or fulfill. We've had a good life together, even if for most of it we've been little more than content companions."

"I do love you, Hamish," she said. "How could you believe otherwise? I can't imagine how you would have reached the erroneous conclusion that—"

Mr. Pringle folded his hands, rested them on his lap, and stared at them as he spoke. "I shouldn't have gone after him that night. I certainly never intended to harm him."

"Don't, Hamish," his wife said. "Don't say another word. It was an accident, nothing more."

I looked at her face. She was calm, resolved. There was no sign of anger in her eyes. Her brow was smooth. It was then that the final pieces clicked into place.

"I'm not a violent man," the vicar said. "It's not in my nature, but sometimes, one's emotions spiral beyond one's control. We humans are all fallible, all sinners, all in need of infinite forgiveness. When I realized the truth of my situation, I knew I had to act. I could not sit back quietly any longer. The child was not mine."

Now Mrs. Pringle's face crumpled and a sob escaped from her lips. "I never meant—"

He reached for her hand; this time, she did not pull it away. "No, no, of course you didn't. You mustn't cry, Caroline. It's I who behaved despicably. When you started to pay attention to me, all those years ago, I couldn't believe my luck. I fell for you wholly and loved you more deeply than I ever thought a man could love a woman. It was unconscionable that I didn't better consider you in it all. You were young and it was time for you to marry. I was the least objectionable of the available options. You weren't made for farming, were you? You made a practical decision; I let my heart carry me away. It wasn't fair to you."

"No, Hamish, that's not it at all. I—"

He took her hand. "It doesn't matter now, does it? We're in a right pickle, and it's all my fault." He released her hand, rose to his feet, and stepped toward Colin. "It's time I make a full confession, but I'd prefer to do so in private, man to man, if that's acceptable. I must take responsibility for my actions."

I watched Mrs. Pringle as he spoke. Her face looked like smooth marble, incapable of movement. She said nothing, so the task fell to me.

"I don't think that will prove a satisfactory way forward, Mr. Pringle," I said. "Honorable though your motives are, remember what you only just told your wife: that you must pursue justice, no matter how difficult it is. You did not kill Mr. Gordon, but I do believe that his death was largely accidental, was it not, Mrs. Pringle?"

Tears streamed down her cheeks. "I was so angry, so very angry. We'd been looking through the rocks on the shore of the loch, searching for ones with runes carved in them. At least he was, because he didn't want to hear what I had to tell him. He wouldn't meet my eyes, couldn't bear to look at me. So I picked up a large stone and threw it at him—"

"Stop, Caroline," Mr. Pringle said. "There's no need for you to continue. It was an accident, nothing more."

"No, you were right when you said it's time for a full confession, but it needs to come from me, not you. Would it be all right, Mr. Hargreaves, if I took a moment to collect myself? I'd like to splash some water on my face and change into a less frivolous gown. It shall only take a few moments. Then, I will tell you everything."

I answered for my husband. "I think that's an excellent idea." Colin looked surprised and started to reply, but I silenced him with a slight shake of my head. He told her to do what she must. I waited approximately five minutes before I followed her to her bedroom, where I found her sitting at her dressing table, an empty cup in front of her. Next to it was a copy of *Jane Eyre*.

"It was the hemlock, I presume," I said, motioning to the cup.

She nodded. "It's intolerable to go on like this. What I've done is beyond abominable. I can't let him stand by my side during a trial and execution. He's already suffered enough."

"Will you tell me what happened?" I asked.

"Hamish was right about so much. I did marry him because he was the least objectionable of the available options. I never loved him, not the way he loved me, but neither was I unhappy. I enjoyed my husband's company well enough, and we shared a comfortable life. I'd made my choice and was content to live with it, at least, that is, until Angus Sinclair returned to Cairnfarn. Or Daniel Gordon, I suppose. It's a blow to know he never told me the truth about his identity. I thought we would never hide anything from each other. I never doubted he was the adult version of the little boy I knew so many years ago. Hamish and I held a small dinner party to welcome him to the village. It was a perfectly ordinary evening until the gentlemen came into the sitting room after having had their port. As Angus crossed through the doorway, our eyes met. It was nothing deliberate, just a passing coincidence. I realize how absurd it sounds, but we couldn't stop looking at each other. From then, I thought of nothing but him."

"Did he feel the same?" I asked.

"I assumed not," she said, "but about an hour after our guests departed and Hamish had gone to bed, I was still downstairs. I knew I wouldn't be able to sleep. I'd never experienced anything remotely like the surge of emotions consuming me. The moon was full and the sky clear, so I went into the garden, hoping the cool air would somehow shock me into being able to return to my ordinary life. He was there, waiting."

"Waiting? He expected you would come out?"

"No. He'd started to walk back to his cottage, but had turned around, unable to tear himself away from me. He was standing in the garden, content to know he was looking at the building where I was. We embraced, but then pulled away. Neither of us wanted to embark on an illicit affair. For three months we did our best to keep apart. We hardly spoke when we saw each other at village functions and made a point of never being alone. Then, one day, I was walking back from the castle, where I'd had tea with His Grace's great-aunts, and I ran into him on the path. There was no one else nearby. He touched my hand and it was as if the heavens opened up and showered stars on me. We went to his cottage . . ." Her voice trailed off. She closed her eyes and continued.

"Afterward, he gave me a bit of rum. Since then, I've always associated the taste of it with joy. It's why I sought out the recipe for Glasgow punch, so that I could drink it on occasion without causing comment. From that day, we could not bear to be separated. I'd never imagined love could run so deep, that it could be so all enveloping. We were both preoccupied with guilt, but despite that, couldn't bring ourselves to stop, no matter how hard we tried. And we did try, Lady Emily, I swear we did."

"Surely you knew it couldn't go on forever?" I asked.

"Not that way, it couldn't." She pressed her palm against her eyes and sniffed. "I was desperate for him to be mine, all the way mine, and I knew he felt the same way, but we saw no way to make it happen. Then I discovered I was with child."

"It was not your husband's?"

"I can't be certain," she said. "My guilt over the affair was so pressing, so unbearable, that the only way I could relieve it in the slightest was to shower Hamish with attention and affection. We were never closer than during those months. It was as if Mr. Gordon was the third leg of a stool, making it possible for my marriage to stand steady. It's appalling, I know, but it's the truth. The child might have been Hamish's, but after more than ten years of marriage with no such result, I find it unlikely."

No doubt she was correct.

"Irrational though it sounds, I was elated," she continued. "This could prove the catalyst for Mr. Gordon and me to be together. Not legally, of course, but I knew he would not abandon his child. We could flee Cairnfarn and start a new life somewhere far away, where no one knew us. It would be a blow to Hamish, but I . . . I assumed he would recover. At the ceilidh, I told Mr. Gordon we needed to speak urgently and in private. We went to the shore of the loch, a place where we'd often searched for rocks carved with Viking runes. It was something we could do together without anyone suspecting there was anything untoward between us. I told him about the baby. He did not react the way I anticipated."

"What did he do?" I asked.

"He was horrified," she said. "Talked about how awful we'd been, about how we'd betrayed Hamish, about how it had to stop, once and for all. He said I should pretend it was my husband's child, that I should take it as a second chance and make a fresh start. He was always so fixated on second chances. He said he'd all but squandered his, embroiling himself in an affair that was morally wrong, but that this child gave us the opportunity to correct course, to make things right.

"I couldn't believe what I was hearing," she continued, "but the more I pressed him, the more he dug in. He'd been looking for rocks

260

as we spoke and found one with a rune carved on it. He gave it to me and said it was a parting gift. For a moment, I was stunned, but then it was as if someone had opened up my chest and ripped my heart from it. The pain was unbearable. I started weeping and could hardly breathe, but he offered me no comfort. His voice was cold and he told me to go home. That was when the anger came. It was like a glowing ember at first, but soon it engulfed me. I picked up the largest rock I could lift and threw it at him. He stepped back and avoided it. So I threw another, and another, and another. Eventually, I struck him with one, and that emboldened me. I kept going, throwing more and more, coming closer to him. He backed away and tripped, hitting his head on a boulder as he fell. I ran to him, knelt by his side, and saw that he was breathing. His eyes were open. He reached for my hand.

"For an instant, I thought everything would be all right. That he would admit he'd reacted badly, apologize, and say we would make a life together. Then he told me that he could never see me again. I picked up another rock, bigger than the others, lifted it above my head, and brought it down as hard as I could onto his temple. He did not speak again.

"Part of me felt as if I were watching it all from above," she said. "I could hardly believe what I was doing. But when I saw he was gone . . . that there was no more breath . . . then I was filled with a new kind of rage. I'm not the sort of woman who goes about murdering people, Lady Emily, yet that is what he'd made me become. I was infuriated. If he'd only done the right thing—been willing to stand beside me and his child—but he'd proven himself a coward in the end. I wanted him destroyed, gone, nothing left. I pulled his skene-dhu from his stocking and stabbed him with it, over and over. I hardly knew what I was doing. Then I started to feel a sharp pain in my abdomen and sticky warmth between my legs. I knew what was happening. I'd killed my child as well as its father. My rage evaporated and grief took its place. I kissed his forehead, placed the carved rock he'd given me on it, and went to the loch. I washed the blood from my hands in the water and splashed my face. Then I stumbled back to the village hall, but didn't go inside, only told a young man standing by the door that I was ill and to fetch my husband and the doctor. I didn't wait for either of them to come, but went straight home and got into bed. I lied to you when I said I heard the clock strike eleven. I needed you to believe I was here before he had died."

She closed her eyes and stood up. "My legs are beginning to feel numb. I think I'd best go to the bed. I took more hemlock than I gave Mrs. Mackie"—she stopped, sat on the bed, and gulped a sob—"I didn't want to kill her, but I wasn't brave enough to face what I'd done. Everything was spiraling out of control. I thought I'd diverted attention from myself by hiding one of Mr. Fletcher's shirts in Maisie's room and felt reasonably comfortable until Mrs. Mackie saw me outside the cottage."

"Why were you at the cottage?" I asked.

"He'd told me about the quote from *Jane Eyre* on his watch and said it was the perfect description of how he felt about me. I'd transfixed him. He lamented that the watch was missing. He didn't tell me about the fire, but claimed that a pickpocket had got it from him on a dark night in Edinburgh. I longed to replace it, but I knew I couldn't buy something like that in the village. People would notice. Instead, I got him a copy of the novel and wrote an inscription in it. An intimate, personal inscription. After Hamish told us about Dr. Harris's watch, and you were all talking about *Jane Eyre*, I knew I had to retrieve the book. I couldn't let you find it."

"You just happened to have hemlock with you at the time?"

"No," she said. "I'd taken it from Irene's cottage while she had you hiking up the Smithy. I could no longer live with what I'd done, but I'd not yet mustered the courage to act. I kept it with me, convinced that I would know when the moment came to drink it."

"Yet instead you gave it to Mrs. Mackie."

"It was a terrible thing to do," she said. "I'd just reached the cottage and was unlocking the door—Mr. Gordon had given me a key—and she was there, walking along the path. I didn't notice until she spoke, asking me what I was doing. I told her I'd lent him a book and had come to fetch it. She asked about the key. I said His Grace had given it to me, but I could see she didn't believe me. I asked her to come inside, laying it on rather thick about how I felt uncomfortable going into a dead man's home. Then, when I was looking at the bookshelves, I pretended to feel faint. She offered to make tea. I insisted that she have a cup as well. She brought the pot into the sitting room and asked how I take it. I told her white with no sugar, but after I took a sip, I said that the milk was making me feel nauseous. She went back to the kitchen to get me a fresh cup. While she was gone, I poured some of the hemlock into her tea."

"Did you know it would take so long to act?"

"I didn't. In fact, I assumed she would die there, in front of me, quickly, and I'm ashamed to say that I wondered if that would make it possible to convince everyone that she'd killed the gamekeeper and then, unable to live with the guilt, herself. Until that day, I'd no idea how deep my capacity is for evil."

"She didn't need to die," I said.

"No, she didn't, which makes me unworthy of anyone's forgiveness, only condemnation. I hope that by ending my own life, I'll at least make things slightly easier for Hamish. Don't fetch him, not now. I don't want him to see me like this." She lay back, her eyes closed. "It's becoming hard to breathe. It shan't be long now."

I sat with her until the end, holding her hand. There was no justifying any of her actions, but showing compassion wouldn't cause anyone pain, least of all her husband. When he realized what she'd done, instead of turning on her, he'd tried to confess to her crimes, ready to take her punishment. He wouldn't want her to die alone.

34

Tansy

1676

The man who had asked if I, too, was a witch or only a thief shoved me aside and stomped into the cottage, followed by the other five ruffians. Rossalyn was still in bed. With no ceremony, they wrenched her out, refused to let her change out of her nightdress, bound her hands behind her, and marched her into the street, where they flung her into a waiting wagon. I braced myself, waiting for the same treatment, but it did not come. Rossalyn met my eyes as they drove her away, but she did not shed a single tear. Her face had gone gray and she looked terrified.

Finella's efforts at protection had come too late. The women must have been seen under the moon and mistaken for witches, and Rossalyn somehow implicated as well, no doubt because of the objects I'd taken from her. I dressed as quickly as possible and ran to Finella's cottage, but no one was there. Had she been arrested as well? I fairly flew back to the center of the village, where groups of people stood outside their homes, worry writ on their faces. I asked them what they knew, but no one would speak to me, so I went next to Cora's. Relief flooded me when she answered the door and let me in. I'd been so awful to her, so needlessly cruel, but she didn't set upon me with accusations. Instead, she listened as I told her what had happened.

When I finished, she suggested that we go to Agnes, so we trudged along the sodden ground—it was raining, of course—to her cottage. She was waiting for us when we arrived, standing in her doorway. I wondered how she knew we were coming.

"It's very serious what you've done, Tansy," she said. "You gave Finella all the evidence she'll need."

"Finella? She's in no need of evidence," I said. "She's trying to protect me, and all I did—"

"I would've thought you're far too smart to trust her," she said. "How did she manage to manipulate you so easily? Pretend to be your friend? Pretend she cared about you? She's never cared for anything but herself. You forsook two women who did care, who were your friends, only to drown yourself in a sea of falsehood."

"What has Finella done?" Cora asked.

"She was found early this morning tied to a tree near the loch," Agnes said. "She'd been forced to stand on a witch's book—a gateway to evil—balanced on a rock. Nailed above her head was an upside-down crucifix. A wad of filthy fabric was shoved into her mouth so she could not call for help. Rossalyn's wedding ring was wrapped in it."

Agnes didn't wait for me to answer the question. "You gave Finella each of those items, did you not?"

"Yes, but only to see if Rossalyn was threatening me. There is a group of village women who practice old rituals. They were to meet at midnight and hold each of the objects, which would enable them to see if there was evil in Rossalyn's heart. I was so afraid, so unsettled after the daisy wheels and the poppet." I turned to Cora. "I'd already been feeling insecure about our friendship and then I started to doubt you both. I thought you might accuse me of witchcraft in order to win the laird's favor."

"There was no group of women meeting in Cairnfarn last night," Agnes said. "I think it's safe to assume it was Finella who hung the daisy wheel on your cottage and put the poppet in your bed, Cora. She's lost her mother and her mother's income, which means she cannae afford to stay in her home, filthy and disgusting though it is. We all know the new laird shares his father's view of witches. No doubt she thought identifying his hated stepmother as one would lead to a reward."

I wanted to protest that no one could believe Rossalyn was a witch, but I was not so naïve as to think serious—let alone well-founded—evidence was necessary in such cases. Testimony that stirred up hysteria was the only thing required to secure a guilty verdict.

"I've been a fool. I . . ."

"I'm sorry you never realized the friend you had in me, Tasnim." I'd never seen Cora's eyes so hard. Her glare chilled me. "All we can do now is try to stop Rossalyn from being convicted."

"The laird brought in a witchfinder yesterday," Agnes said. "He was the man who found you, Tansy, and returned you to the cottage. Would that I had known that sooner."

"What can we do?" I asked. "I'll confess everything to the laird. He won't reject the truth, surely. He can punish me if he wants. I've—"

"You've done enough," Agnes said. She turned to Cora. "We can try to make the laird believe Finella is the witch. If she hangs, she's no one to blame but herself for stirring all this up. Tell me exactly what she asked of you, Tansy."

I went over what Finella had said to me, leaving out no detail. I knew it was not right to falsely accuse her of witchcraft; it would make us no better than her. Stopping one evil with another is not justice, but letting Rossalyn face trial and execution would never be acceptable. I couldn't live with that guilt, yet as I could offer no better strategy, I acquiesced to Agnes's plan.

When we reached the castle, Agnes demanded that we see the laird. He agreed so quickly that, for a moment, I felt a sliver of hope as a servant led us into the Great Hall. Ewan was sitting in an imposing chair at one end of the room. There was a long table on either side of him. A group of MacAllister men surrounded him, laughing and talking and taking no notice of us until their laird saw us and motioned for them to be quiet.

"The friends of the witch," he said. "You're either courageous or stupid to come here. Why would I believe any defense you might offer? Either you're part of her devil's circle or you're under her spell. For the sake of your souls, I hope it's the latter."

"It's neither," Agnes said. "Finella Logan is a selfish, greedy, unprincipled fool who thinks making outlandish accusations will increase her material standing in the world. I cannae imagine that you, our laird, would fall for such tactics."

"Finella Logan isnae asking for anything," he said. "I've never spoken to her before today, but I'm told she works hard and is an honest, God-fearing lass. She certainly didnae ask to be taken prisoner by a witch and cursed."

"Cursed?" Agnes asked. "How so?"

"For an hour after she was found, she could not speak, only bark."

"And you believed this?" Agnes tossed her head, looked to the ceiling, and huffed. "How do you know she wasnae pretending?"

"Why would anyone pretend to be incapable of speech and bark like a dog?" The men around the laird laughed, but I could feel a nervous tension prickling through them.

"As I said, she wants to improve her circumstances," Agnes said. "She—"

I interrupted. "Would it be possible to see the evidence found with Finella? In my country, we do not tolerate witches. I know what to look for, I know how they can trick the honest souls around them." This was all lies; I knew nothing, but I could read the way Ewan was looking at Agnes. He had no sympathy for her. The strategy she was employing in hopes of freeing Rossalyn would never work.

He hesitated before answering me. He pressed his lips together and frowned, bringing his eyebrows together tight above his nose. He pushed his hands into each other, cracking the knuckles. "I suppose it cannae hurt."

One of the younger men was sent on the errand, and returned a few minutes later with the objects I'd taken from Rossalyn, and a grubby rope.

"Finella states that the witch read from this book of spells," Ewan said. I could see my mother's ribbon peeking out from the top of it like a bookmark. I had no doubt it was placed in *Macbeth*. Something wicked this way certainly had come.

"That is no book of spells," I said, "but rather plays, plays enjoyed by the monarchs of Britain."

"Why then did you steal it from my library? Finella has confessed to having seen you do it. She saw you drop the parcel from the window. She defended you, saying you knew not what you were doing, that Rossalyn was the only one possessed by evil. After she read the spell, she placed the book on a rock, forced Finella to stand on it, and tied her to a tree. She chanted in a strange language—the language of the devil—and forced a rag into her mouth. Wrapped in the rag was the gold ring my father gave that woman in marriage. I dinnae ken what that means in a spell, but—"

"The rope was cut?" I asked, picking it up and examining the still intact knot. I didn't want him to keep talking about spells. Doing so would only make him more afraid. "Why was that?"

"To free her," he said, "which should be obvious, even to someone like you."

Someone like me. Rage started to boil in me. "Surely that was unnecessary. There's no sign of a knot, which means it must've been tied with a slipknot. Finella could have freed herself at any time."

"No doubt she was afraid the witch would torment her further if she tried," Ewan said. "It was likely a test."

"Surely a God-fearing woman would have the courage to flee a witch." I shook my head.

"A God-fearing woman would know the dangers she'd face when confronted with the devil's servant." The man who spoke strode into the hall with an attitude of supreme confidence. Later, I would learn his name: Robert Haskins. He was tall, with long legs and narrow shoulders; he stood straight and proud. I recognized him as the man I'd seen on the path near the loch, the man who had carried me back to the village after my ill-fated attempt to attack him. "I wondered, when you fell on the path in front of me, if you were possessed by some demon."

"You see that I am not," I said.

"Yet you share a home with a witch."

"Rossalyn MacAllister is no witch," I said.

"I will prove otherwise, and when I am done, I shall turn my attention to you." He turned to the laird and dipped his head in a sign of reverence. "If you would be so good as to bring the accused here,

I can get on with it. There's no sense delaying. We do not yet know the range and depth of her powers. She may even now be casting spells."

Ewan ordered two of his men to fetch Rossalyn. While we waited for her arrival, Finella entered the room. She was dressed in a gown she could never have afforded. She approached the laird and knelt down in front of him. They exchanged some murmured words and she then disappeared into the increasingly crowded room. Servants from the castle as well as dozens of villagers were streaming in through the doors. News of the witchfinder's presence had spread quickly; no one would want to miss the impending spectacle.

Soon after I'd lost sight of her, Finella sidled up next to me, gripped my arm, and whispered, "You'd best remain silent or I'll accuse you, too."

"Did you hang the daisy wheels on our cottage?" She nodded. "And the poppet?"

"I slipped into Cora's house when she'd gone outside for water. I hid under her bed until she was asleep. I put the poppet next to her and let myself out."

"Why?"

"I've nothing more to say." She twisted my arm, hard. "Tell no one I had Rossalyn's things and I'll tell no one it was you who gave them to me. We stand together and live free, or listen to each other's necks snap as we fall from the gallows."

For a moment—a longer moment than I'd like to admit—I considered what she'd said. There could be no doubt that a word from her would consign me to the same fate as Rossalyn. Finella had been canny, manufacturing it so that the best strategy for me to save myself would be to protect her. But what use would living be if I stood by and watched such injustice? No one who had suffered what I had could do anything of the sort. I said nothing to Finella but did my best to gather my thoughts. I would not get more than one chance to make things right.

There was a commotion as Rossalyn was brought into the room and placed in front of the laird. She was still wearing her nightdress, but her bearing was regal, her face a mask of calm defiance. Haskins stepped forward, holding a slim wooden box in his hand. He opened it and removed a needle, approximately three inches long, with a brass handle.

"I would prefer to do this in more private circumstances," he said, "but will do the bidding of the head of the MacAllister clan."

"The witch will be examined before us all," Ewan said, "so that we may witness the proof of her guilt. I will have no one left in doubt on the matter."

Haskins lifted Rossalyn's arm, pulled up the sleeve of her night-dress, and examined her skin. He then repeated this procedure on the other side before crouching down and lifting her skirt. She stepped back, glared at him, and with one sweeping movement pulled the nightdress over her head.

"I shall happily stand here naked before you so that all can see I bear no devil's mark," she said, turning to face the audience and then back so she could look Ewan in the eyes. "I have nothing to hide."

I had helped Rossalyn dress enough times that I knew there were no visible markings on her body. No birthmarks, no warts, no scars, nothing for Haskins to find. Not that the truth would stop him. He focused in on her left shoulder blade, stepping forward and pulling out a glass so that he could look closer. He nodded, made a clucking sound, and raised his needle high above his head. He paused there, theatrically, and then brought it down with such force that when he landed it on her skin, she fell forward.

"The witch falls in the hopes that we will think her mark is not insensate," Haskins said, "but we will not be fooled." He shoved her down flat, her face against the cold stone floor, then crouched next to her and raised his needle again. This time, he did not move with speed nor excessive force. Instead, he lowered it gently and barely touched her shoulder blade before sinking the point into her. She did not move and made no sound. He pulled it out and repeated the action three times. When he was done, he rose to his feet.

"I'm not a man who takes any joy in his profession," he said, "and would not do it if I didn't believe in its importance. Our Lord tells us *thou shall not suffer a witch to live*. Who am I to stand in the way of divine justice? I didn't choose for it to fall on me to be the one capable of identifying—"

I pushed my way forward through the crowd until I was standing in front of him. "Did you not?" I wrenched the needle out of his hand. I knew Rossalyn. I knew how little tolerance she had for pain. A torn cuticle set her on edge. There was no way she'd be able to lie silent and immobile while being stabbed with a three-inch needle. So I held Haskins's device in front of me. He moved to grab it, but before he could, I pressed the tip of the needle against my finger. The needle slid into its brass handle.

"Och! Everyone quiet!" one of the men standing near me shouted. "Do it again, lassie."

So I did.

And again.

And again.

And again.

273

And then I asked the man to give me the brooch holding his plaid in place over his shoulder. He did. I knelt down next to Rossalyn, who was shivering on the floor.

"Forgive me," I said and stabbed her with it. She shrieked in pain and coiled away from me. I turned to Haskins. "It seems your device is inadequate. There is no devil's mark on Rossalyn MacAllister." I untied my cloak and handed it to her. She was still shaking, but managed a smile as she covered herself.

"Enough," Ewan said. "Enough."

I spun around so I could look him in the eyes and stepped close enough that I could speak to him without the others hearing. "Yes, it is enough, and you have the power to stop it. There are no witches in Cairnfarn, only petty sinners who like gossip. Send Haskins away in disgrace and reclaim your authority over your tenants."

"I have never ceded an inch of my authority," he said through clenched teeth.

"You did the moment you let lies and rumors replace truth and common sense. It's not too late to change course. Take back control. Refuse to tolerate hysteria. You'll find your tenants more productive and your holdings more valuable. You won't lose workers to the gallows like they did in Balieth and you'll earn the trust of all who live on your lands."

He looked uncertain, but I saw something in him I knew I could exploit, an expression I knew all too well from the years I spent with my second master, a man who was fundamentally weak and afraid, who would listen to the loudest voice.

"You may accept that it is wrong to let a witch live, but surely it is at least as bad to execute an innocent soul," I said. "By exposing Haskins as a fraud, you will have saved countless people. The king himself will be in your debt, for he is a man who cares about justice.

He would not stand by idly if he discovered someone willfully maligning his subjects and leading them to their executions."

The fact was, I knew virtually nothing about the king beyond his name, Charles II. I could only hope a laird in the wilds of the Scottish Highlands didn't have much more knowledge than I. On that count, it seemed I was right.

"How did you know the needle was false?" he asked, eyeing me with suspicion. "Perhaps you are the witch."

"You spent enough time with your stepmother to know that she can't bear so much as a stubbed toe. I've heard you comment on it more than once, the last time when you grabbed her arm in our cottage."

"Aye, that is true."

"So now, you will do the right thing. Denounce the liar, Finella Logan, and make Rossalyn's innocence known to all."

He sneered. "I willnae let her profit from this. How am I to know she didnae manufacture the entire scandal herself?"

"She won't profit, but I shall," I said. "I have saved you from dishonor and disgrace. Haskins would have been exposed eventually, and all who stood by him shamed when they're revealed as gullible fools. As thanks for sparing you that humiliation, you will give me enough money to return to my homeland and set your stepmother up there in a household of her own. You need never deal with her again."

"Where is your homeland?" he asked.

"Tunisia."

He nodded. "That may be far enough away to suit me. It is to my benefit to send her somewhere she can cause no further trouble. I order you to make the trip with her and ensure she does not return."

I would have liked to correct him and force him to admit that it was I, not he, giving the orders, but decided it wasn't worth doing anything that might jeopardize going home. What Ewan MacAllister believed meant little to me, but there was one person who needed to know the truth: Rossalyn.

Cora, Agnes, and I took Rossalyn home. She was numb, shocked, and couldn't stop shaking. We gave her a bath, a new nightdress, and a cup of tea. Cora made soup. I mainly kept to myself, quiet, waiting until they had left to speak to Rossalyn. I told her what I'd said and what Ewan had promised.

"I can't go with you," she said, shaking her head. "It wouldn't be right. I'm the reason you're still here, which makes me wholly unworthy of your friendship and help. I never sent any of the letters you wrote to your family. I liked you and wanted you to stay with me. I didn't have many friends among the MacAllister women and couldn't bear to lose you. It was selfish and unforgivable."

I felt as if I'd been struck a physical blow. For years I'd worried my family had forsaken me. If not, had something catastrophic happened to them? I expected rage to consume me, but inexplicably it didn't. Rossalyn had always been selfish. Admittedly, she'd taken things to a shocking extreme, but as I looked at her, I felt something other than anger: pity. She was pathetic, a person who'd always got what she wanted, who'd lived so long with entitlement she knew no other way. Explanations could never justify her actions, but there's something far more freeing, more empowering than anger or revenge: forgiveness.

Which is not to say I forgave her. Not then, at least. But I could see the possibility in the future because I, who had suffered so much, was a far stronger person than she. I had no desire to punish her; all I wanted was to go home. And so I did, accompanied by my former mistress, with enough money set aside to send her back to Scotland.

She would always be free to leave, no matter what Ewan MacAllister wanted. What he had done, what she had done, what my masters had done destroyed too much of my life. I would no longer let any of them have power over me. I would never sink to treating another person the way I'd been treated, and I would never let anger and hatred consume me.

Which is not to say I forgot.

I always remembered.

Always.

And I would be the better person.

Always.

35

1905

Colin and I sat with Mr. Pringle until Dr. Cameron—fetched by Effie—removed Caroline's body from the vicarage. I hated the idea of leaving him alone, but he assured us that solitude was what he needed, at least for now. Back at the castle, we gathered Jeremy and the Greats in the library and told them all that had transpired at the vicarage.

"It's the most appalling thing I've ever heard," Jeremy said. "Terrible business, of course, but it has all the marks of the sensational literature of which you're so fond, Em. A randy vicar's wife and her noble husband, ready to face the gallows in her stead. A reformed criminal posing as someone else at last gets the justice he'd evaded. But poor Mrs. Mackie. I'm broken up by it all. Cairnfarn will never be the same."

"It will recover well enough," Miss Adeline said.

"Places always do," Miss Josephine said.

"It survived the witch hunt, after all," Miss Adeline said.

"Without a single execution," Miss Josephine said.

"Which does make one wonder if it ought to be considered a witch hunt," Miss Adeline said. "No one actually suffered as a result."

"The accused parties might not agree," Colin said, "unless in the aftermath they had the opportunity for a fresh start."

"Pringle's the one who needs one now," Jeremy said. "I told him I'd secure another living for him if he couldn't bear to stay here, but also assured him that the community would rally round. He's done nothing wrong and ought not have to leave his home. I'm pleased that he's agreed to remain."

"We take care of our own in Cairnfarn," Miss Adeline said.

"Always have," Miss Josephine said.

A voice floated from behind the heavy velvet curtains on the far side of the room. "Were there really witches in Cairnfarn, Your Grace?" It was Henry, of course, a notorious eavesdropper.

"Henry, what have I told you about listening to conversations you're not meant to be a part of?" I asked.

A second voice replied. "It's my fault, Mama. Having found his body, I wanted to hear for myself that Mr. Gordon would have justice."

"Tom?" Colin and I asked in unison. I would never have suspected Tom, our most well-mannered son, to be capable of such underhanded behavior.

"The fact is, it's not his fault either." Richard's voice floated from behind a curtain further along the wall. "I've collected a fair amount of evidence that suggests we've all been spellbound by fairies. Initially, it appeared they were working in conjunction with the very unusual Cairnfarn kelpies, but when I found their flag—"

"You found a flag?" Jeremy grinned and leapt to his feet. "A fairy flag?"

"Yes, Your Grace," Richard said.

"Come out, all three of you, and for heaven's sake stop calling me Your Grace. I'm more or less an uncle to you all, wouldn't you agree, Em?"

"Well—"

He interrupted before I could continue. "I'm not sure I'm particularly interested in your opinion on the matter. From now on, I'm Uncle Jeremy, and if any of the three of you grows up to be even half as useless as I, I'll leave you my dukedom."

"That's not how hereditary aristocracy works, Bainbridge," Colin said, as the boys emerged from their hiding places.

"I shall apply to the king and have him make an exception," Jeremy said. "Old Bertie knows I've witnessed enough of his embarrassing moments that he'd never have the cheek to deny me."

"The king does things that are embarrassing?" Tom said, his eyes wide.

"Kings are the most embarrassing," Henry said, "because they know they can do whatever they want. I'd quite like to be a duke, Your Grace, er, Uncle Jeremy."

My friend narrowed his eyes and motioned for Henry to come to him. "You've got decent potential, but your father's blood might prevent you from realizing it. I shall keep a close eye on you."

"This is an excellent way forward," Miss Adeline said.

"Particularly as your brother Jack and darling Christabel have never managed to produce a son," Miss Josephine said.

"Six stunning girls, though," Miss Adeline said.

"One more beautiful than the last," Miss Josephine said.

"What a relief," Jeremy said. "Now you can both stop harassing me about getting married."

"A son would be the best way forward," Miss Adeline said.

"It always is," Miss Josephine said.

"One more word on the subject and I'll flee to London and shan't return to the Highlands again. Given how fine I look in a kilt, you'll never be forgiven by any of the girls in the village. I'm a critical part of the scenery."

"Given how fine you believe you look in a kilt, you'd never pass up the opportunity to wear one," Colin said. "The village girls need not worry."

"Could you please tell us more about the witches?" Richard asked.

"There weren't any in the end," Jeremy said, "but in the aftermath of the trial, the head of the MacAllister clan acquired the Shakespeare First Folio now housed in this library. Apparently it was evidence against one of the accused. I'm no lover of Shakespeare, but even I wouldn't claim it was a gateway to evil. Of course, I don't understand most of what the bloke wrote, so perhaps I'm wrong on that count. There's a ribbon inside, marking the page in *Macbeth* where the witches cast some odious spell or another. It's said to have belonged to the young woman who exposed the whole thing as a fraud."

"Was it a fraud?" Richard asked.

"It was," Jeremy said. "Apparently the laird brought in an English witch-hunter who was nothing but a charlatan."

"That's rather disappointing," Richard said.

"Not for the accused," I said.

"Of course, Mama, I didn't mean to suggest otherwise, only to say that it would have been most interesting to learn there had been active witches in Cairnfarn. They're not all evil, you know. Many provided useful services to their communities."

"You were only just telling us most of them weren't actually witches," Henry said.

"That's quite true, however, there were some who—"

I heard a strange rustling sound coming from across the room. "What is that?"

"Nothing, Mama," Henry said. "It's only that Cedric was looking so miserable this morning in the cold and the damp that I thought it would be best to bring him inside. The Highlands really aren't a proper place to keep a crocodile."

"The castle isn't a proper place for him either," I said. "He has a perfectly comfortable enclosure in the menagerie."

"Yes, but the monkeys have been tormenting him," Henry said. "They're so clever they can get out of theirs and into his and when they do—"

"Return him to the menagerie at once," Colin said, "before he damages any of the books."

"Yes, sir." Henry pulled a petulant face, but did as ordered. He collected the crocodile from underneath a long library table at the far end of the room. Looking as indignant as possible, he started for the door, his brothers and Cedric trailing behind.

"A moment, please," Jeremy said. "Richard, you haven't finished telling me about the fairy flag. I've always been mad with jealousy that the MacLeods have one at Dunvegan. When it's flown, it makes them invincible, but it can only be used three times. If you've found one for me—especially if it's good for more than three goes—there might be competition for my dukedom."

"But you said it should go to someone useless." Henry crossed his arms without dropping Cedric's lead. "Discovering a fairy flag is nothing of the sort."

"Quite right, my boy, quite right." Jeremy turned to Richard. "Do you want the dukedom?"

"No, Your Grace, er, Uncle Jeremy, not particularly," Richard said. "I'm hoping to become a scholar."

"A scholar? Dear me, that won't do at all. We'll find you a spot at Oxford and leave Henry and Tom to duke it out, so to speak."

"Put a stop to this at once, Bainbridge," Colin said. "None of the boys is going to succeed you."

"We'll see, Hargreaves, we'll see."

The boys were all giggling, a clear signal none of them was taking the matter seriously, as they marched out of the room in procession with the crocodile.

"Delightful lads," Jeremy said. "Almost makes one want children of one's own."

"That would require a bride, Bainbridge," Colin said.

Jeremy sighed. "Must you bring me crashing back to reality?"

"There's always Miss Victoria Cholmondeley-Hamilton," Miss Adeline said.

"You almost proposed to her once," Miss Josephine said.

"No one could argue it would be anything but a brilliant match," Miss Adeline said.

"I'm told she still carries a torch for you, despite your disgraceful behavior," Miss Josephine said.

My jaw dropped. "I've never heard the story."

"And you won't be hearing it now," Jeremy said. "I've not another word to say on the subject."

* * *

The next morning, I awoke feeling none of the relief that generally follows catching a murderer. It still troubled me that we didn't know what had become of the real Angus Sinclair. Then, halfway through breakfast, I remembered something. I shot from the table and ran to the stables, where I found Sandy, Mr. Gordon's young friend.

"You told me the gamekeeper made you a box for your treasures," I said. "Did he give you any treasures as well?"

"Aye, he did, madam. Just the one, a ring."

"A signet ring?"

"Aye."

"Could you fetch it and come to the village with me?"

Soon we were sitting with Dr. Harris in her house. Tears streamed down her cheeks as she listened to the boy's story.

"He got it from the man who saved his life," Sandy said. "Saved it twice, in fact. They met in a pub in Edinburgh and got to talking about second chances and the like. The man was just as obsessed with them as Mr. Gordon was. He'd grown up in a little Highland village and left it for the city, where he found a life he loved. Said that sometimes he missed the place he was born, but that he had no regrets. Mr. Gordon told him he was in a spot of trouble, and the man encouraged him to make a fresh start as well. Said he should leave his old life behind and dedicate himself to good.

"That was the first time the man saved his life," Sandy continued. "Mr. Gordon knew if he stayed in Edinburgh he would've come to a bad end, so decided then and there to come to Cairnfarn. Then, only a little bit later, while they were still sitting in the pub, the whole place burst into flames. They raced to escape, but a beam from the ceiling crashed down and pinned Mr. Gordon to the ground. The man pulled it off him and helped him get out of the building, saving his life a second time. Once they could breathe again—the smoke was fierce and thick—they both went back inside to see if anyone else was trapped. They helped a barmaid and a man who'd had too much to drink and then went in another time. It was then that the other man collapsed. Mr. Gordon dinnae ken what happened, but the man wasnae breathing. Then the man's coat caught fire and it started consuming his whole body. Mr. Gordon pulled the ring off his finger to keep as a memento. To remind him what a gift it was to get a fresh start. He didnae ever wear it, though, and gave it to me after we became friends." He'd been staring at the floor as he spoke, but now looked up at Dr. Harris. "Of course at the time, I thought he wasnae Mr. Gordon, but Angus. Now that I know my Angus was really someone else, it's obvious the other man was your Angus. I've heard you were to be married to him."

Dr. Harris nodded. "That's true."

"Then you should have the ring," he said. "It's too big for me and I've got no real use for it."

"I'd like you to keep it," she said. "Use it as an inspiration to live a good, honest life."

"So not change my name and get a fresh start?"

"Live in a way that ensures you'll never need one."

I was glad to have been able to give her some closure. When I returned to the castle, I found Irene had left for me a packet of tisane she said would help with sore muscles should I ever again decide to climb one of Scotland's Munros.

"I'd like that very much," Colin said, after we'd retired to our rooms that night. "Your cheeks rosy with exertion, the wind blowing your hair. We could find a quiet spot on the summit—"

"So far as I can tell, there are no quiet spots on summits." I was sitting at the dressing table, brushing my hair. "The wind is quite fierce. My hair would be an absolute catastrophe."

"I've always been fond of you disheveled," he said, coming up from behind and putting his arms around me.

"There are better locations to find oneself disheveled than the top of a mountain."

"Are there?" He kissed my neck and sent shivers through my body. "Where would you suggest is preferable?"

"Here and now." I put my lips on his. He lifted me from the chair and carried me to the bed while nimbly undoing the pearl buttons on my nightdress. No sooner had he lowered me down than we heard a knock on the door.

"Papa! There's a terrible emergency!" It was Henry. Of course. "Cedric is nowhere to be found. I know I fastened his enclosure securely. The monkeys must have let him out. I'm certain it's all a dreadful conspiracy of theirs. Would you please be so good as to help me find him? He can't survive a night in the cold."

Myriad questions raced through my mind. Why was he still awake? How did he know Cedric was missing? Had he gone to the menagerie after midnight? There were countless more, but I voiced only one of them, as Colin pulled on his trousers.

"How many years until they go to Eton?"

Author's Note

The beauty of the Scottish Highlands is breathtaking, as is its history, rife with clans, folklore, and castles. It's a place I've always loved, but the inspiration for this story came from the "Moorish Lasses," two enslaved North African women seized from a ship by privateers and given as gifts to James IV. They lived at court, serving as ladies-in-waiting to the king's daughter, Margaret. They participated in court life—one of them, Elen, was named the Black Queen of Beauty at a tournament—but were treated as status symbols, the ultimate accessory for a fashionable household. It appears that they attained their freedom in Scotland, but what did that mean? How could they ever hope to get home? We know very little about them, so I wanted to imagine what the life of someone in similar circumstances might have been like. I hope I've done justice to them with Tansy.

Between 1563 and 1736, people in Scotland were accused of witchcraft at rates up to five times greater than in the rest of Europe. Matthew Hopkins, the notorious self-styled Witchfinder General, collected "evidence" against hundreds of them. He pricked skin with needles and knives (often with retractable blades), used sleep deprivation to get confessions, and administered a gruesome swimming test to many of his victims. The suspected witch (usually a woman), arms and legs tied to a chair, would be thrown into a body of water. If she floated, she would have to stand trial. If she drowned, she was innocent. Slim consolation to the dead and her loved ones.

The sailor who brought animals to the menagerie at Cairnfarn is based on my husband's mother's uncle, who had a habit of collecting exotic beasts while at sea and bringing them home as gifts for his sister in Northumberland. Not in possession of a menagerie, she would take them on the train to London and donate them to the zoo. Oh, to have witnessed the scene . . .

Sources

Dunbar, John Telfer. 1964. *History of Highland Dress*. Philadelphia: Dufour Editions.

Foster, Elizabeth, and Christopher A. Whatley, eds. 2010. *A History of Everyday Life in Scotland 1600 to 1800*. Edinburgh: Edinburgh University Press.

Goodare, J., L. Martin, and J. Miller, eds. 2008. *Witchcraft and Belief in Early Modern Scotland*. London: Palgrave Macmillan UK.

Griffiths, Trevor, and Graeme Morton, eds. 2010. *A History of Everyday Life in Scotland, 1800 to 1900*. Edinburgh: Edinburgh University Press.

Habib, Imtiaz H. 2020. *Black Lives in the English Archives, 1500–1677: Imprints of the Invisible*. London: Routledge.

Hutton, R. 2011. "Witch-Hunting in Celtic Societies." *Past & Present* 212 (1): 43–71.

Kaufmann, Miranda. 2011. "Africans in Britain: 1500–1640." Dissertation, Oxford University.

————. 2018. *Black Tudors: The Untold Story*. London: Oneworld Publications.

Kennedy, Allan Douglas. 2016. "Crime and Punishment in Early-Modern Scotland: The Secular Courts of Restoration Argyllshire, 1660–1688." *International Review of Scottish Studies* 41 (November). https://doi.org/10.21083/irss.v41i0.3581.

Logan, James, and R. R. McIan. (1845) 1980. *The Clans of the Scottish Highlands*. New York: Crescent Books.

Miers, Mary. 2017. *Highland Retreats*. New York: Rizzoli Publications.

Moss, Stephen. 2020. *Highlands: Scotland's Wild Heart*. London: Bloomsbury.

Niebrzydowski, Sue. 2001. "The Sultana and Her Sisters: Black Women in the British Isles before 1530." *Women's History Review* 10 (2): 187–210.

Acknowledgments

Myriad thanks to:

Charlie Spicer: insightful, inspiring, and a heck of a lot of fun to work with.

Andy Martin, Sarah Melnyk, Hannah Pierdolla, and David Rostein. The best in the business.

Anne Hawkins, agent extraordinaire.

Laura Bradford, who knew Angus at the beginning.

Brett Battles, Rob Browne, Bill Cameron, Christina Chen, Jon Clinch, Jane Grant, Nick Hawkins, Elizabeth Letts, Lara Matthys, Carrie Medders, Erica Ruth Neubauer, Missy Rightley, Renee Rosen, and Lauren Willig. Love you all.

Alexander, Katie, and Jess.

My parents.

Andrew, my everything.